IN ALASKA
WITH
SHIPWRECK KELLY

IN ALASKA
WITH
SHIPWRECK KELLY

A North-Western Story

DAN CUSHMAN

Five Star Western
Thorndike, Maine

A Five Star Western published in conjunction with Golden West Literary Agency.

February 1996

First Edition

Five Star Standard Print Western Series.

The text of this edition is unabridged.

Set in 11 pt. News Plantin by Jason Johnson.

Printed in the United States on permanent paper.

Library of Congress Cataloging in Publication Data

Cushman, Dan.
    In Alaska with Shipwreck Kelly : a North-Western story
/ by Dan Cushman.
    p   cm.
    ISBN 0-7862-0534-2 (hc)
    1. Klondike River Valley (Yukon) — Gold discoveries —
Fiction. 2. Frontier and pioneer life — Alaska — Fiction.
I. Title.
PS3553.U738I53   1996
813'.54—dc20   95-23524

IN ALASKA
WITH
SHIPWRECK KELLY

Chapter One

"What's the big deal?" asked Kelly when he came in and saw the cake.

"Why, it's your birthday!" said Pa. "Can't you keep tabs on your own birthday?"

They didn't even have a calendar and he wouldn't have known how to work it if they did. Banks and stores at Buffalo gave them away at Christmas, but there was generally a big blizzard about then, so there you were!

Kelly must have been near onto six feet tall, and Pa said he'd better stop growing soon or he'd have to walk around the house bowlegged. In contrast, Pa was all twisted around from getting tromped between forge and anvil. He was a ferrier, and sort of famous at it, but he couldn't walk the way he was facing, or mount a horse except on the off-side, like an Indian. At times he seemed to resent how tall his son had grown.

"Patrick Eugene Kelly!" Pa said, as if introducing him from some prize ring. How Kelly despised that Eugene! The initials: P. E. Kelly! What if the fellows at school found it out? P. E. Kelly! "Pee, Kelly, pee! You want your bladder to bust?" Fortunately, there wasn't much school. It was way over at Storm Coulee, a five-mile ride — when they found a teacher. They'd hire some girl, maybe from back East; but they had dances at the school, and pretty soon she'd quit and marry a cowboy. He might have fifteen cows, which he'd gathered as strays; and she'd file on land, too, and they'd be ranchers. The teacher seemed willing to take her chances, so that would be the end of Kelly's education for the year. One time he had gone down to Douglas with the folks. His two married sisters lived there and Pa had gotten work at a blacksmith shop. However, Kelly was late for the school term so they had put him in a grade where his legs stuck up on each side of his desk, and he sort of held it in his lap, like grub time at the roundup. He had quit and worked with Pa, getting a dollar a day.

Pa had no trouble with the Stockgrowers Association because he ran horses instead of cattle (where the money was). Next year Kelly had just forgotten about school and had cowboyed for the T P Ranch. Mainly he "rode the wide circle," meaning he saw to it the cattle didn't stray too far and probably have their calves branded as mavericks.

It was an open winter, but later on a snowstorm blew in and it was a doozie. The snow came from the northeast, from Montana and Powder River, all flat as a floor. It wasn't cold but the snow covered him and his mare, old Sadie, from nose to tail, and weighted his hat down so he had to empty the brim like a shovel. He got lost and finally came to the Big Horns range, a solid mountain wall, rising right out of the prairie. There was a terrace with much fallen stone, and bushes with the leaves gone, bullberries and the like, a good enough trail if you watched out for the thorns. Some of the so-called Canada olives had thorns as long as cactus that could put your eye out. Finally, he tied to a bullberry tree and crawled in a slot cave somewhat higher and deeper than the rest where soft rock had been washed out from under a harder one, until finally it got too dark to see.

There was this strange sort of stink. It wasn't skunk or mink, but it was animal of some sort, like one had crawled in and died, but not exactly like that either. It was just sort of sickeningly sweet. Also he felt a lot of slick stuff on the floor. He had it all over his hands and wiped them on his chaps. They were hair chaps, white angora, with long curly hair.

Then he got to hearing a strange sound as well. It was like someone walking through a thin mud. So, finally, he lit a match, and good God, there was a great, big, old bear! It was a sow grizzly and she had two cubs, new born, which she was licking. He'd nearly crawled right in and made it a threesome!

He held the match a while; she didn't seem to pay heed. What she was doing was licking them into shape. Bears get born just globs, like pieces of liver, and the mother had to form bears of them. Kelly knew better than to move. He didn't even blow out the match. He let it burn and fall. Then, scarcely breathing, he backed off, a bit at a time, and made it outside into the wind and snow. And old Sadie wouldn't let him mount. It was the slickery stuff, the stink of it. It was all over him. He tried to get it off with handfuls of snow, and moved around downwind until finally old Sadie let him on. She was still none too happy, but she didn't buck, and mares will always head home. She took him right into the barn where he unsaddled, and what a reception he received at the T P bunkhouse.

The winter crew consisted of six fellows beside himself. They were playing cards and no sooner had he closed the door than they let out wails and imprecations as if they'd been raised in a clover patch. They wouldn't even let him get his chaps off; and finally Mrs. Taylor herself came out to check on the uproar.

She took him straight away into the big house and had a tub of water heated, and saw to it he had plenty of soap and a long-handled brush, and she gave him some of her husband's old clothes to wear till his could be washed and boiled, leaving only his chaps. They had to be buried under a caved-in cutbank for about two weeks.

"Well, I see you got home," Pa had said, without even a thank you for giving Ma ten dollars, which was half his wages, and also a whole two-quart crock of butter which Mrs. Taylor had churned. Pa had said, crabbed as usual, "If you'd been here, you could have helped me with Sam Felton's bay team. Real Kentucky driving horses! And he brought them special to be bronze shod. It's about the best advertising a man can get. But I had the whole thing to do alone, stove-up as I am, having to pull myself around on a dolly. . . ."

Pa's specialty was to shoe, but not with iron or mild steel that were made malleable at the forge and burnt onto the hoof for a close fit and likely to damage the hoof, turning it into a sort of rotten cork. He used bronze, which could be put on with very light heat. A horse could actually be cold shod. He bought advertising in the papers to that effect but few responded. He advertised that a rider could cold shoe right on the range with only one simple tool, a rasp and hammer combination costing three dollars with leather case, but not many went for those either.

He was naturally bitter about it. Sometimes he'd go sit in the barn and not come out all day, even to eat, and Ma would have to go coax him. Ma said you couldn't imagine, seeing him now, how he used to be before the accident. Kelly did, however. He had a real good memory of things when he was little, and how Pa used to be straight and tall. Kelly didn't know how they would have gotten by but for a very peculiar circumstance. Pa had homesteaded on land that the U. S. Army once considered for a summer cantonment, and had drilled a well — water that was the best, ice-cold and not a hint of alkali. But in spite of this, the road was surveyed a mile to the west, and the stage company put its station at Duck Coulee with a reservoir that caught run-off water, scarcely fit for horses. The station master was supposed to furnish food as part of the fare. He did, but he had married a big, morose sort of foreign woman who knew how to cook little but a heavy bread and salt pork and beans. The beans were fine in cold weather; frozen, greasy, they could be sliced and fried; but in the summer when most people traveled, they turned sour. However, she kept right on serving them. Nothing went to waste. It was awful! Everybody said so, drivers and all.

One day the driver turned off and drove by way of the Kelly place to fill his water bags, and Ma had just baked some of her famed dried peach pie, and she treated. Pretty soon it became a regular thing. She put up a sun shade and table, and started charging twenty-five cents. Sometimes she made as much as two dollars a day. But Pa didn't like it a bit. He felt aced out by his wife. Here he was one of the finest ferriers in the land, shoeing with genuine bronze, yet maybe a whole week with only one customer. However, Ma went right ahead selling the pie, and they even got put on the new government map as Peach Pie Ranch. She always served the driver free.

Chapter Two

It worked out real well for Kelly that he was from Johnson County, the "rustlers' county," and Pa was in horses, not cattle, because Kelly got asked by some Association ranchers to act as their rep at a number of the "outlaw" roundups. There had been bitter disputes and some shooting the years previous and few Association men were willing to risk their hides. So Kelly went with a whole fistful of certifications, and from some pretty big outfits! He was paid a dollar a day, plus twenty-five cents for each calf claimed, and he didn't have to wrestle or brand a single one. He just stood there and made his claim, disputes being settled by a committee of three — a Johnson County man, an Association man, and a stock inspector. No guns were to be carried on the person. They all said how well he'd done, not having to shoot even one man.

That fall he rode in the north Johnson beef roundup and was later asked how he'd like to join in the big DeSmet and Sheridan drive to Billings, up on the Northern Pacific in Montana. Which meant he could also ride to south St. Paul as a 'puncher to punch-up any fallen stock. One dollar a day plus expenses, and ride back by Pullman sleeper. Once the cars were inside the yards at south St. Paul, your duties ended. The buyers took over, inspected the brands, and paid off by mail to the registered owners, as shown on the official brand books, and the 'punchers were turned loose on the town.

Well, Kelly guessed St. Paul had never seen a bunch like came on that trainload from Billings! They bought beer and decked themselves out in funny hats and masks that had strings you could pull, making a big, red tongue flop out. They scared the city people half out of their wits and, of course, there were some older 'punchers who had made the trip before to take the newcomers in hand to see the bars, bawdy houses, stage shows, and the rest.

They saw some beautiful theatres and houses of pleasure. A man named Archie Warren, who owned the Bank Saloon in Billings, had given Kelly the address of the famed Alhambra, all polished marble and alabaster, statuary, naked nymphs, mahogany bar, teakwood floor and pillars, grand piano and French bevel mirrors such as he never knew existed. And he met a nephew of the owner, Mr. Studdsworth P. Blackmore, who truly fit the name. He was a very powerful man with black, curly hair, much coated with pomade and about forty years old. Studdsworth P. Blackmore was a salesman of fine liquors, Warren and his famed Bank Saloon, the Montana distributor.

"Here, grab hold of that!" said Mr. Blackmore, sitting down at a table to arm-wrestle. Kelly did, and he put Kelly's arm back as if he were a child.

Mr. Blackmore's father had been an English army officer in India and he himself once a captain of Sepoys. "Finest troops in the Empire," he claimed. Not only that, but Mr. Blackmore was a citizen of England *and* the United States both! Voted Republican in the United States and Liberal in England. England was where he bought his suits. Nothing like a Bond Street tailor. "Perfect forty-six," he boasted. "Haven't changed in ten years. I could cable and have a new suit, perfect, in six weeks' time!"

It was certainly a strange bunch who hung around the Alhambra which, fine as it was, stood in a rough part of town. There'd been an article in the Minneapolis paper that it should be closed

13

down since it was little better than a den of thieves, mainly from Chicago, even members of the Black Hand. But the St. Paul *Pioneer Press* lashed back, saying Minneapolis, "our satellite village across the bridge," should first do something about its yearly incursion of Scandinavian lumberjacks who ran rampant and were cheated of their wages.

Shady denizens or not, the Alhambra had *real style,* with an orchestra, or trio, the best he'd ever heard, violin, flute and harp, which played numbers such as "The Herd Girl's Dream" and "Over The Waves." The owner, an aunt of Mr. Blackmore's, lived upstairs and was seldom seen, said to be sick in some strange manner that was turning her to a sort of green stone, living mainly on Turkish food and a liquor known as Chartreuse made only by certain monks in Europe whose formula had been kept secret for eight hundred years.

When Kelly got back to Billings, he was absolutely strapped for money, so Mr. Warren at the Bank Saloon said he could winter there and do odd jobs at twenty-five cents per day. The depot freight house was without a night clerk, so he could probably bunk there in his office and Mrs. Gibbs might let him graze at the beanery for doing chores. Also at the saloon there was a free lunch, if he didn't make too good a thing of it. "Those sausages come by express from Milwaukee!" Mr. Warren said. Ditto the black bread, or pumpernickel.

"You'll be required to put on a clean blue chambray shirt every day, and clean trousers twice a week, and drop the dirty ones in the laundry basket" — the Bank Saloon was the exclusive agent for the White Swan Steam Laundry of Bozeman. And it would be Kelly's task to wheel the clothes basket to the train, and get the new one, using the express cart. The saloon would be good for his first set of clothes at the Mercantile.

"You won't have any gaboons to clean," Mr. Warren said. "The swamper does that, but you have to see about coal in winter

14

and tend the stove when not in school. And there'll be no calling people by their first names, not even the town bum, is that clear?"

Kelly said yes. Ma had told him he could start calling grownups by their first names when he got to be twenty-one and voted the Republican ticket. Mr. Warren thought that was pretty funny, being a member of the Republican Party himself, but the policy remained fixed.

Once squared around he went up to the school. It was housed in a box-like building, two stories, basement and belfry. Also there was a room midway where the superintendent had his office. Not a soul in the hall. Just the smells. Actually a quiet stink. Each room had two doors, one to the room proper and the other to the cloakroom where he could see by the clothes which grade was which. As far as he knew, he'd do well to rate grade five. He tiptoed down the cloakroom and peeked in the far door, which was at the back of the room and, as he feared, the desks would never have fit.

He saw one fellow about his size hunched over, knees up on each side like a grasshopper, sort of holding the desk in his lap. He was some ranch boy who had missed a couple of terms and probably had forgotten what he'd learned when he did go, so the teacher would ask something and the fellows half his size, and the girls with their braids and hair ribbons, all waved their hands to answer, but the teacher insisted, "No, we'll let Homer answer this time." Of course he didn't know. Homer sat there, obviously wishing he was back at the ranch. "An adverb, Homer, modifies a verb, adjective, or another adverb," the teacher said and poor Homer wished she'd ask what a hackamore was. On that he could tell her a thing or two! "A hackamore modifies a boreal, a brow-band, or another guide leather." But unscholarly things that really made you a living never came up. So he just sat there looking open-mouthed and stupid.

15

Kelly peeked in some other rooms, including the Latin school, which was in a sort of half-basement, full of fellows his size. There were all sorts of X's and Y's on the blackboard. Then he saw the man in the office looking at him, so he slinked out.

"I'm way ahead in some things and way behind in others," Kelly said to Mr. Warren, "so I figured I might write away to a school I saw advertised in the Chicago paper. Here it is. The Burlington School of Science and Arts, Burlington, Iowa."

According to the ad, everything was taught through grade school and Latin School, Trade School, and Science. And it said, "Diplomas certified by the Superintendent of Education, Burlington, Iowa." Also, "Credits Accepted by Leading Colleges," and "send for one free placement examination. Let us determine your proper educational placement. Many need corrections in certain restricted areas only, and many plans of study are available."

Kelly assured Mr. Warren: "I've read *The Count of Monte Cristo* all the way through, but I don't know shucks about adverbs. Practically memorized the brand book, repping for the small outfits." Kelly laughed about it. "Had to, to keep from getting shot. I'll bet I know the alphabet in more positions than any teacher in the county."

Mr. Warren thought that was pretty funny. "You know it from the side of a cow, all bent around, and not on a nice, flat blackboard. Listen . . . take this ad over and show it to Carlyle, and see what he thinks."

This scared him, because what he meant was Kelly must show it to a lawyer at Forbes, Forbes & Carlyle, a firm that represented the railroad and included the biggest lawyers in the state: Carlyle in Billings, Jack Forbes in Helena, while Bob Forbes liked to travel back East. People used to call the latter "Bob Ford, the dirty little coward," on account of the song about Jesse

16

James, but he'd just laugh and say, "Well, you hadn't better hang up any pictures."

Kelly was a bit timid about walking in, but Carlyle, a tall, thin man with graying hair, took the ad right out of his hands and said, "How much you think we ought to sue these scoundrels for, cowboy?"

It was a joke, so Kelly said, "Nothing, so far! They ain't got any of my money yet."

Mr. Carlyle read it through, and asked Kelly about what schooling he'd had, the books he'd read, and concluded: "Send for their free test. When it comes, I'll read it, and have you sit down and answer it. I'll see how you do, and compare that with what they say. They're in this to make money, not to improve the world, so they may try and sell you a lot of courses you don't need."

Kelly sent for the test, took it, and had Mr. Carlyle make up his mind about how he did which, Carlyle said, was pretty fair, the problem being he belonged in about grade three some places and college in others. So Kelly sent it and got back the results that, of course, were very favorable (how else could they make a living?) and Carlyle said, "Hell, let the tail go with the hide! Take the upper grade." Kelly did, and had to pay extra for materials which included some books he could keep to start his own reference library.

As expected, his main trouble was with grammar, the parts of speech, but Carlyle said not to give it a second thought. "Edward Gibbon himself never said, 'I'll use a verb here, and a subordinate clause there,' or 'this is a collective which I should use as a singular.' You learn by habit and the way to do that is by reading good stuff, Addison, for example. Or Lamb, who sounds simple but is really very adroit." Mr. Carlyle believed if a child learned to walk the way the teachers tried to make him learn grammar, he'd still be crawling at age ten. Could

17

you imagine a lawyer arguing a case and trying to diagram his sentences?

"So read good writing, even good newspapers, like the New York *Tribune*, alone, and about half out loud." And he gave Kelly a couple of books to try out, one by Addison and the other by Mark Twain, *Tom Sawyer*. Kelly took very good care of the books, reading them during quiet hours at the saloon, careful to say the words silently and, after he'd read some pages about three times, he found himself saying things the same way. He saw how good grammar got to be a habit.

When possible, he would sit in the law offices and watch Lenora Hess, who drew up briefs, partly with pen and ink in a truly beautiful Spencerian hand and partly on one of the new type-writing machines (which he first mistook for a sewing machine), and he would read, mainly from the law library, things like *Nature and Source of the Law* by Gray and *Ancient Law* by Raine, which was tough going but still more interesting than one might think.

One day he was reading when Madame Riddell, proprietress of the Venus Hotel upstairs in the building next, stuck her head in the door and said, "Hey, stop moving your lips!"

Kelly shouldn't have, but he said it was how the lawyers had told him to do it, and she gave those lawyers the very devil. "It makes him look like Sid Schmidts," she complained. Sid was sort of a town bum who sat around squinting at the paper and reading half out loud.

Jack Forbes was there from Helena at the time, and he took Kelly's side, probably to test Madame Riddell's mettle, because she had a voice like a trombone. And oh, would she cut loose when called on to protect her girls! Jack conceded she might be right as to the law cases, which were scanned quickly for information, but when one read real quality writing he should move his lips, because good speech would then become photo-reactive for him.

18

Madame Riddell saw some of Kelly's penmanship and said it was a shame, and she insisted he take a bundle of old letters one of her girls had left (it turned out she had committed suicide) and he ought to practice by laying a tissue over them and copying. He did try, but it only stalled him. Mr. Gerrigan, head bartender at the Bank Saloon, had the real system. He had Kelly learn to print, copying the newspaper type, upper and lower case, and keep doing it until he could print as fast as he could write, and the letters would join up as a matter of course. And there he'd be, writing that looked very good and could be read, every word!

There were regular jamborees at The Venus. It had front and back stairs, both enclosed, and some of the leading citizens were said to have their own keys to special locked doors. There were also tales about the Roman Circus where some innocent young cowboy, fresh from the range, was told he had drawn the lucky number and hence his sport was free with some visiting beauty. Well, she would lead him a merry chase stark naked, while all unbeknownst to the cowboy it was watched through secret slits in the wall for one dollar each.

Kelly never saw this stunt himself, but he was told the "visiting beauty" was a girl named Annie who seemed very young and quiet, slim, with a great mass of dark hair. He'd go up there to deliver things from the saloon, liquors or champagnes, and the girls would say, "Here he is, Annie!" but she'd stay out of sight, and Madame Riddell would say, "Leave him alone, you harpies!"

Kelly stayed around the saloon mainly to do his chores and errands, and to study. The Institute had some very clever ideas. One was a geography system for which he received, besides a book, cardboard maps of the continents, die-stamped to be broken apart, shaken up like dice in a box, and then put together, each country named and what products it produced, also the race, population, and its flag. Kelly would spread the pieces on a card table and all the fellows would have a go at it.

Hornaby, who ran the town's biggest store, saw it and said, "Why I spent a whole two years studying geography in school, and never learned as much as this overgrown cowpoke has in a week!"

They also had a slick way of learning the times tables and carrying them around with you. This consisted of a varnished cardboard square with numbers one to nine up and across, top and side, and squares from two to eighty-one, which was nine times nine. "Why good God, they slouch along from grade three to grade six teaching them their times tables at that damn school of ours," said Hornaby.

And somebody would say, "Yes, that's where our tax money goes!"

Chapter Three

There was a lot more work when it got cold and the big stove had to be fed. It was a coal stove. There were coal mines close to town, but Mr. Warren used only the best which came from the north in the Bull Mountains, about twenty-five miles by road, where they dug the famous Bear Creek coal. It gave off much black smoke but more heat and no clinkers and little ash. It was on the road to Roundup and to the Judith Basin, the Musselshell, and the badlands where rustlers still hung out despite expeditions of whole armies of vigilantes. The fellows said Kelly should write up many tales about these vigilantes, seeing he had won a "superior" rating for rhetoric from the Institute.

"Why don't you?" encouraged Mr. Warren. The lawyers said Kelly should take notes, sort out each man's tale as he told it, and organize them all later. Kelly did spend some time at this, asking and listening, and writing it down in his freight-office bedroom after closing time, which for him meant ten o'clock even though the saloon stayed open until twelve. He also worked at it on Saturdays and especially on paydays.

You really knew when payday came at the railroad. Some of the men would gamble away every cent they had earned, and next morning their wives arrive, looking for Mr. Warren to get the money back. Well, he'd return it, provided they'd lost it at The Bank and hadn't spent it at The Venus. Often they'd spent it with the girls and would go home and lie, saying they'd gambled it away at The Bank, in which case Mr. Warren would be very polite and say no, they must have spent it elsewhere. He wouldn't say where, although they'd come right out and call him a liar. Eventually somebody would tell them, and it must have been a terrible blow to them as wives. There was drink and gambling at The Venus, too. They had faro and similar games on big nights, and music, but the implication was they'd been cavorting with the demimonde, paying for what was to be had at home, free. And they'd have special music and foods, oysters from the East coast and crab from the West, and girls dressed to the nines! Salesmen with the finest silks would call, and the girls bought lavishly, as did Madam Riddell.

Mostly, Kelly sat around the saloon and watched the men play cards, eating one sandwich from the free lunch — always when Mr. Warren was there. He didn't want to graze on the house in secret, and every afternoon at a quarter to five Mr. Gerrigan, the head bartender, would ask him to go to the drug store for his medicine.

Mr. Gerrigan was tall, with the most silvery hair, and he wore the whitest of starched shirts, jackets, and collars with always a dark blue tie and diamond stud. He never drank on the job, only when somebody invited, and he took a nip of beer — about twice the size of a whiskey glass. Then, at a quarter of five, he would lay fifty cents on the cigar case and it would be Kelly's job to go up to Stepp's Pharmacy for his prescription. Stepp would go in the back room and return with a folded paper of powders which he put in a paper sack, and give Kelly five cents change. Kelly would hustle back and deliver it at the cigar counter, and Mr. Gerrigan would put the powders away and say, "This is for you," and gave Kelly the five cents.

"Thank you, Mister Gerrigan," Kelly always said.

At exactly five — they had railroad time, set by telegraph — Mr. Gerrigan would balance the till, write down the figures,

22

and turn the bar over to Tom Willard, the night-shift man. He would take off his white coat and drop it in the soiled laundry, change to suit coat, pocket the sack with its paper of powders, and leave for his room at the Globe Hotel over the hardware store. In about forty-five minutes out he would come, all changed, swinging a walking stick, and somebody watching from The Bank would say, "Well, that sure fixed him up!"

Where he went was to visit his lady friend, Mrs. Celia Blanchard, milliner. Most nights they would have supper at the Hong Kong Cafe in a booth with the drapes closed, smoking heavy Turkish tobacco, Player's Ovals, silk-tipped, which had to be ordered special. But Mrs. Blanchard, being a decent woman, couldn't be seen doing it in public.

So passed the winter.

Kelly graduated from Burlington with a "superior" rating and received his diploma, step one. He was now eligible for the Latin, or High, School for which he had laid aside the money from his daily wage and tips from errands and by wheeling baggage from the depot in the railroad hand cart. Then something happened that really rocked him.

He knew something was wrong when he came to work. There were men standing around and watching. Something was going on at the front stairway of The Venus. Two carriages were outside, one belonging to Art Follick who was combination coroner and Justice of the Peace, and the other to Dr. Garfield.

"They found her sitting in a chair with the bottle beside her," Kelly heard someone say. "They could smell it. Like almonds. Prussic acid."

"She was all dressed up, just sitting there!"

Kelly knew, with a terrible knot inside him, who it had been even before somebody said, "It was that Annie girl, the dark, quiet one."

Then a fellow named Harboldt whom Kelly had never much

liked said, "Aw! Those whores! They're always killin' themselves."

It was like being kicked in the stomach.

"You!" said Warren. "Leave my place and don't come back."

Harboldt, shocked, looked around for support, but Warren wasn't the man to give the same order twice. He hooked a thumb at the door, and Harboldt slinked out. He stood outside a while, and Warren went back to whatever he'd been doing. Kelly was sure proud of him that day.

"They don't argue with Warren!" Mr. Gerrigan said later. "Used to run a place in Deadwood. Partners with Sheridan in Butte. Hired Hickok one time . . . lookout for their faro bank."

"Wild Bill Hickok?"

"The same. Fired him, too!"

"Holy smokes!" said Kelly.

The suicide had really shaken Kelly. He had to get off by himself. What he feared was that they might ask him to be a pall bearer. He didn't have anything suitable to wear. At any rate, such fears were unjustified. Mr. Warren, the local newspaper editor, a retired rancher named Kid Reid, and others served. They rode in a special carriage. The undertaker and Mr. Carlyle led the way on foot, then came the hearse, and Madame Riddell and all her girls in their finery in two carriages, also buggies with gamblers, bartenders, some railroad men, and others Kelly didn't know, and a big contingent on foot, Kelly among them.

Mr. Carlyle was to deliver the oration at the grave, no minister having come forward. If they'd had a resident priest and she'd been Catholic, Kelly wanted to think he would have handled it, but all they had was a priest or brother who came up every other week from the Fort Custer Agency. There was a receptacle to drop money for a memorial of carved marble with a granite base. Kelly dropped in a silver dollar.

He stood sort of at the back of the crowd. It was very quiet and nobody smoked. It was so quiet you could hear the winter birds stirring in the cottonwood and box elder trees, still leafless with buds just starting to swell. You could smell the trees and the river. From far away, a train whistled.

Carlyle spoke in a beautiful, clear voice, and not one bit woebegone to forgive this poor sister this and that. What he did mainly was read from a text by Robert Ingersoll, "The Great Commoner," about life being but the rock that "separates the cold and silent vale of two eternities," and how "we try in vain to call beyond the depths, but nothing answers save the echo of our wailing cry." He spoke for about five minutes, also quoting Pascal in French: *"Le silence éternel de ces espaces infinis m'effraie,"* which he translated: "The eternal silence of those infinite spaces terrifies me." Kelly liked especially how Carlyle had pronounced silence — sort of like see-lawnce, with the accent on the last, long syllable. All this was quoted in the newspaper, and Warren said afterwards with considerable satisfaction that all "preachers were given something to shoot at!"

Kelly could drop a silver dollar in the monument fund partly because he had discovered a new source of income, not unlike the one Ma had with her dried peach pie. Every day at a certain time the westbound Limited, the Northern Pacific's crack passenger train, stopped for a major cleaning, watering, and fueling. Express was unloaded in carts. The blackest porters in the snowiest of jackets stood by the doors, tending the steps, and passengers, particularly those in the Pullman Palace cars, would get off to stretch their legs.

"Son," said a Billings arrival, "I wonder if you'd go in the coach and bring me my Saint Paul paper." He gave him the seat number, and Kelly had no trouble finding it.

"Whyn't you clear all these papers out?" a porter said. "They just lie and get stomped on."

Hence he started going from end to end in the train, day coaches

25

often more productive than sleepers, gathering all the dropped and sat-on newspapers, a huge armful, sometimes requiring two trips, and took them to the room off the beanery where the waitresses ironed things — he could smooth and even damp-iron them like new, after the girls showed him how it was done — and he sold them around town. Subscribers who got theirs through the post office had to wait longer.

It seemed everybody in Billings came from somewhere else, and one day a fellow rose right up out of the barber chair at Murray's, lather and all, to say, "Wait! Is that the Fergus Falls *Spray-Clarion?*" It was his old home town and he hadn't seen a paper in months! The same happened with the Wadena *Jezebel*. What a name! So he got to watching for papers from all sorts of places, asking fifteen cents for them, saying they were rare and it was a hard job finding them.

Not wanting to sign up for Latin or Science school, Kelly decided to take the detective course from the Chicago School of Detection. Since there wasn't much to do between lessons, Kelly answered an ad to become a railroad telegrapher. A key and sounder were included, but Kelly found he had to furnish his own batteries, which were expensive. Fortunately, the depot night agent was employed by Western Union and gave him his old ones. You could drill holes near the bottom and set them in brine which boosted them back to full power, but they didn't last so long. Kelly practiced, and spent time on the railroad key, when cut off from the line.

"For God's sake, don't ever practice unless that switch is cut or you'll get the Limited wrecked," the depot night agent warned, but he was happy to leave Kelly in charge while he sat around in the local beanery to josh with the girls and drink coffee.

Kelly's detective course wasn't much. He had in mind becoming a railroad detective and riding all over for free, but the school wanted him to practice shadowing suspects, which in Billings might get you shot.

"The size you're growing, Kelly, they'll make you a yard bull," said Stephenson, one of the night-shift bartenders.

Well, they had his money, so Kelly finished the course, and along toward spring somebody left a freight-house window open, and two tramps got in and stole a case of Three Star Hennessey. Kelly happened to hear them and saw them hustling across the tracks to the river with their loot. He went for the night marshal. ("Don't attempt to make arrests yourself," the course had warned, "quickly contact the proper authorities.") Anyway, they were caught. They'd drunk up about half of one bottle and were tipsy. The funny part was the brandy had been expressed to The Bank! It made Kelly sort of a hero. Anyway, there was no more laughing about his detective course.

The telegrapher course was much harder. Kelly got so he could send, slowly but fairly accurately, but he couldn't take. He'd sit around the depot and hear the sounder going, the operators up and down the line talking to one another. Or they'd cut in on the news line to see what was happening. One night, with nothing better to do, the depot night agent cut in on the Associated Press news wire and transmitted an account of how Patrick "Horseshoe" Kelly had captured the Three Star Gang of Brandy Bandits single-handed. He added that Kelly was a graduate of the Chicago School of Detection. When Kelly heard about it, he thought it would only go down to Miles City where they would know it was a joke, but it was relayed on to Chicago because it had a Chicago angle. A Chicago weekly printed the story with pictures, paying the sender five cents a word. Of course, it wasn't actually Kelly's picture. It was just some cut of a handsome young fellow they picked up out of the files, but **PATRICK KELLY** (thank God they didn't know about the Eugene) **THWARTS BRANDY BANDITS** was the headline and the article mentioned his being a graduate of the Chicago School

27

of Detection (whose advertising the paper carried).

This story was circulated far and wide. "Kid, you're famous!" one transient said upon meeting Kelly. "I read about you in Spokane Falls!"

Chapter Four

They were doing a lot of carpentry work at the freight house and Kelly feared he might be shoved out, but such was not the case. The company mining engineer, Jack Ridgeway, was having a small lab built for the coal tests he ran — how much carbon, shale, ash, sulphur, iron — which affected its use for the new power-grate locomotives.

"Encroached on you, Kelly," said Ridgeway, who was about twenty-five years old.

Kelly took to him first thing, in spite of his dude accent, Philadelphia by way of California. Ridgeway (he said to call him Jack) got out a small transit. It was actually a compass with the E and W on the wrong sides — Kelly didn't know why — and a mirror that folded back, and a high front sight. After about two minutes, Jack told Kelly he had his declination all wrong, which meant the magnetic pole. He himself had until lately been up to his butt in mud where they were hydraulicking in California and was glad to be up north where the summers weren't 110 degrees in the shade.

"Well, we had it fifty-odd below some years back," Kelly told him, "so it will average out."

"When that day comes, I'll be far gone," Ridgeway said.

Kelly gathered that nobody traveled like a mining engineer. If there was a wholly evil climate in the world, they'd be sent there.

"You wait!" Ridgeway continued. "They'll strike platinum in the Arctic Circle. Why? Because there's no law of God nor man north of the fifty-three."

After being allowed to work the hand transit, and try to get through his head why the E and W were reversed, Kelly showed Ridgeway his multiplication square. Ridgeway said it was the slickest thing he had ever seen and what he himself needed, seeing he couldn't add or subtract on a slide ruler. He could divide, do square roots, cube roots, and of course all the trig functions, but no addition.

Kelly looked at the slide rule and thought he'd go crazy before learning even what things were for, let alone use it. But Ridgeway said nobody used all the scales. They were there chiefly so an engineer could show off and maybe get his pay raised.

Then he said, "Wait a minute! Here's one I'll give you." And it was an old one that had been stepped on, but could be fitted together with glue, good as new. Jack said he'd been using it just by holding it together by thumb until he got a new one.

Ridgeway had arrived at a flush time. Kelly hardly got to spend an hour at the saloon all day because of the commercial travelers. It was 'stock-up period' for the stores, getting ready for the cattle shipping. Kelly was kept on the go, wheeling a depot cart around for the traveling men, many of whom came only once per year when the merchants put in kingly orders for the finest quality goods. Back East, Kelly was told, farmers bought cheap-jack stuff, but cattlemen demanded only the best. By God, when you were out on the long lonesome, you didn't want gloves busting at the seams — hence only the finest buckskin by the bale of forty-eight pairs, assorted; also sides of the best leather for saddle strings, oak leather soles; canned milk by the case (cattlemen never milked a cow); kegs of vinegar, boxes of dried fruits, kerosene which always was loaded on the side of the wagons in case it got loose; and wagons in tandem which required

"Finished. Reading law down at Forbes and Carlyle."

So much for that!

Eventually, things settled down. The rains came just enough to stop the coal drilling, so Mr. Ridgeway left for some other job. The Northern Pacific had mineral deposits of many kinds, a plethora of riches, all coming with the land grant. Kelly put in for the position of a railroad detective, using Ridgeway's name as a reference, also Mr. Blackmore's. He had already talked to Mr. Carlyle who was mildly favorable; Carlyle had said he guessed Kelly would have to get it out of his system, and he would write a letter. When no letter was forthcoming, Kelly thought nothing would come of it, but one day Mr. Van Schuyler, vice-president of the line, arrived in his private coach, checking the Billings cattle yards. It was one of the line's main sources of revenue, and danged if he didn't ask Kelly to dinner — at seven o'clock — and he was feasted on iced potato-cream soup, squab with truffles, and wines, French pastries similar to Ma's pie except for more crust. It was all served by the blackest Negro waiters, with faces that looked like fresh-polished stoves clad in the whitest, stiff-starched jackets Kelly'd ever seen. And a different wine for each course, and how about a cordial? So Kelly said, "Here goes," and asked for green Chartreuse.

Did that snap their eyes open! They had it, and Kelly took the little-bitty glassful down in one swallow. Yow! He felt like he'd been struck by lightning. They were all watching him, and he sat there not turning a hair. Later he learned it was 110 proof.

"How was it?" Mr. Van Schuyler asked.

"Fine!" said Kelly. But he decided to confess. "I'd heard of it. Always wanted to try it out. Heard tell it was an elixir. Looked it up in a book in the lawyers' office. Forbes, Forbes, and Carlyle." Kelly wanted to get the name in, them being the company's law firm.

"I think Elixir Chartreuse is something like 130 proof. You

could get on as a fire-eater."

Kelly didn't really expect anything to happen with his detective application, Van Schuyler notwithstanding. He was sure Schuyler thought of him as just a big, tall cowboy, staring sort of pop-eyed at the world. However, about two weeks later Kelly was summoned to St. Paul with a letter containing a railroad pass, although not Pullman or chair car, just the day coach. As it turned out, Kelly arrived with five others just as green as himself, or worse. He was accepted for training, along with two of the other five.

The training wasn't much. Mainly it had to do with the filling out of forms, and not to do this or that. He was issued a gun, a double-action Smith & Wesson .38, which was a good piece of equipment. He was then instructed never, never to fire the first shot. In fact, it was just as well not to fire at all, because in a train coach a flying bullet was likely to get the company in a costly lawsuit because, even if you hit your target, a robber say, you were as likely to hit a passenger. Kelly was made to store his Tipo hat and riding shoes, and had to be garbed from the railroad stores. He got a badge, a card-in-isinglass certification, and was put to riding on day coaches — not on the main line, but little spur lines.

Kelly was to buy his ticket on the train and keep tabs whether the conductor issued a punched ticket, or just put the money in his own pocket, in which case Kelly was to get the number on his cap and report him. In other words, he was a spy, and he didn't take to that at all. Then he was switched to a Pullman, which was more complicated. Fellows would board with fake tickets, or just hand-written notes, and get berths, and you had to keep watch if the conductor at one division point had words with one on the next and indicated the passengers for whom the fix was on. Kelly had heard about this before, but it was hard to catch them doing it. He wondered what they'd say if he braced some conductor and demanded his cut or otherwise he'd blow the scheme, but of course he didn't. The truth was, they generally spotted him for what he was, a young fellow in a cheap company suit who didn't generally have a Pullman ticket, so he didn't actually catch anybody. Just got treated like dirt.

The head of security called Kelly on the carpet, saying he didn't seem to be working out but, nonetheless, he was going to promote him to Detective First Grade and let him carry the loaded pistol in a holster. It was a latch-down holster, not the sort anyone would use if he relied on being fast on the draw. Kelly was also issued some heavy winter garments. The reason for this was soon plain: he was to ride outside on the tender, back behind the coal where the water was stored, to guard against robbers taking over the train.

It sure was cold back there, with a lot of snow and rain. It would mix with ash and blow down on him. Sometimes he got so numb and blind from cinders and gritty rain (it didn't even need to be real rain, the steam would turn to a dirty wet ice and coat him over) that he had to squat down and get a hand-hold and pray not to go to sleep for fear that he would fall between tender and baggage coach. When he couldn't stand it any longer, he tried to move in with the engine crew, but they would run him out. He never saw men so mean as railroad engineers. They didn't knuckle under to anybody, not even the conductor. An engineer was as close to being a monarch of the rails as there was, and they drove the firemen of which there might be two on the fast runs. One fireman, just plain tuckered out from shoveling, had said to his engineer, "What time is it, Mister Johnson?" And did the engineer look at his watch? No, sir! He pointed to the steam gauge and said, "There's your watch . . . nine hundred pounds."

It got real cold, down around zero, even when there was warmth blown from the engine and from the heavy steam pipes connected to the coaches. You couldn't imagine all the things that coupled the engine with the rest of the train. Kelly learned this well because one fearfully cold and steamy night he got down in the "blinds" for shelter. This was the "blind baggage," the great door to the baggage and mail coach, next behind the engine. In fact, "riding the blinds" was a noted boast of the real fast-train hoboes, or stiffs as they liked to call themselves, the elite. At any rate, that night it dropped down fearfully cold; it was in eastern Dakota, between Watertown and Sioux Falls, and they were weaving and clanking along at about fifty miles an hour. Kelly fell into a sort of trance. When the train ended that part of its run, Kelly was found by a couple of yard bulls, or railroad police. They ordered him to get down, but he couldn't move. His back had become frozen to the door. So they jumped in and started beating him with billies and, when he still couldn't get out, they pulled him down across the couplings with one terrible two-man yank, tearing the back right out of his mackinaw. Then, when he was on the ground, they still weren't finished, but tried to make him stand up by kicking him.

"On your feet, you long-eared son-of-a-bitch!"

"I was froze fast!" Kelly pleaded.

He tried to tell them he was there as a detective. To prove it, not locating his badge, he pulled his revolver instead. Did they give him room then! The yard bulls were armed with clubs, not guns. The railroad didn't want bullets flying around the yards, killing some waiting passenger.

Still in his backless mackinaw (and armed), they led him to the Railroad Hotel where he ate two orders of sausages, eggs, and hotcakes, slept for twelve solid hours, and got up in time to ride the cushions back to St. Paul. When he was unable to see Mr. Van Schuyler, he packed up and boarded the westbound, using badge and gun as his ticket. Not wanting to drag his tail into Billings, where everybody would ask questions, he detrained at Miles City. He managed to hire on riding for the Slash D, a horse outfit in the Powder River country, and stayed on there for over a year, making his fame as a cowboy during the following winter.

How this came about was due again to a very heavy snowstorm — one far worse than the one that had driven him into the cave with the mother bear and her two cubs. It came before Christmas, once more the first heavy storm of the year. Kelly and a brace of 'punchers, Charlie Fallon and Jack Snow who was called the "Two Dot Kid," rode into Miles City. They crossed the railroad tracks which were so banked over with snow you couldn't see the rails. Miles City had an electric light plant and it was all ablaze — lights looking big as wash tubs through the storm. They rode up to Bufton's Powder River Bar. Tying their horses' rumps to the wind, in they went.

Kelly happened to be wearing a pair of Mexican Peso-roweled spurs, actually silver dollars made big for the Oriental trade, each filed to sixty-four long points and bored to hang loose so they'd jingle. Kelly striding to the fine Circassian mahogany bar, Tom Bufton's pride and joy, tossed one leg over the edge in joy and relief. With a war whoop, tip-toe with snow on the sole making him six-six if he was an inch, he swung that spur and brought it around in a big sweep, pivoting the while, imprinting on that bar what was known as an unwound watch-spring curve. That night Tom Bufton was nearly mad enough to get his forty-five out and shoot Kelly.

Bufton tried then, and for weeks after, to polish the scars off, but pretty soon people were coming just to see it. Even passengers off the Limited stopped to look, among them a professor who declared it to be the perfect diminishing calculus spiral curve, heretofore deemed unattainable. It was photographed and reproduced by the new photo-engraving process and as such published far and wide, many times with a pen and ink drawing of Kelly in three-quarter profile. It was "Horseshoe" Kelly all over again!

"Well, some of us are born famous, and some of us have fame shoved on us!" Kelly concluded.

Chapter Five

Kelly kept composing careful letters to the Chief of Security of the Northern Pacific, asking for his back pay, with no answer. He even wrote Mr. Van Schuyler personally, but all letters were a waste of stamps at two cents each until George Sample, the postmaster, suggested he put "cc: Forbes, Forbes & Carlyle, Attys., Billings and Helena, Montana" at the bottom. Kelly did, and did he ever get an answer!

"Dear Patrick," the V. P. wrote, telling how he regretted the oversight and all about Kelly's letters having been misplaced by lesser talents in all the hurly burly. They sent the money, which came to $88.60, and he still had the revolver.

About the same time out of the blue Kelly also heard from Jack Forbes, asking him to drop in at the Helena office. He had an idea the attorney might get him on as a probation officer, or something, at the U. S. Marshal's office with which Forbes was very close. Carlyle, still lawyer for the Northern Pacific, gave him a pass good for ninety days and Kelly wasted no time getting to Helena where he rode by omnibus up famed Last Chance Gulch, Helena's main street, and was let off in front of a stone building of impressive façade. He then went three stories up by hydraulic elevator to the law offices that occupied half the floor and simply reeked of importance.

"Kelly!" Jack Forbes cried in greeting. Kelly had come at a very good time. It seemed that since McKinley had been elected

41

over Bryan for president, Montana had a new U. S. Marshal who was absolutely desperate for deputies, one of which fit Kelly's description exactly. "Yes," said Jack Forbes, who had moved to Helena permanently, "only the best for the new United States Marshal!" There were certain formalities, such as informing the marshal himself, but Thomas S. O'Connell, newly appointed U. S. Marshal for Montana, surely wouldn't "turn his back on a man named Patrick Kelly."

As much as anything, it went to show how the railroad stood politically. Jack Forbes took Kelly around and introduced him to O'Connell, a fine-looking man, fairly bristling with portly charm, who seemed to make a habit of handing everybody a cigar.

"This is the man I've been telling you about," said Forbes.

"Welcome aboard!" the marshal said. It was just that easy! Apparently, big holders such as the Northern Pacific and the mining interests were each entitled to at least one deputy because all Kelly had to do was sign some forms and take an oath which was performed before Judge Millbank.

Afterwards they sat around talking about something or other up in the Flathead country where the homesteaders who had flocked in with the Great Northern were having trouble with the Flatheads. The Flathead reservation had been moved from the Bitterroot, prime ranch and timber land, to the wilder region up north which was more to their liking because of the fish and game. There was even a buffalo or two. But there had been a mix-up, as usual. The reservation had been tossed open to homesteading "by the Swedes" with the result the Flatheads' allotments under the Dawes Act had run head-on against the Swedes' claims under the Homestead Act and the new timber claims besides. There had been shooting with no fatalities as yet, and lawsuits, generally concerning water rights. So far the lawsuits were in the state courts.

"Nothing has been brought here, thanks be to God," said Judge Millbank. "We hope you're a good man with our red brothers, Marshal."

After a second, Kelly realized he was the Marshal. "Oh, I get along with the Indians, all right," he said. "Every time I go home I ride right past Custer's grave. It reminds me to be careful."

That was how it started for Kelly. He was given a brass badge, and the lawyers fixed it up so he could live in the Montana Club — which wasn't a club like the Masons or Odd Fellows, but only a place where the mining and cattle kings and the big merchants ate and sometimes roomed. How much it cost, he didn't ask. It seemed understood that the cost might be something the lawyers and their clients would worry about, so Kelly moved in.

"Understand, Kelly," Jack Forbes said in the sternest of voices, "you are now an officer of the U. S. Department of Justice and of the federal court, and in no manner, shape, or *praescriptum* are you to favor any railroad whatsoever!"

"I'll work on it," he said.

The very next day he got sent off, not to the Flatheads but to Fort Benton, the old-time head of navigation on the Missouri River. The fort was now much outflanked by the new Montana Central railroad. It didn't go into town, but followed the high prairie hills with a view of the river, so you had to take a hack one mile to the city proper, a fact that had the residents much embittered. But it was a real nice town, old and cool and shady by the great river, with many mansions and lawns belying its wild reputation (one shooting per day on the average, at least during the steamboat season). Kelly was to take into custody a Cree half-breed charged with attempted homicide, an act performed up north in the Marias River country.

Kelly didn't know all the facts. Apparently it was a homestead-

43

allotment dispute, the same as he'd been hearing about, but this case involved a Cree-French half or quarter breed, a Métis. This man, a tall fellow named Louis LeMo and also known as The Piegan Kid, was deemed to have some Piegan, or Blackfoot, blood as well as French and Cree. It was because the Piegans were a U. S. tribe that LeMo had been registered such and, hence, had been able to file on an allotment. It was this filing by LeMo and his ten-year-old son by a Piegan woman that had caused the trouble.

"You new, U. S. Marshal Kelly?" asked Louis LeMo. "Me, Piegan Kid. You call me that, heh?"

"All right. Piegan Kid it is!"

"So. You good man. You know how I know you good man?"

"How you know I'm a good man, Kid?"

"Because I read about you in paper!" It shouldn't have surprised Kelly that this part-Cree, part-French, part-Piegan and part God-only-knew-what else would read a newspaper, but it did. "I read about you make great sign, calculus curve, with Mexican spur in bar. You do that?"

"Yes, I did it. But I claim no credit. Pure accident. I came in from a snowstorm with ice caked on my boots, giving me an added inch, and I was wearing Mexican spurs."

"Sure, but you do this thing, M'shu' Marshal! Deep inside brain," he tapped his head, "you savvy?"

"Sure, I savvy."

"You surprise I read newspaper? Read English, United States, French, Cree, Latin, whole works. Read Square Cree, you savvy? This ol' tam writing, my people. Métis, French-Cree. Also Piegan. Ol' red-coat police chase my people down from Canada."

He pronounced it with the accent on the last syllable. Indians did that, even if they weren't French. Because most Indian names were accented on the first syllable, the Indians accented European names on the final syllable.

"Kid been here, this country, long tam. Keep books for Sisters of Providence at Fort Shaw School. You savvy? They French Sisters, Holy Sisters Providence, Mother house, Montreal. They speak French, lak Kid. Keep books in Square Cree and French, both. What you call double entry." He laughed. "This joke!"

Kelly laughed. "Why two sets of books?"

The Kid glanced around as if he suspected eavesdroppers. "So can burn one set books ol' government come snoop! Ver' private thing, Sisters' books. Ver' rich order. Plenty money from ol' Canada-Pacific, Great Northern, both. Built hospital, care for sick. Those fellow, Lord Strathcone, Jim Hill, Jaypee Morgan, ver' thankful to Holy Sisters! Give them plenty land, you savvy? Ol' church, Pope, also government fellow in Washington, Ottawa . . . they maybe lak get hands on Holy Sisters and money. Ho-ho-ho! Play hell, read Square Cree books!"

"What if you got hit by a stray bullet?"

"Then they still have, maybe, English, French book."

Kelly couldn't help thinking that this fellow might not be above saving his hide by burning both sets of books, because what he had here was one smart Indian!

The Kid evidently guessed this and said, "Oh, ver' great sin . . . what-you-say? . . . stack deck on Holy Sisters. Kid suffragan brother! You know what that is? Say Mass when priest not around. They send, maybe Irish priest. Irish priest get ver' lonesome at French-Indian mission school. Pretty soon he just up and leave. Maybe just turn up in San Francisco, Saint Paul, Minnesota. You know? So Kid say Mass. 'When two men have bread in my name, there I be also.' " He crossed himself. "This right in Holy Book, Marshal! So it okay I say Mass, hear confession. Those Sisters! Ha! They have no sins! Have impure reflections, you savvy? Kid listen behind screen. Give ten Our Fathers, Hail Marys. Also say Mass for the dead. Requiem in Latin! Know all masses in Latin. Every tam you learn one language, next come easier. Say Mass for Ascension Thursday, Pentecost, whole works. Ol' Canada, she plenty mad those Sisters have all that land, gift from railroad. Always try charge tax! Canada Pacific Railroad lend them lawyers. You have friends, lawyers, Marshal? You maybe get me lawyers down in Capital. You do that?"

"Sure, I'll see to it you get a lawyer. Best in the whole state."

"By gare, you friend of Kid! They try hang me, maybe for shoot those fellow. Damn Swede. He jump my son claim."

"He didn't die, Kid. He's up and limping around."

"Very bad thing he do, try jump allotment. I have lil' boy, you know? Also squaw? Up on Blackfoot reserve? We all get land, allotments under Dawes Act. You savvy? He try jump ver' best part. Water rights, too. You get me good lawyer, Kelly?"

"The best!"

Kelly took a great liking to the Piegan Kid. It was actually fun hearing him and realizing that he, Kelly, could understand French, Latin, Cree and Piegan when it was strung together with English and some sign language. He resolved to get a lexicon of French and English. He would learn just the basic words. Whenever you bogged down, you said "God-damn" or "lak-so, you savvy?" And you looked a man right in the eyes and knew that he understood. When the Kid glimpsed the first sign of bafflement, he stopped and had another go at it with different words and signs.

"They call this *lingua franca*," said Kelly. "Your language."

"Who say this?"

"The French. I read it in a book."

"What book this?"

"*The Count of Monte Cristo*. It was written by a Frenchman named Dumas. Doo-mah."

"Sure, I know a man one tam, Dumas. Not same man. This fellow he know notheeng. He drive what you call Red River cart. He haul freight all way to Fort Walsh, Canada, you know?"

"Yes, I know."

"This long-tam ago. Kid maybe twelve year ol'. Ol' Canada Pacific, she chase all Cree 'breeds off land. Ver' bad thing my people, ol' railroad." He brightened and said, "Good thing for Holy Sisters, Montreal. Ol' Archbishop, cardinal, Montreal . . . he walk quiet around those Sisters! They have plenty land!"

Kelly could see he was very happy to see the Sisters wielding all that power. Kelly said, "Ol' money, she make the mare go."

"Oh-ho! You head, she work all tam. You carry those slide rule! Land surveyor, he carry slide rule. Some tam you teach Kid. He maybe teach you Square Cree. You going put Kid in jail?"

"We'll see about it. Talk to the lawyers."

"They get good marshal when they find you, Kelly. You get Kid, by gare, free train ride to Helena."

"Food, too. Good meal on the dining car. Compliments of ol' President. Great White Father in Washington. You savvy?"

"Sure. Also Teddy Roosevelt. He little white father. He live one tam over in Dakota? Run cattle? Cowboy?"

"He played at it."

"Sure."

Kelly took the Kid back to Helena where a young U. S. Attorney took over. The damned fool had him locked in a stone jail. Kelly could hardly believe it. He called on the Kid and found an altogether different man from the one he had picked up in Benton. It had never occurred to Kelly that he'd actually be locked up. You never locked up an Indian. Jailed Indians would die. You'd come around one morning and they'd be dead. No reason — just dead.

Kelly got the key and paid the Kid a visit. They played some *bezique,* a French game similar to seven-spot dix pinochle. Kelly lost two dollars and left at dark, about nine.

"Well, good bye, Kid."

"Good bye, Kelly."

Kelly locked the door, or almost — he left the lock bolt caught outside the arbor and, next morning when they brought breakfast, the Kid was gone and the bed had not been slept in.

"You can see the lock was turned," Kelly said. "It was that damned arbor. It must have caught the bolt. Well, all hell can't find him now!"

The U. S. Attorney was shrill-voiced, angry. It was his first case and Kelly, "that damn' shavetail marshal," had let the prisoner escape. It was Kelly's first round with the term shavetail which he learned was an Army term for someone just commissioned. They used it for bob-tail mules, too, and it was not exactly flattering. Kelly made no defense, that is, not directly; but he did remark to the judge that it might be lucky because if you lock up an Indian, particularly behind stone walls, why, one morning you'd come in and find him dead. No cause. No strangulation. No wound or contusion. Just dead. Well, what then? A dead Indian. In this case part Piegan! The Piegan-Blackfoot claimed to be a separate nation. Had their own treaty with the Department of State! All this occurred to him as he ran it around in his mind, like dice bounding around the sides of a craps table, and he said, carrying out the metaphor, "It's only a question of time before it comes up snake eyes."

"The judge is very upset," Marshal O'Connell told him later, loud and stern so the shavetail U. S. Attorney could hear him. "But you're new at the job, and I'm taking that into consideration."

Kelly was properly chastised but that night, when he returned to his quarters at the Montana Club, there was a bottle of Irish malt whiskey on the table, its source a mystery. That was Kelly's first case. The young attorney was very short with him, but the others were more understanding and the word went around that he was very good with Indians. Indian cases were not coveted by other deputy marshals, so they fell to his lot. He was particularly engaged with the Flatheads. Their land and water-right cases more than exceeded all other tribal legalisms combined. The water flowed clear and cold. Homesteaders claimed a certain number of "miners' inches," and the Flatheads pointed to their treaty which said "as long as the streams do run and the winds blow. . . ." White farmers wanted to irrigate, and the Indians wanted to fish. Dams and weirs were built, and the Indians, seeing the trout and salmon gasping, tore them down. Charges were made. Briefs prepared. County judges found for the white ranchers. The Indians appealed to the federal court in Helena. This decision, in turn, was appealed, ending time and again at the appellate in San Francisco. "The voice may be the voice of Jacob, but the hand is the hand of Esau" was a comment often made.

The implication was that Kelly wanted it so, wanted the free trip to San Francisco, Indian in tow. "Esau" liked to attend the plays. He tried to look wearied and out of sorts on his return, but it was hard not to mention such names as Maurice Barrymore, John Drew, Maxine Elliott, Modjeska, Weber and Fields, the Flying Sullivans, William Gillette. The Indians always wanted to go in summer, which was the San Francisco winter, fine and cool when the New York theatres were sticky hot. All in all it worked out very well.

Chapter Six

The seasons passed and Kelly fell in easily with being a deputy U. S. marshal. He didn't mind at all working with the Indians, a task no one else wanted. He didn't mind at all taking their side against the damned agents — and you had to wonder who *they* thought they were representing? He enjoyed it when the agents appealed the decisions of the state court, and he had to take some chief to the U. S. appellate court in San Francisco. He complained about it, of course, but the Indians asked for him, and he said it was little enough for a white man to do, considering the hash they'd made of things with their reservation, letting it be mixed in with the homesteads like two decks of cards.

In town, he liked to hang out at the assay offices. Helena had three, including the U. S. Army office where, monthly, they cast ingots of pure gold — generally, these days, from one of the big hardrock mines. There were placer mines, however, and some very rich vein outcrops which generally played out at about thirty feet. "Blowouts," the miners called them.

One day at Miller Bros. he saw a piece of pure gold. It had come from the riffles of a sluice on Nelson Gulch but was fresh from some vein and had some of the original quartz attached. The assayers beat it out with a hammer and took a small bit for assay, which ran a surprising 985 fine. It was worth $115, and Kelly bought it from the owner saving him the brassage fee charged by the government.

Never melted, still in its natural state, with streaks and layers, it was truly a thing of beauty, much purer than the usual Nelson or Last Chance gold, and worth a premium at the gold beaters in Germany who preferred the natural over the smelter product when that pure.

Kelly learned quite a bit at the assay offices, just standing around and listening. Anyway, he took the specimen to Goodman, the manufacturing jeweler on Main Street and told him he wanted him to make him a badge, and did Goodman spread himself! What he did, more or less following the official design, was to fashion a shield with a star underlay. By beating the gold, not melting and casting it, the natural lines Mother Nature had given it were retained, save the very slight impurity of what the assayers had said was bismuth. At any rate, it was pure gold color in one light, with a purplish iridescence in another; then, under the little balls of the star portion, the jeweler had inlaid some square and oblong bits of lapis lazuli which looked like sapphire but were darker, a more dense blue. Painters like Rembrandt had used it, sparingly, in making their blue pigments. So said Sol Goodman when he showed it to Kelly from several angles, in lamplight and out in the sun; and he engraved a motto in Latin — *Semper Paratus* — which Kelly had himself looked up. It meant "always prepared." Similar to *Semper Fidelis*, only not so common. His own name was engraved, quite like his signature, carefully drawn in Spencerian.

Kelly was reluctant actually to wear this badge around the federal offices, outshining the U. S. Marshal himself, but he wore it as the train moved out of the depot. He wore it and his Tipo hat, tan whipcord, pegged trousers, with stockman's walking shoes which buttoned down the sides (folding buttonhook on watch chain), and a twenty-one-jewel railroad watch, in memory of his old railroading days. The coach window gave a view of

51

the country, broad mountains ascending and descending the Continental Divide, bypass to the Pacific side. One could tell the Pacific slope by the trees, the grass, and the quality of the atmosphere. Blue shadows lay in the gulches.

Kelly went to the smoker and rolled a cigarette of damp, cut-leaf tobacco kept in his parfleche — his Indian money belt of moose bladder and squaw-tanned leather, a gift from the Flathead tribe to show their gratitude to him as protector of hunting and water rights. Chief! White Chief! Yes, they had called him that after his last of several journeys to the great court in San Francisco. The parfleche had but recently held the golden badge; now it held money. The moose bladder, packed with dry grass, would keep him afloat in the deep waters of a mountain river, but was seldom so worn. If not left flat, people might think he was wearing a truss. It also, when freshly rolling cigarettes in tan papers, left the faint odor of the Indian smoke process. He preferred not to think of it: beaten by paddles, smoked in willow, urinated on, and God only knew what else. But, as was said, the sausage fancier should never watch it made! Rembrandt's pigments, for instance. Lapis lazuli well enough, but green? The green of Rembrandt came from copper plates buried in manure piles, poison vertigris, death to how many French and Flemish peasants that the Rembrandts might have the perfect green? Ah, yes. Rose and thorn! The jasmine under which the cobra lies! Kelly thought of life, death, and of eternity as he gazed from the smoking-coach window and saw the dark cliff and white froth rapids as the Little Blackfoot River went by. The Seattle papers had been full of it the day before: **GOLD IN THE KLONDIKE!**

Klondike? There was a new one. It sounded like some place in Holland. Little boy stuck his finger, or something, in the dike and saved the nation. Every year it seemed there was a new gold excitement up in the Yukon. Last year some fellows were in Seattle with their Indian wives tossing nuggets out of hotel

52

windows. Riots ensued. Windows were pressed in. Men cut by glass. The famed totem pole knocked down. Newspapers warned that gold the size of a .45 bullet would weigh twice as much, specific gravity of lead being ten and gold twenty. Sent everybody scrambling to learn what specific gravity meant. Kelly knew, of course, and could point it out in his *Handbook of Chemistry and Physics*, the dog-eared, imitation-leather copy Jack Ridgeway had given him along with, at various times, the slide rule — stepped on — and hand transit with broken glass. Last year, as he recalled, the argonauts and their Indian wives were from somewhere called Carmacks. This time, Klondike.

"It happened last year, too," a man said. "Indian wives tossing nuggets out of the hotel windows. It's whizeroo, if you ask me. The ship owners start a stampede to Skagway or some place, so they can sell passage and supplies."

Kelly tended to agree. Last year Gold Bottom sounded like a reasonable location, but this Klondike was a bit hard to swallow. The dike part made it sound like it was all ready for you to move in and start panning the gold, the hard digging already done.

"There was a strike at Eagle," somebody said. "That's right on the Yukon River. You can go there by river steamer."

"Sure, but by way of the Arctic Sea! They'll get twice as much money!"

And wouldn't you know it! There was an article about Blackmore! *The* Blackmore, "heir to the famed Alhambra in St. Paul." And in stud-horse print: **WELL KNOWN LIQUOR DISTRIBUTOR TO MOVE FAMED ALABASTER PALACE** — apparently stone by stone, beveled French mirrors, mahogany, teak grand piano, by way of Seattle up to the Yukon and thence to Dawson City.

Kelly recalled that John Healy, late sheriff of Chouteau County, had after his defeat for re-election gone to Skagway and thence to St. Michaels at the Yukon's mouth, and purchased a steamboat.

Healy seemed to be pretty *well heeled.* Money he'd laid by, running Fort Whoop-up in Canada, the old whiskey fort, from which he'd been chased by the Royal Northwest Mounted Police.

It was The Piegan Kid who had told Kelly about Healy and Fort Whoop-up. "By gare, those fellow he think he run whole damn' country. Whoop-up, Whiskey Fort, and sheriff, too. He mak trouble for me Fort Shaw. Ol' Sisters put him in place! No arrest Kid!"

It was funny Kelly should think of the Kid, but then he no sooner had walked in to the office that morning than O'Connell had said, "Your Crees must be in trouble again, Kelly. It seems they attacked Fort Assiniboine."

That had to be a joke! Fort Assiniboine was located near the junction of the Montana Central and the Great Northern — it had been built there for no conceivable purpose except to hold the ground in the Blackfoot Treaty Land, which meant a whole hell of a lot of land. It was forty miles in one direction and half the Bear Paw Mountains in the other, a "hay reserve" for cavalry that never fought a battle.

So Kelly had to leave on the Montana Central. He got off at Pacific Junction where the Montana Central joined the Great Northern main line. Only a station and section house, one tree. In the far distance the fort — weather vanes and finials, gem-green creek bottoms, Beaver Creek coming down from the mountains — the Bear Paws, Chief Joseph's last stand. Kelly looked for transportation. There was none.

"You should have gone on to Bull Hook," the station keeper said.

"Why didn't they tell me that on the train?" Kelly asked, sweaty and annoyed.

"Ask them why they didn't tell you."

How could he? The train had pulled away! There was no choice but to walk.

54

"Look out for the rattlesnakes," the station keeper called. "We had a section hand bit last week."

Kelly walked, carrying the small valise he always took along when not knowing how long he would have to stay. It contained a shirt and underwear, socks, some blank forms he might be called on to fill out and, encased in a wool sock, his new .44 caliber Police revolver. He was given his choice of a Smith & Wesson .38, double action and a Colt .44, and he took the Colt — not just for old time's sake (some said it was the caliber that "won the West"), but because it shot cartridges which also fit the .44 Winchester, model 1873 and one could buy cartridges for it everywhere.

It was hot and very dry. He avoided the deep gash arms of some bad lands and finally, after deciding the Fort must be a mirage, he dropped down on the cottonwood-filled valley, green grass, Army fences, brick buildings, very fine and said to be the best-constructed and most useless fort in the West. He showed his badge to a weary-looking sentry and was waved on to the Headquarters house — all brick, red glazed, with much millwork and the finest maple floors.

After a while the commanding officer, Colonel Harrington, summoned him. Apparently the colonel hadn't an inkling as to why he was there.

"They said the Crees were making trouble," Kelly began.

"No. The Crees are the only ones *not* making trouble."

It appeared to Kelly that the colonel had been asleep on a leather couch. He decided to salute and shake hands, both. He stood until an orderly had placed a chair for him. The orderly, a Negro sergeant, withdrew. The colonel sat down at his desk. He then burst forth.

"Oh! Christ Jesus, have we had a terrible forty-eight hours! Our guard house is full, our infirmary is full, and every jail and medical quarters in Bull Hook is full. This was supposed to be

55

the one fort in the nation that never had a battle. Well, they settled that one for us!"

Kelly wondered who "they" were. The colonel decided that Kelly ought to have a drink, and so should he. He had some English whiskey which Kelly guessed was a gift from the redcoats to the north. It was very good stuff.

"Sorry to have brought you up here, Marshal. Guess the captain thought he needed you in Bull Hook."

"What about the Indians?"

"What Indians? Those Crees? They're camped up Beaver Creek. They had some trouble early on at Bull Hook. They were camped and were accused of some petty thievery. Garden truck. No trouble here. We let them camp on the reserve. Ranchers cause the trouble. They think the reserve is open range. The Indians run some horses. Horses don't hurt the range. Cattle, sheep! We even had poaching bands of sheep." He sat holding his glass and shaking his head. "Oh, we've had the devil's own forty-eight hours in at Bull Hook. The outpost of hell!"

Kelly waited.

"It all started when they sent the colored troops. Infantry. This is a cavalry post! All whites. We had some colored orderlies. Cooks, you know. Then they sent this colored infantry. Infantry! What would we do with foot soldiers? That made us about half black and half white. We had to keep them apart. We never gave them liberty at the same time. Well, what happened, we had about twenty men left here. Officers, cooks, ferriers, you know. The rest all went in to Bull Hook and you can imagine! That damned town. It should be burned. Cleansed by fire. The Great Northern admits it! And by God I will burn it if things like this are left to go on. Anyway they all got drinking and they fought. They wrecked one damn honky-tonk. I'm glad! I wish they'd torn it to the ground. They have some Negro whores there, and they won't take on a black man, either. Oh, no!

56

They've raised themselves in class!"

Kelly had to laugh about it, and the colonel decided to laugh, too. The whiskey made him see some of the funny side.

"They fought in the honky-tonks and they fought in the saloons; they fought in the streets and in the alleys."

"Just the soldiers?"

"No! Bull Hook got into it. Cowboys. They thought it was fine. Some of those fellows grabbed the chance and rode horses right into the bars and honky-tonks. They were the only ones armed. They shot around in the air, and shot out some lights. None of our men was armed. None that I know of. Nobody killed. Not as yet. The so-called county hospital is filled. We sent our doctors in. Bull Hook has three doctors, and some practical nurses. It's settling down now. Our men are back, except for a patrol, and about eight in the infirmary. Oh, jeez! Sorry we sent for you. I guess Lieutenant Givens. . . ."

"Well, we thought it must be the Indians. They've been causing trouble here and there. Canadian cases, no reservation. They were camped for a while on the Butte dump, and in Helena."

"They're pretty well situated up Beaver Creek. They catch fish and rustle a cow or two, strays that get on the reserve, our hay reserve. I'd as soon they did. Teach those cattlemen a lesson. They think it's open range. No, I don't mind the Crees. You acquainted out there?"

"I know Louis LeMo, the so-called Piegan Kid. He used to work as bookkeeper and general factotum down at Fort Shaw Mission. Sisters of Charity. Technically he's not Cree. Piegan. Well, he's Métis, that's a racial designation, a third French." Kelly laughed. "I guess you can't be a third anything but, if you could, he'd be it. Officially he's Piegan. Registered. He wanted to take out a claim under the Dawes Act. He has a wife up there on the Piegan-Blackfoot reserve. And some children. They all took out claims. But he likes to hang out with people

57

more French. Got into some shooting trouble. Had to put him in jail. Released. Own recognizance."

"They come around here some and sell things . . . moccasins, medicine bundles, buffalo horn hatracks, you know. I don't mind them at all. By God, I wish Jim Hill would move out of Bull Hook and burn the town. Give it to the French Crees!" The colonel laughed. "I feel better," he said.

Chapter Seven

Kelly borrowed a horse and saddle — an Army saddle, not the sort he was used to, no horn, but plenty of places to tie things — and rode up the creek to the Métis camp. There were old Army tents and Indian teepees, some wickiups — generally called wake-ups which was what you did in them, early, with sun and sometimes rain or snow coming in.

The kids gathered around, tall boys, characteristically slim and alert, smart — oh, the Crees were smart! Dogs, more of a shepherd than a northern husky breed, barked. They had learned to stay away from horses — horses kicked the hell out of them, and the rider was generally handy with a quirt, a real long one that sent them howling. There were probably women and there were children, but most of the women hid in tents or in the brush while the men and children came forth at sight of a stranger. Kelly knew some of the "chiefs" by name — Little Bear, Medicine Calf, and Louis LeMo, the Piegan Kid.

"Kelly! You come up here, long way!" The Kid had a very strong French accent and pretended to lack English entirely if it served his purpose. He knew he couldn't get away with that as far as Kelly was concerned. "You come all this way to see your frien' Louis LeMo? This mak me ver' honored!"

"I thought you fellows were on the warpath . . . attacking the fort."

"Oh, those soldier! Black soldier, white. They fight lak' hell at Bull Hook. No. Kid, he stay long way off. Get in no more trouble. You come up here about big fight? You worry about Kid? You my good frien', Kelly! You leave those jail door unlock. You do these thing for me, Kelly!"

"Yes, and that shavetail United States attorney from back East practically went into convulsions. He would have had my badge!"

"Hey! Goddam!"

"I told them they can't lock up an Indian. I told them a damn' Indian would die. They do, too. Oh, *you* wouldn't. Your French blood would keep you going. They had no cause to hold you, anyway. Nothing that would stand in court."

"Sure. You my frien', Kelly. Some tam Kid, he pay you back. Maybe give you good Cree horse for ride to Klondike. Inside Passage. We have heem, maybe forty, fifty pretty good horse. Maybe sell at high price for Inside Passage. What you think this Inside Passage, Kelly?"

Good God, it had even reached the Métis camp! It should be no surprise. The French Crees were known as the Jews of the Indian world. Ever since the H. B. C. arrived — Hudson's Bay Company, "Here Before Christ" as the old joke put it — the Inside Passage had been water on their wheel. The Kid knew more about the Klondike than anybody. No, it wasn't any place he'd been, or his people had. The name was new to him, but it was just up from Fort Vermilion and he did know about Fort Vermilion.

"You ver' great white fellow, Kelly! Ver' great rock man, geologist!"

"You ought to get on keeping books for Blackmore." It was what Kelly really had wanted to see the Kid about. It was just a hunch he had.

"Who this fella, Blackmore?"

"Oh, he's a liquor salesman I know. He inherited a big, fancy music hall in South Saint Paul. Well, not so big. But a work

60

of art. All alabaster, French mirrors, teakwood, grand piano, the works. He's knocking it down and moving it to the Klondike. By Great Northern to Seattle, by ship to the Yukon river mouth, and by steamboat upriver to Dawson."

"Must be ver' rich!"

"It will cost more money than I thought he had. Must have inherited it from his aunt. She turned to green stone from living on elixir Chartreuse."

"Sure, you good fella, Kelly. This you trouble, too nice fella. You give man shirt off you back, Kelly. You leave jail door open for Louis LeMo! You don' forget you frien's, Kelly. This ver' fine thing. I do you big favor some tam, Kelly!"

"Sure, I know you will. I'll do you a favor if you'd like to get a job and go to the Klondike. If I see Blackmore, I'll tell him to hire you, keep books. You speak French, Indian! Know all about redcoat police. Keep two sets of books, one for him and one for anybody that tried to come around snooping."

"He big crook, Kelly?"

"No, but he has a whole pack of cousins and relatives who may have claims against the estate. They could tie him up in court. But he's no thief. If he were, I would be a fine U. S. Marshal to be boosting him." Kelly added, "Reminds me of my own dear father."

Kelly slept at the fort in the guest accommodations and rode in to Bull Hook with the colonel in his carriage. He had a look at the damage. It seemed to be nothing much. There was some broken glass, mostly being swept up and replaced. Only one man was still in bed. He was a white fellow with a broken leg. The wounded had been brought by ambulance to the fort infirmary, but the broken leg was harder to move. The colonel cursed him out, telling him, "Conroy, you finally got what you deserved." But he left him a supply of tobacco. He was obviously relieved it hadn't been worse. "Two or three dead black men would have

61

been a disaster," he stated.

Kelly sent Blackmore a letter recommending the Piegan Kid and then decided to ride over to have a look at the glaciers of the Lewis Range. He rode over the St. Marie's Pass, and luxuriated in a log lodge at Lake McDonald. He visited the Piegan Reservation. He returned to Helena by stage via Flathead Lake and Missoula.

Helena, like every place on his journey, was excited about the Klondike and the Inside Passage. Flathead horses had doubled in price. Teams especially were in high demand — one heavy team had gone for a reported $375 while saddle horses, just good old-time remuda stock, commanded upwards of a hundred in Calgary. And now there were buyers coming from Seattle! They proposed taking horses to pull heavy freight on the White Pass above Skagway where there was a surveyed railroad route. Heavy freight could be taken by sled as far as Lake Bennett, on the Canadian side. People now talked about Lake Bennett as familiarly as they once did about Lake Erie. They sure made Kelly feel ignorant and out of it. There was said to have been a box carrying a ton of gold swung to the Market Street Wharf in San Francisco.

Spokane, he read, was stripped of horses. Hardly a dray running. Merchants had to haul their freight by depot handcart, which was right in his line. There was another Inside Passage, narrow, north-south lakes, some two hundred miles long, and maybe two miles wide. Horses could be taken, herded along the shore, for use in the portages.

Kelly hadn't truly come to realize — as one might say, subjectively — how big the Klondike was until he saw in the Sunday *New York Herald* that Diamond Jack was on his way thence with Lyla, the "Maid with the Flaxen Hair," and bringing the famed Orloff diamond. It was Borneo orange-yellow, 10.3 in hardness on the Mohs scale, the hardest bit of substance on earth and with the power to glow in the dark. This had been demonstrated in Tiffany's, in a night-blackened room, fading only after a full hour. Yes, Diamond Jack was on his way, with Lyla, with the Orloff, via Seattle and White Pass on the *Olympia.* Cut in segments after arrival in Skagway, this pleasure boat *Olympia* would be transported over the railroad grade and the White Pass, over the lakes and rivers, down not up the Yukon, a saving of two months in time, to be rebuilt and bedazzle the Klondike. Dawson City, that was the name of the town. Named for George Mercer Dawson, of the Canadian Geological Survey, if any were in doubt as to how big Klondike was thought to be.

The land was truly in a state of expectation. Gold in the Klondike had taken Cuba and the war threat off page one. It was the *fin de siècle* and the dawn of the first century to start in two in one thousand seven hundred years, although the calendar would still read 1900.

"Kelly. Telegram! Marshal Patrick E. Kelly?"

The brakeman knew who Kelly was, but he liked to call it out anyway. It was ever an event when a telegram was taken on the fly and for a marshal! Kelly thanked him. One did not tip a flagman, signal man, or brakeman.

"Thank you, Bob." Kelly made it a point to know their names.

"My privilege, Marshal."

Everyone watched him open the flimsy to see whether, perhaps, some bank robber would be taken.

> **Be at the Chequemegon 8PM.**
>
> **Blackmore**

With no change in expression, Kelly put the telegram away in an inside pocket. Arrogant bastard. Presumptive bastard might well be the correct term! Very doubtful parentage. Kelly had never believed all that about the English Army officer father, or the captain of sepoys, dual citizenship. A strong offense is

63

the best defense. And Blackmore was offensive! Be at the Chequemegon at such and such a time! At least he'd asked him to a good restaurant. The Chequemegon, named for the bay on Lake Superior, was Butte's finest.

A gentle trip through the high lake country to Spokane Falls, and still an hour before midnight. Spokane (most people dropped the "Falls") was going full blast as he'd never seen it at that hour on week nights — full blast, and not a room to be had. The town had declared itself terminus of the British Columbia trench route to the Klondike. Crazy! The world was going absolutely crazy. Kelly slept outside on an unused express cart until somebody woke him — and rather roughly — gee-hawing the cart by its long let-down handle.

"Got to get off, cowboy! This is no lower berth."

A damned depot express smasher. Kelly had a good mind to place him under arrest. What could the charges be? *Lese majeste.* It meant attack on the king, actually, but it could well be taken to mean attack on the authority of the United States Department of Justice.

He had a chance to wash up before the eastbound arrived, but his journey back didn't work out well at all. There had been a freight derailment tearing up whole rods of track and the train got into Butte after seven o'clock that night. Kelly had time for no more than a quick shave, a bath, and a visit to the cleaners where he waited shivering in the barrel while his clothes were sponged and pressed. Butte, at its mile altitude, was suddenly cold when the sun set. Blackmore, of course, was always on time, and not above lecturing a man who wasn't. However, it was also Blackmore's humor to forgive all. He had been one of Kelly's sponsors. He had recommended him to the railroad. He had introduced him, a gawky cowboy, to the finer things in South Saint Paul. Kelly was glad to respond in kind.

"Every time I open a paper, S. P. Blackmore! Alhambra sawed

up into shipping segments! You were the talk of Fort Assiniboine! The colonel at the fort was enthralled to hear I even knew you!"

Of course this was a damned lie, but Kelly had mentioned him to the Piegan Kid, the man who could use his skills in keeping books of two kinds, the known and the unknown. He assumed Blackmore had come down on the Montana Central, a branch of the Great Northern.

"I was there but I didn't have time to pay the colonel a visit," Blackmore conceded. "I did take your suggestion to see the so-called Piegan Kid. His French-Canadian experience! Accounts in all languages! We'll have to stop calling him Kid. Business reasons. Lacks dignity. We have a class operation here, Kelly. The one and only Alhambra, rising over the log and rough-plank dreariness of Dawson City. The Klondike."

Kelly mentioned Diamond Jack McGowan and his boat-gaming palace, the *Olympia*.

"With his boat and his diamonds? He'll never make it. Diamonds or picnic boat. Taking an excursion ship over the pass? And the insurance company will never sit still while he carries the diamonds. The Orloff? Paste! Good God, it's all a promotion! But us? We'll have the real thing!"

Kelly liked the sound of the "us." It meant he was in. Just *how* he had yet to learn.

Chapter Eight

They retired to one of the private dining rooms where Blackmore ordered up a very good dinner. He seemed in the best of moods. Kelly gathered he assumed that Kelly was late because he had stopped at Sheridan's famed gaming house on his way from the depot.

"Now here is this lottery ticket. Only a formality. Matter of business."

It was a pink lottery ticket with date and number, and with a flourish, drawing out an indelible pencil and bearing down hard, Blackmore endorsed it with his very bold and practiced signature. He added, "Pay to the order of Patrick E. Kelly." Kelly wondered how he had learned about the "E."

"The Skipper asked it be done this away." Very few people knew Sheridan well enough to call him "The Skipper." Blackmore gave Kelly the lottery ticket. There was a "now that dinner is finished, let's get on with it" in his manner. "I'll wait for you here in the lobby." The Chequemegon had a lounge filled with newspapers and magazines where early arrivals could wait for their parties to arrive. "Sheridan, if he pleases, can explain the particulars. You may wish to turn it down. That's up to you. To the two of you."

With more than a slight tingle of curiosity, Kelly walked to Sheridan's. The place was busy, as always. He wondered whether he should offer up the signed lottery ticket to Sheridan personally.

He went in the gaming entrance, past the crowded pan games, the noise, tobacco smoke, through the now almost empty horse room with all the blackboards — win, place, and show indicated, the odds. A single telegraph sounder clicked with no one heeding.

"Hello, Marshal," said the counter man.

"Hello, Bill."

The horse race lottery was going full blast. It actually had nothing whatever to do with racing. It was really a version of the Chinese lottery, 100 numbers, 100 squares, and balls that fell from a machine, ever turning. You could make from five to fifty thousand dollars for each twenty-five cent card. The real Chinese lottery with the Chinese characters, one to 100, payable down in Chinatown were sold by Chinese outside for one dollar. You heard tales about men coming around after years and being paid without hesitation. No doubt the same was true of Sheridan's, but he had size and glitter, not the dense smells of the mysterious East, bunks and China girls to fix the pipes. You could get a head on just walking inside those dives. To each his own. The lottery was favored by any number of good Irish Catholic miners. "A man needs something after the drip and heat of the deep levels!" Sheridan had once said.

Kelly went to the main counter.

"Hello, Claude."

"Oh, hello, Marshal." He looked at the ticket with its endorsement. It was apparent he had been informed. All seemed to check. He went inside an office and took some time, probably opening a safe. He came out carrying a very heavy manila envelope with clasp. A small square of sealing-wax dangled on a silk string. The clasp stood unbent. Kelly recognized it as a safe envelope for ore samples, although such envelopes found more use holding checks and currency. In the present instance the clasp was unused and Claude drew out a thick pack of financial instruments of one kind and another: certified checks, vouchers, and most proudly gold vouchers against the Alaska Juneau Mining Corporation.

"What do you think of those?" asked Claude.

They were larger than the rest, barely fitting inside the envelope, and heavy. They were heavy with gold. The scroll decorations were all gold, and not any of your thin gold leaf that flutters in the air, but gold of thickness and color as one might see crowning some rare altar cloth. Good Lord, you could burn those vouchers and pan them and still have a quarter or eighth their face value. Backing the golden decorations, there was in purple a picture of the mine itself, buildings climbing from dock and sea to tunnels into the mountain. The paper, if indeed it was paper rather than some stiffly pressed linen, had as if it were needed a gold seal and several signatures. On the back Sheridan's name was inscribed, and his own. Pay to the order of — Patrick E. Kelly.

"By the God, that's money!" said Kelly. "I'd hate to be carrying these in a shipwreck!" All the checks and vouchers were made out to Patrick E. Kelly. All needed his signature.

"Skipper around?"

"Yes, he's at the helm."

Kelly passed through the mid part of the great room, past the elevator shafts where the wives and mistresses of Butte's finest might ascend without the intrusion of the public eye to the third-floor Sky Room, a world to itself where one left the ordinary usages of society behind, classless except for wealth. Of course, no one was barred, but the average "pan" player would feel hopelessly out of place, even though his corpus and manners might be ignored. Butte, where the mucker of today might be the millionaire of tomorrow, was a democratic town.

Kelly thought briefly of such things as he heard the elevator pass in its metallic cage very slowly, raised like a barber chair by a round steel pillar deeply set, a slow ascent as quiet as velvet and descent as well — not dropped like a pile driver as the hoistmen up on the hill were not beyond doing when told, "Go easy, we have a senator aboard today!" just to show him he was living in a democratic country. You could hear the "E-e-e!" as he found himself free-falling into the depths. But here female voices, the good cheer and heightened tones, told Kelly the elevator held a stylish group of both sexes who had had a few and anticipated pleasures more. He entered the men's world of hearty smells and the noise of the restaurant and the longest bar in the world. He passed toward the front, rising to various levels, a step here and a step there, through the odors that would identify each even with one's eyes shut, past the seated and standing crowd, food, beer, whiskey, brandies and tobacco, all backed by the appropriate backbars and mirrors, mounted animals, a gratifying chaos until he found Sheridan reading his newspaper, one newly come from New York. He always scanned the page dealing with ships' arrivals. He was an old-time sailor, sail and steam, with flipper hands that in their way recalled the sea.

"Oh, Kelly," he said, not looking up, delaying to finish some item. He put the paper on a shelf behind him. Sheridan never paid only partial attention; he gave every person his all or none. He shook hands with one of his flippers, a grip soft but vested with the memory of great strength. The grip told you that Sheridan would still be somebody to contend with "if the seas ran red."

He leafed through the checks and vouchers, looking at each of them front and back. He hefted the gold certificates from Alaska Juneau. There were vouchers from the Royal Trust. "These may be handy in Canada, if there's any trouble in exchange."

Apparently he assumed Kelly was Klondike-bound. He went through them all, Wells Fargo Bank, orders against Mackay Telegraph, Clark & Sons, Butte, Old National, Seattle, and a number of Sheridan's own certified valid at any Federal Reserve, all with Kelly's name on them, and his alone. Not a damned one good without his personal signature.

He handed them all back and told Kelly to count them, which he did. Ten thousand on the bottom. It was the most money he'd ever had in hand at a single time.

"I would assume you have come to an agreement with Mister Blackmore," Sheridan said. The assumption naturally flowed from his cashing the lottery ticket which was evidently part of a unique sort of contract: Blackmore and Sheridan — and Kelly. Entrepreneurs, venturers by unsigned contract into a new land. "Those are all made out to you, personally, and only in the event of your . . . ah . . . demise or mysterious disappearance, revert to the payer . . . me. I will leave instructions for reversion to your dear mother in Wyoming, or next of kin. I'll need the proper address. Each will require your endorsement. Not now, Kelly. Never carry an endorsed instrument. Look at those Alaska Juneau vouchers! By the great horned spoon that's beautiful money!"

Then Sheridan said with some firmness, "Now, Kelly, don't forget you're a United States Marshal here and in Washington and in Alaska, wherever the starry flag shall fly. And I would be much surprised if you're not a marshal in the Dominion as well. This rush seems to be shaping up worldwide as the biggest since the Rand in Africa. The mounted police will need you to deal with our own nationals. Don't assert, but stand ready. I know you'll do that anyway, but I wanted to drive the nail home. That badge of yours will be hard to ignore."

Kelly had to ask about Blackmore. How did he figure — exactly?

"Oh, I thought he'd explained. At all events you'd want to get verification from me. You'll be in for ten percent. We haven't a scratch in writing, but it is understood . . . I'll have forty-five percent in consideration of the banks, faro, and roulette, as a matter of course, but others too as the land demands. Mister Blackmore will have forty-five percent, in consideration of the building, the liquors, and transportation." He planted both hands and looked down on Kelly, not because he was so tall, but because he stood on a slatboard of some sort to ease his feet. When Sheridan walked about, one could see that his feet, like his hands, were splayed, requiring slits in his shoes, but he seemed always to stand. There was no stool. He walked with a sailor's shuffle learned under sail, not steam.

"Come to it," said Kelly, "you with forty-five, and Blackmore with forty-five, I'll hold the controlling interest."

If Sheridan was concerned, he didn't show it. "Right now, it's a shot in the dark. Frankly, I think Blackmore is staking his bets and hasn't seen the horses. He's the one making the gamble. Imagine, sawing that building into winch-size cargo! He's had men there since early spring."

"In Dawson?"

"No, inside somewhere from Juneau. Buying spruce barge timbers. Seasoned wood. Some big mills up there. He was short of money. On cash. I was surprised when he came to me."

"You staked him?"

"No. I'm backing the banks. He felt it was a smart move to hire that friend of yours, that Cree-French fellow . . . used to keep books for the Sisters. I wouldn't have touched the deal if I hadn't found out the Cree was trusted by the Sisters. And I wouldn't have touched it if you hadn't been willing to go along. Sheridan's is not an eleemosynary institution, Marshal."

Kelly vowed to memorize that word. He said, "I put the bug in his ear anent the Piegan Kid. Louis LeMo. I trust him. He's as crooked as a diamond willow cane, but I trust him. Well, what I mean. . . ."

"I know what you mean," said Sheridan. "You know what

he's capable of doing."

"Right! And why Blackmore wants him. He wants him because he can keep two sets of books, one in Arabic figures and one in Square Cree."

"Square Cree?" It was news to Sheridan and there wasn't much about figures he didn't know.

"The old-time writing. Not fifty left in Canada who can read it. I'd imagine the Kid made up some of it on his own."

Sheridan's great body rippled with a silent laughter. "But you can trust him!"

"Sure. Put it this way . . . if you know a gambler can deal seconds, you can trust him in a way. You always take it into consideration."

"All right, that's why I want you on the ground. When it comes down to the case cards, it may be there won't be any Alhambra at all. It may sink. It could very easily be stalled at Saint Michaels and never make it up the river. But we'll still have you, and me, and the bank."

"La banque! Toujours la banque!" Gad! how Kelly liked to say things in French. It had real style! Once he was in Canada — *vive la Canada!* He resolved to learn French.

Sheridan was finished with the vouchers and with his plans, which were not plans, actually, only a setting forth into a great unknown.

"If I were twenty years younger, Kelly. . . . Well, I have you. You are Sheridan. Beyond the boundaries, you are Sheridan! Good enough? This is the gambling business. Law of averages. Faro, roulette, wheel of fortune, Rocky Mountain, baccarat, chemin de fer. I think it's more important to have the number one faro bank on the Klondike in a tent than the number two palace, Alhambra, or otherwise. We don't know who or what we'll be up against. Diamond Jack will be there. You'll have to make Sheridan's something to outshine that daughter, diamonds or no. I was looking at her picture in the Sunday theatrical. They had her on page one across four columns, from the fold up. Glaze paper. New color process."

Kelly knew what he was talking about. " 'The Girl with the Flaxen Hair. Her fingers move like lightning, her diamonds dazzle the eye!' "

"Right! Sheridan's will have to put up real money to counter that. But we'll give it a go. The biggest bank will still be the biggest bank."

Kelly thought — *and backed by a pipeline into the richest hill on earth* — but didn't say it. It was one of those things you never alluded to.

"You'd better get going. Blackmore will be over there, wherever he is. Remember, 'you carry Caesar and his fortunes.' "

One never expected this gross, gaming-house keeper with his vast, cow-like face and his flipper hands and feet, with his cigar turning a quarter part to limp lamp wick, to be quoting Plutarch. There was a lesson there somewhere, and Kelly would think about it.

Chapter Nine

Kelly was surprised that Blackmore would show such anxiety as to wait for him outside the Chequemegon. He had been pacing up the fairly level side street and back again, and probably seeking a spot from which he could see the front door of Sheridan's.

"Well?"

"Let's go inside. I was kept standing. He spends the whole time standing on those big splay feet of his! Did you notice how he cuts slits over the toes? You'd think, with his money, he could have them bench made. Soft Vici-kid."

Blackmore was in no humor for such things. "Did you get it?" he asked impatiently. "The money! I'm no prize bull to be sticking your banderillas in, Kelly!"

"Let's go inside and be comfortable. We need light and a counter."

Blackmore was not eager to go inside under the light at a public restaurant counter where he might not care to raise his voice. This Kelly knew and hence his insistence. He wanted to hand over the vouchers in full view and testimony. He sensed Blackmore had not seen them and that he would not be pleased to see each made out to Kelly, requiring his signature alone. He was likely to ask that Kelly sign over perhaps half, and deliver them forthwith. This Kelly had no intention of doing. His answer would be merely, "Why, certainly, we'll take them back to Sheridan for instructions." He knew very well that Blackmore wanted

74

no such confrontation.

Blackmore heard him without moving, so Kelly walked to the Chequemegon's door which he held open, and held open, until at last his partner without nod of thanks passed inside. Blackmore would have continued on to private quarters, but Kelly fancied the broad counter in full view and hearing. He sat down and spoke to the waiter.

"Hello, George."

"Hello, Marshal," said the waiter, sixty with a lifetime of skills, deft, unhurried, yet fast.

Blackmore, with violence causing the stool to creak, sat down beside him.

"My treat," said Kelly. "Coffee."

He knew just coffee would annoy Blackmore still more after the dinner he had provided. However, the man decided to laugh.

"A real high roller!"

"Oh, I'd go for the apple pie, but I'll have to watch the pennies from here on. Mister Sheridan has put me on a very restricted rein. I'll have to note down each expenditure, no matter how trifling." He added, "Of course, the coffee comes from my own pocket."

Blackmore waited to see what Sheridan had provided. So Kelly took the vouchers from the envelope and handed them over. Blackmore went through them, looked at each, front and back, made perhaps a mental computation, and laid them down.

"I'll have half of those, Kelly. And they need your endorsement."

"No. I intend to endorse each as used. This represents, so far, my ten percent share of the enterprise. Sheridan was specific and, when Sheridan is specific, Kelly does not argue. Do you know what he said, Blackie? He said, 'Kelly' . . . with a big ha-ha, of course . . . 'Kelly, this leaves me with forty-five percent, Major Blackmore with forty-five, and you with ten. The two

of you would make a controlling fifty-five. On the other hand'
. . . remember this was the Skipper talking . . . 'on the other
hand, Sheridan and Kelly would likewise make a controlling fifty-
five. Why, you own the controlling interest!' And then he said
something about being glad I was a United States Marshal."

"Marshal?" Blackmore said savagely. "You'll be nothing more
than a man with a golden badge worth thirty-six dollars and
fifty cents on the Canadian side."

"A badge like this will not to be taken lightly on British Canadian soil when more than half the stampede is likely to be
U. S. nationals."

Blackmore sat, looking at the vouchers and the endorsements,
many actually printed with Kelly's name, not just inscribed. The
Sheridan orders. They seemed to have been ordered up for Patrick
E. Kelly. The Alaska Juneau certificates and the others had it
on the back, in Sheridan's fine, Irish school-hand: Pay to Patrick
E. Kelly.

"It will be your responsibility to deliver the horses, Kelly!"
he said finally. "God knows how I've been able to carry the
financing this far. Cedar timber, barge bottoms, steamboat fare.
And all the responsibilities in South Saint Paul. There was to
be a railroad from Skagway over the White Pass. What there
was of it sank. Seventeen hundred feet of climb in seventeen
miles, with switch backs from Skagway, a hundred feet per mile."

"That railroad is now on the maps," said Kelly.

"Well, they tried to put an engine on it and it sank into the
spring holes. Hot springs, never mapped. Hardly noted until the
snow came. Dead Horse Pass! That's the new name for the White
Pass. There's one stretch of a quarter mile you can walk on
the carcasses of dead horses! And the thaw hasn't started!"

Hence Blackmore had gone to the only man he knew with
the gambling money, Sheridan. He had tied up his own money
sawing and moving the Alhambra, building barges, shipping sup-

76

plies via the Yukon at its source.

"All the champagnes and brandies will have to go by barge, and be there when the building and fixtures arrive," Blackmore continued. "We'll need at least thirty heavy horses on the dock at Skagway. Everything will have to be at Bennett for the breakup. Then the Yukon rapids. The White Horse! I have one of the best pilots in the north. There may be a tramway. Otherwise, we'll have to shoot the White Horse loaded or, if we can find enough small boats, lightered. *Bateaux* men will be there from all over the North. Everything will have to work, clickety-click. We'll have competition, of course. Diamond Jack McGowan is on his way. He's in Seattle, and may be gone when we get there. Him and his Orloff diamond!"

Blackmore said "Orloff" with contempt. "The Borneo yellow?" he continued. "Taken from the idol's forehead in India by a Russian soldier. Bought by the empress. The one who gave herself between the silken sheets to half the officer corps. Some captain ended up with the Orloff. If true, he really must have had what she needed. He must have had it hung on him like a stallion." He lowered his voice. Women frequented the Chequemegon. "There was a real man for you! He lost it gambling in Paris. That's how Jack got it. Oh, he has the genuine Orloff. It was displayed in Tiffany's window. He'll make you and your golden badge look like fifteen cents!

"He's bought that damned excursion steamer and is having it towed up from Puget Sound. Under cargo. Liquor, gaming equipment, diamonds. A shipload of diamonds, if you'd believe the reports. Don't ask me how he plans getting down the Yukon and through the rapids with an excursion boat. He'll try to pull it up on the shore in Dawson City and go right into business. A damned fool . . . but you have to admire that kind of a gambler!"

"He's to be backed by the Czarina and you'll be backed by Butte Hill?"

77

"Right. And I'll take the Hill every time!" Blackmore went on. "I never believed it about the Orloff. It would have to be insured. Jack's in debt. He'd have to use it as security and, if the insurance company wouldn't let it be shown in the Tiffany window without guards, they wouldn't let it be taken down the Yukon! In any event, I'll have to have those horses on the ground in Skagway. You have the vouchers . . . you have the responsibility!"

"They'll be there," assured Kelly.

In Helena again Kelly did not deny his intended destination. "I'll drop in at the Appellate in San Francisco," he promised Marshal O'Connell. "It might be I could get a mission and collect *per diem* and expenses."

"Yes, send us a postcard from the Klondike!" said O'Connell.

"There's not a U. S. Marshal in all of Alaska," Kelly said. "It's not even a territory. It's a possession. The only representative the U. S. has is a Collector of Revenues in Sitka." Kelly had inquired of a federal lawyer and this news had surprised the boys at the office as much as it had him. "Officially, the laws of Oregon extend."

"Oregon!"

"It was the closest state when Alaska was purchased."

They shook hands.

Now for the horses! The high line was stripped of horses. How about south to Wyoming, even Colorado, the hot sands of Arizona? Kelly stopped for a visit in Billings, just to get the lay of the land. He visited a couple of days, and took the coach to Sheridan, to the old homestead where the folks were summering, still serving the ice-cold mountain water and dried peach pie. Pa had some pretty good advice about horses. He had clipped an article from the *Equine Gazette* by Professor Brigham Y. Stallcup, Dean of Animal Husbandry at Utah University, about a breed of powerful horses known as the Baltic Grays, bred for the Lithuanian knights of olden days who fought through the frozen marshes during the religious wars. Under full breast and head armor, with knights astride and themselves armored, a ton of steel, still nothing could stop them. They had been blessed by the Pope. Some said by the devil.

When the warfare quieted down, the peasants tried to use the horses for plowing and heavy hauling, but the hard mouths and stubborn nature of the beasts which had made them a success with the knights proved not so advantageous for farming. Pull they could, but turn they wouldn't. They'd keep right on through hedge and fence, and finally the peasants gave up. They were turned loose, pretty much, and sort of ran wild for a time until they were brought to California in numbers to use in the mucks of the hydraulic mines.

Kelly rode to Utah and visited the dean. Yes, he had seen them, had done some tests on them, in fact. He'd actually ridden a couple with no trouble at all. It was their hard mouths. He laughed, being Mormon. "Blessed by the Pope. Urban the Eighth, or something. No insult intended!" he hurried to say, remembering the name was Kelly.

"And none taken."

Their use ended when the hydraulic mining stopped. Farmers didn't like to wake and find their fields flooded with a foot of mud and, of course, the gold diminished. A non-renewable resource, unlike agriculture. The Mormons had been wise in putting their faith in the latter.

"They sold the horses to farmers down in the central valleys," the dean said. "Temperatures of over a hundred degrees. They proved next to useless. Finally turned loose in the hills. When I was there, a man tried to sell me a team for a hundred dollars. Too hard-mouthed for farming. But point them in the right direction. . . ."

"I want them for the Klondike. The White Pass, actually, a lot of icy spring holes."

"Then they're your beasts. For them it will be like going home."

Kelly expected the herd to have vanished, if not into the hills then into the hands of horse buyers, but the demand of the Inside Passage and the White Pass had not yet washed up on these desert shores. He could buy cheap. He hired drivers, mostly Mexicans, at a dollar a day and shipped via flatboat from Stockton, then tidewater to San Francisco Bay. Starting with forty-three of the brutes, he arrived with forty-one, two having died mysteriously after being lifted in a horse sling to be shod. Kelly was in his element, arguing with ferriers. They had to send for special shoes with screw-in calks, California being unprepared, at least in the hot central valley, to shoe horses for ice and snow.

Leaving the horses in the charge of Mexican drovers waiting a flatboat, which had to be brought up from the bay, he visited San Francisco. He had been told to look up an old friend of Blackmore's, Judson "Jug" Macure. Judson Macure — only if you knew him well enough could you call him Jug. Like Kelly, he was a law-and-order man, but without a badge. He reigned at The Majestic, one of the better places on the Coast — the Barbary Coast. The Majestic was a first-class establishment where gentlemen went for a variety of pleasures and emerged unscathed. The *unscathed* part was Jug Macure's responsibility, and his pride. He was skilled in the over-the-shoulder lift, a rapid transport outside, turn at the curbing, facing the door, a quick unload, depositing his gentleman butt-down on the curbing undamaged. It was a fact that customers actually returned later to express apologies and gratitude for the efficiency and *care* of it all! Jug Macure had been a policeman on a ferryboat, a guard against bay pirates, then under the *nom* "The Cro-Magnon Kid" had had a short career in the ring, losing by knockout in the third to a tall and skinny blond Norwegian sailor. But he had found his true talent at The Majestic where he saved his money and planned one day to marry his landlady, whom he always took with him to the theatre, sitting in the high gallery.

Kelly while in town, waiting at the Appellate, might have taken a "hostess" or "actress" from one of the better houses, well and modestly garbed for the occasion, with midnight dinner of oysters on the half shell, or the famed Humboldt crab, at some food palace on The Wharf afterward. But there was still a ship to consider. Few carried livestock. Boats in drydock gathering barnacles were called forth for passenger service. Kelly would have had no trouble getting passage for himself, but the horses! However, he was again in luck. The steamer, *Jacob Swain*, had been in the salmon trade, hauling loose cargoes of humpback, or Northern Whites, a slippery, slithery, fragrant tonnage, to coastal ports to be canned for the Asiatic and African trade. "White or pink salmon, of the second grade, guaranteed not to turn red in the can," Jug told him. "It's an old joke, Kelly."

God, how the hold stank! But even that was a stroke of luck. Foods could not be stored there. Tourists? Not a chance! However, hard-bitten gold-seekers, machinery, or, yes, horses. At the stern, a ramp from which salmon had been scooped was also a ramp up which horses could be driven, blindfolded and snorting, into the noisome interior. The skipper, who was his own agent, assured Kelly his Baltic horses would find it actually *congenial* — he used that word, and with men and merchants standing in line for Klondike passage.

"He who hesitates is lost," Kelly said to Jug. "This is the mining business and all mining is a gamble."

Blackmore had been very specific about insurance on the horses. Of course, being Blackmore, he had been very specific about a number of things, easy enough when seated at a counter in a restaurant in Butte. Kelly got in touch with several insurance offices selling naval insurance of several kinds: ship, cargo, liability, life and limb, and found a man willing to come down and close. Kelly was expecting him by the hour as he waited for the horses from Stockton. He had had to make arrangements for a tug to bring them across the bay, hence gave little more thought to insurance until they were up the ramp and down into the fragrant, dark hold, especially difficult due to their new shoe calks. It was only then he really gave the underwriter some serious thought.

Jug was all in a lather to go, but he had his landlady to whom he was affianced, and had been for a number of years. She kept his savings for him, and the trouble seemed to be making it available at the bank.

"Oh, I have the *order* for it," Jug said. "I just have to wait until tomorrow." The order was postdated to give him time to reconsider.

"That's fine. The insurance will be settled by then."

There were gold-seekers still making arrangements, many for deck passage under tents and tarps. But the insurance underwriter never showed — or did, got one whiff, and sneaked away again.

"I'll give him another quarter hour," said the ship's master the next day, watch in hand. "Then it's Ho! for the ocean blue. We have to catch the tide."

"To hell with him," said Kelly. "I'll save the damn' premium for myself."

He had a sense of good fortune. He was a man riding the crest! It was one chance in a hundred to find a ship practically waiting, and which accepted livestock. The horses had scarcely snorted when driven into the dark hold and assailed with the stench of fish from a hundred voyages. Good captain and crew, also. Experienced! Knew Northern waters like the back of the hand. None of your first-trippers.

They cleared the Golden Gate and put to sea, a very dangerous coast northward, many ocean currents, deadly whirlpools. Graveyard of the Pacific. Some said it smelled of the Orient — the famed Japanese current! Actually, but for the strong wind, it smelled of fish. Everybody got to singing a song, made up right on the spot:

> **So sail through the misty**
> **Sail through the rain.**
> **And Ho! for the Klondike**
> **On the good *Jacob Swain*!**

The ship settled down to a dogged progress. A pronounced shaft alley chatter ceased to alarm; indeed, the vibration became reassuring. At times the boat would hesitate and then lurch forward, but that also seemed to be an ordained thing.

"The Canadians might board us at Georgia Strait," the mate said. "The Queen's waters."

"Why, that's an outrage," said Kelly. "This is a U. S. ship, sailing from and to U. S. waters!"

"That's what I say! Very hard fellows to deal with . . . the British. Never forgave the U. S. for plucking off Alaska. They had their eyes on it, you know. The Czar sold chiefly to make sure no European power got hold of it. Seven million they paid. Seward's Folly. They took that much from Juneau alone, not mentioning all the fish and furs."

Kelly sought feed for the horses. He had bought some sea-damaged oatmeal from a stampeder headed to Dawson with a mercantile outfit. A crewman gave him an old straw mattress. A person took his life in his hands, going below — the stench, the slipperiness, and the stomping horses, a pit of hell, a nauseous, infernal region! They drank water from buckets, as one cautiously held on to a cargo rail.

Despite the danger of Canadian inspection, the skipper turned into the Straits Juan de Fuca and the narrows where Victoria, the capital of British Columbia, stood proudly in the sunshine.

"Always sunny in Victoria and foggy in Vancouver; but Vancouver has it beat by a mile," the mate remarked to Kelly and Jug.

The skipper did not like Victoria because it was where he might be boarded for inspection and even be required to take on a pilot, a ruse to give some Canadian work, nothing more. But there was no signal.

"They think we're heading down the Sound!" the mate said. "You noticed the skipper turned east. What he'll do next is make a sharp turn north beyond San Juan Island. He'll steer as for Bellingham. Then we'll come back to the ship channel. Strait of Georgia. A few reefs but not much. Pilot's only a waste of money."

All went well. The mist was nothing that required a groping half speed. The water opened out, with the mountains of British Columbia and those of Vancouver Island both in view. And forests. Islands and forests! One had to know where the ship channel lay.

"He's steered it a hundred times!" assured the mate.

It was a long journey, often slowing as if to test the way, feel for the bottom, past canneries and sawmills. Sawdust made floating islands on the sea. There was a day and a night journey down a channel which made Kelly wish they had taken chances on the broad Pacific, but all went well, and a stiff new breeze told when they emerged in the broader waters of Queen Charlotte Sound.

Kelly had been studying the maps up in the pilot house. "If the fog lifted," the mate told him, "you could see both shores. Actually this is the Strait, not the Sound. The Sound gives you open water to Japan."

"Ho, for the Klondike!" said Kelly.

And the crew got to singing a new version of the song:

**Ho! for the Klondike
On the good *Jacob Swain*!**

They expected to put in at the first port in Alaska, Ketchikan, but it required sailing a narrow channel between islands and it was fish-hauling season. So the boat steamed on and came up against the docks at Wrangell, on a point of land. Plenty of open sea.

"Yes, you can go ashore," the skipper said, "but by God we'll leave after the first toot of the whistle!"

Wrangell had fisheries, a cannery, and a yard for river boats. It was outlet up Stikine River, out of Canada, twenty-odd miles east, famed for a number of reasons — gold, its Grand Canyon, the location of Telegraph Creek where the old dream of an American/Trans-Siberian line came to a stop with news of the successful Atlantic cable.

Few went ashore. Few wanted to visit a saloon of which Wrangell had a number or get shaved, however his chin might itch from growth, not with the *Jacob Swain* poised to depart and willing to lighten cargo, if only by one!

They resumed their northward course with a slight oscillation of the shaft sounding like chatter. There were actually a number of vibrations, and one tended to assuage the other, which alone would have made the boat seem ready to fall apart.

"Oh, it's a good ship, the *Jacob Swain*," Kelly told Jug, repeating what the mate had told him. "Ten score voyages into the icy seas, and not sunk once!" And he added, savoring the marvel of it all, "Not a single time!"

The illogic of this caused Jug Macure at last to cry, "Of course not! Sunk *once* is enough! It would be at the *bottom!*"

Actually, the vibration was not so bad now. The engine men had apparently taken time to tighten the bearings. At least to pump in new grease. The whistle blew for no particular reason unless to call forth echoes from the glacial peaks.

"To your right, the Great Coastal Range!" the mate called, using a megaphone. All was white except dark stone at the very summit, too distant for echoes. "To your right, Kate's Needle, altitude: ten thousand and two feet." Not ten thousand, but *ten thousand and two*. Accuracy! It counted on the Inside Passage. Ten thousand and two — that meant above sea level. However, with tides, how did they know?

All waited for Juneau with its famed gold mine, one of the lowest in grade yet highest in profit in all the earth. But the skipper chose not to challenge the narrow channel and steered west, much safer and faster.

"Two hours quicker to Skagway," the passengers were told. "Also we catch the tide up, not down, the canal."

The canal was the Lynn Canal, a hundred-mile gash of the sea aimed like an arrow northward to the three great passes, the Chilkoot, the Chilket, and the White, straight via lake and river toward Dawson City, the Klondike, and rainbow's end: Bonanza Creek — wealth beyond the dreams of avarice waiting only hard work and willingness, the great attributes of the common man.

Chapter Ten

It was morning. The days had become very long, blending into night, the long daylight of the North increased now by the light reflected from glaciers. Kelly was inside the stateroom with shoes off. He was sitting with stockinged feet on the floor. He slept in his long silk-and-wool two-piece underwear and with his wool socks on. He kept the revolver in his bunk, between wall and mattress. He was just starting to stand when a strange grab and lurch caused him to reach for a bulkhead that was not there. He felt dizzy. The ship had tilted.

It seemed so soft, so gentle. It was the feeling he had once had on a bobsled, near the end of its run when it dumped him into the snow. But that was brief. Soon, there was a ripping, muffled growl, very deep in the bowels of the ship. He was on the floor! He was on hands and knees! Things were spilling from the bunks. He got to the door. The deck hatch. Things were spilling all around him. When he could stand, he grabbed the hatch and, sock-footed, got to the deck.

Something was missing: it was the shaft chatter, the rocking vibration that had become part of the ship. He was surrounded by a terrible silence, silence even though punctuated by the cries of men.

"Jug!" He went back inside.

"I'm here." Jug was up and dressed. That was how he slept, with even his shoes on. Unlaced, but on. Not wanting to take a chance with thieves. The ship was filled with hoods. There were hoods Jug knew personally to be on the list ever since he'd been guard on the ferryboats. Pirates on San Francisco Bay.

"What happened?" Kelly asked.

"We struck something. I think we're hung up on a reef." This from a man named Mayo. He was an old Northerner. "We're all right so long as she hangs."

True, the ship had stopped. It had stopped progress forward, but slowly, gently it swung to the port side. As it swung, a second wave from the sea passed along the deck, encroaching the staterooms. Kelly was ankle-deep. He had a cat's hatred of water. Cold water. Above all he hated to step in water, stocking-footed.

"Holy Jesus! Oh, blessed God!" At once a curse and a prayer. Kelly made it outside against a drunken swing of the floor. Water passed in a wave along a slanting deck. He held to the wall. There were things afloat. Shouting voices. Officers gave commands, unheeded. A lifeboat was hanging by winch tackle, and nobody could free it. He felt along the deck. His socks gave traction on the cold, wet surface. Men were afloat. Jug was behind him, holding to his dunnage bag. Always prepared. He packed it every night. But Kelly was in wool socks and silk underwear, drawers and shirt, and parfleche. He could see a shore and high-pillared docks. Unpainted, weather-darkened buildings. Indian huts and totems. The Indians were in umiyaks, digging their paddles. He groped along the rail trying to avoid repeated waves of the cold sea.

Jug was yelling. "Kelly! Come on! Come on!"

His voice had a very strange sound, as if from a great distance. Two of the umiyaks were taking survivors. The paddles flashed. Good God, no! They were driving back survivors!

"Fi' dollar! Fi' dollar!"

Kelly went overboard, feet first, holding the half-submerged rail. The sea did not receive him so much as turn him on his side. Turned on his side, he tried to swim. What he took to be a round, black rubberoid life-preserver floating high, very high, turned out to be a suede leather dunnage bag. He got hold of it. He got one arm over it and a current carried him. The water looked endless across the waves.

"Fi' dollar, fi' dollar!" one of the Indians shouted.

My hat! Kelly thought, but he still had it on. His Tipo de Oro. He heard Jug calling, "Grab on, you damn' fool!" *It's finally come to it,* Kelly thought. *He's found his true name for me.* Jug had always resented his marshal's status. "Kelly! This way! Swim on your damn' side. Use both arms!"

Kelly grabbed the side of a umiyak, which was slippery. One of the Indians rammed him away with a paddle. He wanted money. Kelly had no way of finding money with one hand on the umiyak and the other around the dunnage bag.

"Haw! Kelly, haw!" Jug! The damn' fool thought he had to talk to him in horse. He wanted to laugh. Actually he did laugh, and the cold water strangled him.

"Fi' dollar!"

The Indians suddenly stopped. Jug had drawn his bulldog .41 revolver. The Indians stopped poking with the paddle blades and were helping them aboard. Kelly found himself lying stomach down, looking at a gray bilge that swished and washed into his face. He sat up, and made sure he still had his life preserver, the slick and rather heavy dunnage bag. They kept asking for money.

"I wouldn't give them a dime!" yelled Jug.

Kelly inventoried himself to see what had been saved. He had the badge pinned to his parfleche. His hat, yes. No revolver. It was still in the bunk, between mattress and wall — along with his own dunnage. He found some money in a parfleche pocket and gave a silver dollar to one of the Aleuts.

"Damned easy mark!" growled Jug.

89

Two more were picked up, one of them seventy years old if a day, shipwrecked while heading for the Klondike. Kelly paid for them.

"Probably have more than you do," muttered Jug.

"Don't give it a second thought." Kelly gestured and let them glimpse his badge. *"Noblesse oblige."*

The Aleuts really dug in, hoping they'd get some of the *oblige*, too. A strong current was running down the canal. One could see the horse manes of foam running over reefs more or less lined with the outward tide. The tide would carry the *Jacob Swain* to sea, to the well-named Icy Strait. But the boatmen knew their water and brought the skin boat with its overload of passengers to a dock in front of some gray-black huts along shore. Jug watched to see they were not charged a second fare — a parting backsheesh, or whatever they called it. The Indians had long suffered from the white man's thievery, but that did not mean they should get away with a double fare.

Kelly had sighted what he knew by the smell must be a sawmill. It proved to be a woodsman's camp. There was a small, side-wheel steamboat with smoke rising lazily from the stack, one long, deep-water dock, and two for shallow flatboats, usable perhaps when the tide was full. What looked like a good, old-fashioned Montana-style log house, consisting of one cabin built to another cabin and to another, each indicating a season of growth, had smoke coming from the chimney. It looked like home, and substance. A growing business.

"Pull in here!"

Two men appeared, both Scandinavian.

"By yimminy. You shipwreck fella?"

"From Minnesota?" yelled Kelly.

God, how they laughed. "Yah, sure! Minny-sota!" cried the shorter one.

"Fi' dollar! Fi' dollar!" the Indians kept yelling. Kelly shouldn't have but he was so glad to feel the ground under his feet, he dug into the parfleche, having to half-undress to get at it, and found three more silver dollars, one for each Indian. The silver dollars seemed like a great deal more money than any five-dollar greenback.

The Indians started asking for whiskey, but the taller Scandinavian told them to be gone. "You get us in yale!" Then, turning to Kelly: "You bane spoil those Indian, too much money. You fellas, coom inside."

They went in. The cabin was hot from a tubular, horizontal stove. It ended in a square cook stove. The stove was ruddy along the firebox and up the stovepipe, where it turned to enter a stone and mud chimney.

"Pitch pine heat! We woodcutter. This my partner, Nels Nelson," said the short Scandinavian. "He Swede fella. My name Ole Helverson. I'm Norwegian." He pronounced it Norveejan. "Cut pitch pine . . . sell pitch balls. Saw tops off trees in spring, pitch come out, whole hunnert pound! Two hunnert pound! We sell pitch balls, roll up in pine needles. Quick fire. One match! Skagway. More money as feller get packing ol' Chilkoot Pass. That our boat. She's stand-up engine, steam tug. Har, you stand back, don't get burned that stove. You dry off slow. We hang up clothes. What this you got? This life-saver?"

"That's my medicine bundle," said Kelly. "Moose bladder."

"You policeman? Yimminy! Look this badge, Nels!"

"I'm a marshal back in the States."

"This Alaska. She no state. She United States. Pretty soon territory. I don' know. How you know I from Minny-sota? We spend two year log off Nort' Dakota. You hear about Paul Bunyan blue ox, babe? Year of two winters? That yoke! You talk, no sound . . . all words freeze up solid. Spring coom and by golly sound thaw out, sound like five hunnert people talk, same time! All talk whole winter thaw out! That big yoke down thar."

Kelly gave him a good laugh to make him happy, old as this story was.

Bathed and naked, underwear rinsed in fresh-melt snow water, hung by the stove to dry, Kelly sorted through the suede-leather dunnage bag. Things were wet only in streaks. Gad, the assortment! There were pants of black moleskin velvet, a good fit around the waist, but very short. Two shirts fit, although short in the arms. One could unfold the cuffs, making them a few inches longer, or roll them to the elbows. He chose the latter. A nice set of cuff links, gold and polished green malachite. The shirts were a light gray linen or brindle-wool mix. Fine quality. There was a brimless hat or toque, with a wide, gold-worked headband and a beret top, with a tassel on string. He dug deeper and found pictures, letters, strange neckwear, some gloves of black suede, socks, slippers, scarves, cards, more letters, but not a one he could read, even the printing was strange.

"It's some sort of damn Turkish or Balkan," Kelly supposed. "These people in the photos look Bulgarian. None of them have fezzes."

Jug said, "If that fellow is Bulgarian, you better look out for him. They're mean. I had my rounds with Bulgarians." Jug knew about such things. "And Montenegrins! They're the worst. Oh, God, once they go for you!"

"Well, I hope I find this fellow! I intend to move heaven and earth to return his property. But he can't object to me using it in the case of shipwreck, which this is! I don't suppose I could borrow some shoes? Or moccasins?"

"Sure," said Ole. "You know what skal do? We get you geude mukluks. Also buckskin leggings. Squaw make 'em. Moose-hide mukluks. Heavy back hide! Heavy, like miners' boots down in Juneau! Screw hobnails in. Nels, he know geude squaw. Yust up coast. By old Russian Mission. Take four-five days, get geude fit."

92

"Like a Bond Street tailor? Perfect forty-six?" Kelly said.

"Sure. Yust like tailor. Up canal, Skagway. They think you old-time Yukon man, show up in sailcloth parka, mukluks. Leggings, too! We go up Skagway all-time. Haul wood. Give you free ride, help unload, unload pitch balls."

After eating, bacon thick and greasy and a huge stack of sourdough pancakes, Kelly fell asleep at the table. He woke up alone. Jug was outside with Nels and Ole. He found the coffee, thudding hot on the back of the stove. Suddenly he remembered everything — especially the horses. "God damn! God damn the damn luck! The horses drowned!"

Ole came in. "So all horses drown? What problem? You use boat. Dog sled."

"The problem is I have to face a son-of-a-bitch . . . the owner!"

"Oh, he not have horse? You let him worry about! You stay har, go partners with Nels and Ole. Make plenty geude money, sell pitch firewood. Much better as acetylene."

Kelly learned they used acetylene gas to light the big hotel and many other buildings in Skagway. Carbide, the generator of acetylene, was also being used on the trail, but with mixed results. You dropped some in the snow, urinated on it to start the gas, and tossed in a match. Quick fire! Only the damned stuff melted itself down, maybe five feet or however far the earth was, and went out with a whoof.

"One big God-damn explode!" said Nels. "Maybe he work okay on ice. You put geude pitch ball in gold pan, light fire, much better for trail camp. Ol' Yukon trail go all way Dawson. Sleds, dog team, all-time."

Kelly decided the boys had something. He said, yes, he'd think about their proposition, he and Jug, and decide; but first they had the duty of doing what was right. "A promise is a promise," he concluded. "I'll have to face the son-of-a-bitch about the horses!"

93

With temperatures fluctuating above and below the freezing mark, steam was always kept up in the little, vertical engine boat, stack and boiler, side by side, two side-wheels. "Much better as sternwheel in float ice," Ole said, but didn't say why. The wheels operated deeper but narrower. Perhaps that was it, and it had ice fender guards. There was little float ice, and what there was could be pushed aside.

This was Kelly's job, standing in front with a long, steel-shod pike. You had to take care and brace yourself. That ice was deceptive. If six inches were exposed, then thirty-five inches were underwater. So, when you saw a slab of ice, you set your weight against the pike, boat and ice swerved, and you learned to yell each time so that Ole could compensate at the wheel.

"By golly, you like ol'-time whaler, Kelly! Harpoon!"

The Aleut village was across the canal and around toward Atka, the old Russian mission. The stone church still stood without a window broken or slate gone from the roof. The Russians had really built, and the Indians were careful not to disturb the holy things for fear they'd get the Russians back. Oh, they'd had their experiences with the Russians! Do nothing, nothing, nothing to bring them back!

The Aleut village was of some size, with fifty or more skin-and-wood buildings, revised igloo shapes with spirit signs, suggesting a use of a cross symbol — neither Russian nor Christian, but a variation of both. They were visited twice yearly by the Reverend Easterly, an Episcopal priest from Skagway, and by the Roman Catholic monsignor from Juneau. The Russian Orthodox Church still clung to a foothold with an archbishop in Sitka, but that was far to the south on an outward island where one got the warm winds from the Japan current and from which no archbishop was prone to leave.

The mukluks were fashioned of moose neck to fit Kelly's feet, very thick-soled with belly-hide farther up. They would require a second and third journey. Even though high topped, they failed to meet his velvet suede pants. However, this was rectified by adding buckskin leggings with wrap-around strings, decorated with beaded and dyed porcupine spirit signs. These were special symbols said to appease the gods of the mountain who were believed to live deep under the glaciers in rock caverns and could be heard moaning and groaning at night, especially from the top side.

"I'll listen for them when I get up there," said Kelly. "See if I can make contact."

And then there was the parka! He liked the parka best. It was made from a light brown canvas, looking as though it had been dyed by boiling in strong tea. Actually it was used sail, selected from some unworn section and sold at cut rates for just such a purpose. A parka is unsurpassed for turning the northern wind. It was fitted to hang amply like a small house, but unlike a greatcoat to yield, not provide an obstruction. The only real warmth came from the hood, lined with soft skin and edged by black-tipped wolverine, a very coarse guard fur from tail and back, with most of the warm, under hair plucked away. It had the distinction of resisting frost in some unknown manner, and he was told one could wear the edged hood in the coldest weather without the moisture from his breath accumulating and becoming a bother. It also deflected the blowing wind, guarding one's face. Many old Northeners liked the dark wolverine as a light screen, almost as effective as Siwash snow glasses. These were large wooden shields with holes the size of iron nails which could be adjusted near or far. Kelly had heard that the old-time snow trailers disliked smoked glasses because the necessary metal frames conducted cold to the bone, or warmth from the bridge of the nose outward.

"Wolverine hair double!" Ole said. "Walk into wind. See plenty geude. Wolverine hair no catch frost!"

Kelly didn't say so, but bucking the strong Arctic cold did not exactly figure into his plans. The price for all this — one hundred dollars.

Nels said, "Skagway, she spoil these Indian. When I first come to country, twenty dollar, whole works." To the squaw he said: "Hey, you, Annie! You throw in gift, maybe one pair mittens!"

And she did — a pair of leather mittens, well-chewed and soft, on a leather thong to go down each arm, inside and over the shoulders.

"You now have to give gift."

"Oh, Christ!" Kelly frisked himself and gave her a quarter kilo package of tobacco, very strong, in lead foil, which he'd found in the black suede dunnage bag. By the smell it had been cured in a sweet brandy.

"You bane have plenty cash?" Ole asked. "You say saloon fella build big barge? Big gamble! Okay! What you need is Russian boat nail. Square copper boat nail! Never rust, never get loose in green timber. You know how much ol' rusty ten-penny nail cost last year, in little rush? One dollar each! Whipsawed scows, green lumber, fall apart, sink. Have to burn up . . . get nails."

"They'll know better this year."

"Ho! Those fella never learn nothing. Why you not buy sack Russian square copper boat nails?"

Kelly knew something about square copper nails. They may have been boat nails to this Viking, but they were sluice nails back in Last Chance Gulch. They never loosened. The miners drove them about seven-eighths in and, when they wanted to take the riffles out for cleanup, they simply pulled the nails, washed down the bottom, and then drove them back in, but never all the way.

"Bronze nails?" said Kelly.

"No, copper. Bronze too hard. Make geude bell metal. Russians make all bells for Catholic missions in California. No copper har. Russian bring all way 'cross Siberia. Cache copper boat nails. Squaws use make rings, all kinds stuff. Sell fishermen, chechakho, tell 'em solid gold. Get you sack copper boat nails. Sell 'em for thousand dollar a *pood* up on lakes, top of Chilkoot Pass, White Pass."

Kelly thought he said pound. "You're crazy. How many nails in a pound? Thirty? Forty? Why, that would be twenty dollars apiece."

"No, *pood*. *Pood*, she Russian, like forty pound. You take fifty *pood* . . . she U. S. ton. Fifty-five *pood*, British ton. Long ton, you know? Ol' mounted police inspector, he say nobody go over pass without one ton. They say comestible. You savvy this comestible, Kelly?"

"Sure, something you can eat."

"You take along few sacks potato. You tell those feller how square copper never rust, thicken when drive in. Best damn' boat nail! All kinds boats, iron ten-penny nail, green wood, rust. Boats fall apart. You tell 'em that. You got along fine copper nail! Show your black partner. . . ."

"Blackmore."

"Sure, Blackmore. Show him copper nail! He forget all about lose horse. We offer squaw maybe hunnert dollar. Two hunnert dollar. Buy whole damn ton square copper nails. I help you haul up to Skagway. Tell you what . . . you give Nels and me one your gold certificate, Juneau, buy whole damn ton Russian nails."

"Will they take the vouchers?"

"Nels and me take vouchers! Get plenty dollar, half, quarter. Big, old-time pennies. Big bag coins! Indians think they rich. Four-inch and ten-inch nail. Square copper. You sell one dollar each, five dollar each, when chechakho damn' whipsaw, green spruce boats fall apart."

Kelly decided he'd do it! It would fend off Blackmore in case he got unreasonable about the horses.

Chapter Eleven

It was an all-day journey under cargo — wood, pitchballs, sacks of copper nails — up the canal to Skagway. He looked up the Russian words for inch and foot in the back of the little black book he still had from Jack Ridgeway. The ten-penny size was two *vershook* and the ten inchers were half *arshine*. The half-*arshine* king spikes were a quarter *vershook* thick, while the smaller two *vershooks* were one-eighth *vershook* thick.

He had time to memorize all this and have it on the tip of his tongue because, knowing such things and pretending that other people, of course, knew them too, was important. He wanted to be able, without reference, to reel it off at an instant's notice. It gave the façade of expertise — which, of course, it was. He'd learned that while guiding salesmen around Billings. People sat up and took notice. They'd say, "By God, that feller knows his vinegar!" and would wait for him, wouldn't order from anyone else.

The way to Skagway was a slow, twelve-hour journey, a good deal of that time against the tide. The steamboat was drawing considerable water. One had to watch out for ice from Haines Inlet, which led up to the Chilkat Pass.

Skagway was much larger than Kelly had anticipated. It had more than a mile of docks and warehouses. Many of the buildings looked twenty years old. They stopped at Brunton & Son, Fuels. A sign advertised:

MAGIC PITCH BALLS
ROARING FIRE IN TEN SECONDS

"You leave nails har," Ole said. "This geude place. Watchman all-time."

Brunton himself met them. "Kelly," he said, "these copper nails are a winner! Real boat nails, green timber or dry!"

So Kelly told him about back in Boulder, Montana, a gold town where they built a livery barn with square copper nails, because the only nails they had were sluice nails. About twenty years later when some outfit went to hydraulicking and hence needed to build a big sluice — about ten miners' feet of water per second — a fellow fell in off the catwalk and drowned, just got beaten to pieces, clothes in rags, some of his gold teeth and steel boat nails showing up in the riffle. Well, they had to have those square boat nails and, none being at hand, they burned the livery barn and screened the ashes just to get them!

"They can build their boats of green spruce boughs and they'll hold together and, when they get to the Klondike, burn those boats for fuel and sell the copper nails to the sluice makers at a big profit," Kelly informed Brunton.

Being shipwrecked, he later told Jug as they were walking, might be the luckiest thing ever happened to them. Shipwreck Kelly! He liked that. He felt like a new man. He had experienced a rebirth, as his aunt said she had after she'd gone to hear Evangeline Booth deliver a lecture. He just felt like striding along! Jug had to hip-skip and jump to keep up with him.

There was a two-story hotel, The Skagway House.

"I believe I have a room reserved," said Kelly, standing at the desk and letting the clerk glimpse his badge. "Kelly, United States Marshal. My assistant, Mister Macure. Double bed . . . well, no. A cot, perhaps?" The clerk was nonplussed, and loath to say no. On inspiration, Kelly added, "It might have been

100

made by Mister Blackmore."

"Yes! Blackmore. Just a moment."

The clerk left and talked to the manager who came out, introduced himself as Robert Sterling. There had been an error. But it could be remedied. Mr. Frobes and Mr. Schiff were in the room reserved for Mr. Blackmore, but they could give Mr. Kelly a room with a back exposure, a double bed, or he had a folding cot for the marshal's assistant. Kelly said it would do quite nicely.

He signed the register with his usual straightforward Patrick Kelly. "May I sign for Mister Macure?" he asked and was told it would not be necessary, unless it was the marshal's custom. Kelly shook his head and let the blotter be applied. He knew how to stay in hotels. You stepped back and waited for them to do things for you.

The room, when available, smelled of sleeping men. It was not unusual in boom towns to rent in shifts, and twelve hours was considered standard. The main thing was getting the sheets changed. Kelly, perhaps due to his golden badge, secured the full twenty-four hours.

Ah, a bed! It was truly fine to lie at length in a real bed with his shoes off — or mukluks — although the mukluks, when removed, left his feet smelling like all the smoked herring in Norway. After a time, Kelly got up and checked the bath down the hall. It was a primitive affair, and no hot water. He needed a shave. Leaving Jug to enjoy the bed, he went out to find a barbershop.

"Leave the moustache," he told the barber. He hadn't been wearing one, but that was difficult to discern, against his full growth of whiskers, and he had one when the barber had finished the shave. In the mirror, as he checked the moustache, Kelly saw that the climate was turning his skin dark like everyone else's in the North. He had had the barber's boy go out to fetch

101

for him a stick of Bocabella Castile. It always added class to have your own soap and Bocabella, made of soda and olive oil and not slaughterhouse grease and lye, was *de rigueur*. A man always created a good impression when he showed up at a bath house with his own soap. The boy found it at an apothecary's. Kelly gave him a fifty-cent tip. The more humble the servant, the larger the tip. Of course, the badge made a difference.

"Le badge!" said Kelly to himself. *"Toujours le badge!"* He thought how truly easy it was to speak French. It had come to him at the Cree camp where they spoke the Coyotie French. He hoped Blackmore still had connections with the Piegan Kid. He would be very uncomfortable without the Kid, or somebody, as intermediary. After bathing in the back room of the barbershop, Kelly waited for his clothes to come back from the Chinese laundry where they were hand-washed and iron-dried. Gad! The silk underwear! A man should wear nothing else. Thank God, he'd had it on when the boat sank! His socks still smelled faintly from the mukluks. The black suede pants glowed.

Kelly was quite happy loafing around Skagway, recovering from his journey. The day passed, and another. Skagway was a teeming, tramping circus. One never heard such accents, and saw such strange garbs — Kelly's among them. He rather liked his Northerner appearance in the parka, with the fur fringe tossed back, the mukluks, even the suede velvet pants, too short and making buckskin leggings imperative. In being unique, he was right in style.

The Juneau paper arrived. It was published weekly, and carried by steam launch. And there were the Skagway papers, two of them, the *Democrat* and the *Nugget*, both hand set in very large type. Such headlines! Saving the time of printers, sitting black fingered on their high stools.

The Juneau *Miner* was full of news:

"Colonel Blackmore, late of Her Majesty's armed forces,

Officer of Sepoys" — *Colonel? Cripes, they'd raised him in rank!*
— "said Juneau was most certainly to be chosen capital of
Alaska. Yes, Alaska was to be a territory, and perhaps state-
hood soon to follow!" The colonel was reported to have addressed
this group and that. Juneau was to be the key point to the Klondike, a new railroad, the Alaska, British Columbia & Northern,
was projected by way of Taku Pass, Inkun City, and a hot springs
health resort on Taku Lake. Even Kelly was mentioned. **"Deputy
U. S. Marshal Kelly, and assistant, will meet the colonel in
our satellite port of Skagway, having brought two score heavy
draft horses to pull the supply boats of Colonel Blackmore's
Klondike Enterprise up the abandoned grades of the White
Pass Railroad from Skagway, while the building itself, the
famed "alabaster palace," the Alhambra, cut in segments
with floors, roofs, French beveled mirrors, and all equipment
comes via St. Michael's up the Yukon's mighty stream by
steamboat."**

Oh, God, had he spread himself! Could it be that the sinking
of the *Jacob Swain* had not reached Juneau, less than twenty
miles away? Apparently such was the case. The survivors had
all gone on to Skagway, toward the Yukon, the Klondike, and
not to Juneau. But the news had reached Seattle, hop-skipping
Juneau, for a newsboy was on the street shouting, *"Puget Sound
Northern!* Latest about the Klondike!" Kelly heard his name! "All
about the shipwreck. Many lost on *Jacob Swain*. U. S. Marshal
Kelly saved. Read about 'The Luck of the Shipwrecked Marshal!'
All about Kelly . . . 'The Man with the Golden Badge!' "

He was on page one. In a box. He hustled to buy a copy.
They were selling fast, at one dollar each! (He got a brief, bitter
satisfaction from that . . . Blackmore, in his Johnny-come-lately
Juneau *Miner*, was selling for only two bits.) Kelly withdrew
to what privacy he could find to see what was being said of
him in Seattle.

103

The Luck of Shipwreck Kelly

The luck of Shipwreck Kelly took a turn for the worse when he leased space for two score heavy work horses said to be descended from the steeds of the Baltic knights, "mighty engines of power," in the fragrant hold of the trusty salmon hauler, *Jacob Swain*, bound for Skagway, the White Pass, and the Land of Gold! All went merry as a wedding bell until early on the morn of the 8th inst. when the good ship *Jacob Swain*, engines clanking from a hundred trips, tore out her bottom on the reef near Skagway Inlet, the Lynn Canal, drowning all horses and passengers of unknown number, but sparing Kelly, and partner, Jug Macure, who escaped in their hats and underwear.

Undismayed, the intrepid argonauts arranged a grubstake, courtesy of eminent soap merchant, Jefferson Randolph Smith, heretofore known for purely reverse charities, who now keeps tab, with field glasses, of his assignees, to make sure naught befall as they labor up the incline of the Chilkoot Pass, heavily burdened, accumulating the Queen's minimum of one British long ton, deemed necessary to keep in abeyance the starvation of the long cold from her loving subjects and guests.

Kelly was mad! It was the worst thing that could have happened! When he got back to the hotel room, he read the article through again. He showed it to Jug Macure when he came in.

"It didn't say hardly anything about me."

"Too bad! Oh, I bleed for you! What would you have liked, 'The Eminent Bouncer from the Barbary Shore'? Everybody reads this weekly rag. They rush it up here by express launch. If Blackmore didn't know, he does now!"

Jug Macure was by the window with the paper. "What now?" he asked.

"I say, Ho, for the Klondike! That's where we'd better be headed. Why?" Kelly asked rhetorically, "because with no horses we'll be of no further use to Blackmore! I knew there was some reason I wanted the copper nails." Jug seemed baffled. "Blackmore will try to sue, or something. I'd like to get the goods to Canada. We'll be in a position to deal. Not stay and be arrested!"

"Good God, Kelly!" Jug responded. "You're a marshal. You're the only federal official here. You'll be arresting yourself."

"It's not so damned funny. There's a U. S. Commissioner. There are sure to be lawyers. Show me a place without lawyers! I'd rather deal on the Canada side. We'll be on Chilkoot and he'll be on the White. They're twenty miles apart. One goes to Lake Bennett and the other to Lindeman. All plateau. Those lakes are flooded rivers. Camps all over, sawing wood for boats. I want Blackmore to see how crucial the copper nails are to his damned barges. The main thing is to get over the pass. We'll be in a position to deal. He's stubborn. When he sees he has to have the nails . . . and if not, we'll sell at auction." He stopped Jug before he said it. "No, it's not dishonest. Those vouchers were made out to me personally. That speaks for itself. I have to help him get to Dawson, agreed, but on my own terms. I wish there was a telegraph. I'd wire Sheridan. Anyhow, losing the horses was an act of God. I have to do what, in my judgment, is right. And this is it. If I have to shove it down Blackmore's throat, Sheridan said I have the controlling share. Now I see what he meant. I'm to act for him when beyond the Fifty-three. 'No law of God nor man north of the Fifty-three!' This is the Fifty-nine, plus. We'll be north of Sixty on Lake Bennett. Yukon Territory. Canadian law."

Kelly went out and bought a revolver. The clerk at the Alaska

Commercial brought out a Frontier Colt, same frame as the old
.45, but in the new .32 special caliber. Seven and a half inch
barrel. Latch-down holster. In the North a man needed the range.

"Shoots like a rifle," Kelly told Jug, though he hadn't tried
it out. "Can't let my colleagues of the Mounted see me unprepared."

It fit under the parka, rather high up. A reassuring feel, on
the left side, balancing the parfleche. He bought some sourdough
pants. Canvas, blanket-lined, bigger in the legs. He had to take
off the mukluks to get them on. The velvet pants needed cleaning
again. Some of their dinglebobs had come loose. He left them
at a tailor shop. He had to wait his turn.

"That's all right. I'll pick them up when I get back from the
Chilkoot. Out to try the pass."

They went by way of newly founded Dyea, across some flats,
between the Sound and Skagway Canyon. They hired horses. The
nails would require four trips for men, only one for horses. These
were small ponies of the North, staunch, sure of foot. Nails were
damned hard to carry on your back.

The canyon was the canyon of Skagway River, and a very
mean strip of property. It was a stone gash in rock that looked
volcanic, a series of pinnacles actually that nothing, not even
a mountain goat, could climb. The Chilkoot river was a lot more
than Kelly had imagined, but right now it roared deep under
ice, and icy shelf banks. Most of the timber had been cut, and
a lot of it just to stick down holes in the ice to keep people
from stepping in and ending in the noisome depths. A vapor
rose from who knew what hellish occlusion.

Jug had insisted on making the journey with a fifty-pound
pack, so Kelly did too, conditioning for the pass. Chilkoot Pass
was the most famous mile in Christendom with hundred pound
packs the rule. A steady canyon traffic preceded and followed.
A breeze from the north held the odor of smoke, and the stink

of civilization. This ultimately proved to be smoke from Sheep Camp, a town, and the stench came from slit trenches and backhouses, the latter renting at twenty-five cents for five minutes, heated for your comfort. And you were charged a dollar deposit! There were other camps, tents, and wickiups, smokes from dozens of fires, signs with various stores' and countries' names on them, and men as far as one could see. And there was the pass with a long, dark clot, apparently hanging as still as a picture. You saw movement as on the minute hand of a dollar watch, the hundreds bent under their packs — a scene now familiar in newspaper illustrations throughout the land, indeed throughout the world, still crowding out the war with Spain. To the north were great glaciers with here and there a point of mountain rock. The mountains of the White Pass lay in the northeast.

Sheep Camp was built like a wall, a rough circle of shanty stores, gambling and whiskey houses, and what appeared to be a small circus tent, with part frame and part canvas wall:

MAZIE'S

"There it is," Kelly said to Jug, looking at the camp. The stench almost vanished when one stood in the midst of it. "The eye of the storm," said Kelly.

Chapter Twelve

They drew up at Mazie's. Kelly could hear an organ of some kind, or melodeon, and laughter — girls' voices. Places like Mazie's, even when half-tent with ventilation, always seemed to have that certain smell. Kelly and Jug went inside.

"I'm Mazie," she introduced herself as they entered. She had one incisor tooth set with a ruby, a Ceylon stone, bright rose, about the color of sockeye salmon. Rimmed by a gold setting it was surprisingly bright and, from some angles, one might take it for a pink diamond.

"Shipwreck Kelly! There's a name for you," Kelly said. "I lost a fortune in work horses. Heavy work horses, with snow cleats! Gone. Gone to the bottom! But we made it. Meet Jug Macure, late of the Majestic, Barbary Shore. If you want anybody tossed out, Jug will be glad to oblige."

"I handle that myself," said Mazie.

For having a canvas striped roof, it was a surprisingly substantial place. There were wainscot sides, of a sort, and a floor of what appeared to be sawed larch. It served as a dance floor and was similar to the eastern hemlock. Hemlock was sawed for lots of cheap flooring because it was tough — although giving the worst slivers known.

There was an in-the-slot melodeon which was wound by crank. There were two girls, or had been — one had returned to Skagway and one had gone with a gentleman friend over the pass. Mazie had a Chilkat handyman and a bartender named Finch who, following a bad night, she said was asleep in an adjoining shed.

Mazie sat down and lit a cigarette. "Shipwreck Kelly . . . the man with a golden badge!" He took it off his shirt and let her admire it. "What are you doing here, Kelly? Not climbing the Chilkoot!"

"Why not?"

"It doesn't seem your style."

"It wasn't my style until the horses went down."

She hadn't seen the Puget Sound paper, but she'd read all about him and Blackmore in the one from Juneau. He explained how it was. Sheridan was putting up forty-five percent which gave him and Jug, as she could see, a ten percent control in any dispute.

"Colonel Blackmore! Is he actually sawing up his joint and taking it in by riverboat? That makes my tent and melodeon pretty tame stuff!" She herself hoped to move the best of her fixtures and the liquor and gaming stuff over the Chilkoot at, say, forty cents a pound, at least as far as Bennett City or one of those towns where they were building the boats. If there was transportation, by boat or sled, she would go on to South White Horse. You never knew till you had a look. There was gold coming in every day. Gold from the Klondike by dog sled and measured like silver dollars. "It's the real thing, Kelly! This will be Last Chance all over again. If you're with Blackmore, what are you doing here? Why not the White Pass? That's where the horse freight goes. They have a cliff route there that would make your hair stand! But you said the horses drowned."

"Oh, I'm finally out of horses," Kelly told her. "Now I'm in square copper nails! Russian. Ten-penny, and ten-inch spikes. Worth a fortune. Dollar an inch, minimum. They told me in Skagway that anything could be bought if you had money enough. But a man's foolish to make hard plans before he sees what the

109

conditions are. Diamond Jack McGowan is coming with a boat bigger than Blackmore's scows. And he isn't bringing horses. I shouldn't have, either. It was Blackmore's idea."

Mazie recalled Jug, or said she did. She preferred to talk about San Francisco. She had heard enough talk of the Klondike. Then she let Kelly and Jug bed down in a partially heated storeroom and next day Kelly was in a mood to try the pass. Jug was set to do the whole job himself; it was right in his line. Kelly said no. He wanted to go over with him.

"From what I've been told," said Mazie, "height is an advantage. They say it lets you carry a pack high and clear. They go two or three abreast. Forty cents a pound. That's what the traders are paying. Some very big outfits."

She fed them breakfast. One meal free, after that a dollar a throw. There were no exceptions.

The morning sun was shining with a pale light through the smoke of Sheep Camp, and Kelly looked at his watch. It said ten past ten. Jug, who liked to show off, took two *pood* of nails, eighty pounds, but Kelly took only forty, padded by a straw-filled mattress he bought from Mazie.

"The Canadian police see that mattress and they'll turn you back," Mazie told Kelly. It appeared that Soapy Smith, or one of his henchmen, had gone up with a bag of straw intending to set up some sort of a monte game, and the police had sent him back fast!

"Where's the boundary?" Kelly asked.

"Well, that's the question," Mazie said. "I don't think it's actually been surveyed. You can't mount markers on ice. It creeps. The boundary is where the police up there say it is."

They waited in line. Once started, you were shoved. Men wedged you in line. Footing was the thing. The worst was being crowded in two or three abreast, and not being able to stop. And having somebody's face shoved in your rear end. The footholds were slots in greenish-black ice.

"This ever thaw?" asked Kelly.

But nobody answered. It was best just to keep moving, and slowly. The line of climbers was like a great snake, a python. Once in a while you came to a place where you could step aside, a breather. But Kelly wanted to stay close to Jug. It was not yet noon. Three trips per day? That's what they said. A day of twenty-four hours? It never got dark. Nobody talked. Kelly would ask a question and get no answer, or maybe an answer would come several minutes later. Footing! Footing was the thing. He looked down at the green-brown, urine-colored foot slots.

"Keep going, cowboy," someone said.

He was wearing his Tipo hat inside the parka hood. He never felt right without a hat on. That was a cowboy in him! It was often said that real cowboys slept in their hats. Not true. Well — perhaps once in a while.

Climbing became a drug. It was like sleepwalking. Kelly lost track of time. And then of a sudden there was a falling away, and he was on the final, easy steps. There was no longer a mass of wool-clad men ahead. Nobody's heels when he looked down. No more smell. He was in the open. He could see. Gad, but he had a view. Ice and far mountains, smokes of distant camps. A breeze came from the region he knew to be Chilkat, north and west. He felt like one reborn in a new world. The world of the top, not the bottom. He was thankful for the parka, and the wolverine fur to protect his face. There was a wide scattering of camps and outfits nearby, small and large. The lucky ones would be those who came in groups of three or more, leaving someone always on watch.

There was a police house made of newly sawed square logs with a flag outside and some dog pens in back.

Kelly registered for Jug and himself. When he showed his

badge, it eased matters. He hadn't brought his revolver. It was at Mazie's.

"Your jurisdiction ends at the boundary," said Constable McKay. "But we may ask your help with some of your nationals."

"Lots from the States?"

"Yes, the main bulge, but we have many English and, surprisingly, Australians. Imagine! Other side of the world! We even had a fellow from Canada just the other day."

"Ha!" said Kelly, sensing the joke. "You couldn't send *him* back."

"Oh, yes we could!" said Constable McKay. "Everyone is treated alike. You say copper nails? That will do. We're getting plenty of food. You can pick your own camp. That fence isn't the boundary. It's our deadline between the Indian camp and the freight camp. You can hire a dog sled or find other means. At all events, we'd like to have you sign before you leave for the inside."

Kelly decided to visit around and see if there was anybody he knew. The Montana camps — Garnet, The Bear, Alder had all but emptied, the men having headed for the Klondike. Not all the stampeders were mining greenhorns, as reports would have one believe. Kelly fell in with several men with English accents. Kelly liked the English, particularly those met on the stampede who were not the h-dropping kind but more likely the ne'er-do-well younger sons of good family. He couldn't believe they were the snobbish English his father had described, riding to hounds across fields of the starving Irish and eating fat on Irish food shipped unabated in the dreadful days of the famine.

They all drank too much. Broke or not, the English of good accent drank only the best. He learned to classify them by speech and distinguish the cockney from the "younger sons." He decided the latter had the cockneys beat by a mile. Also, Kelly held to

112

the theory that you could judge a man's breeding by the liquor he drank.

Kelly left for Skagway to face the colonel alone. Jug was to remain at Sheep Camp and continue carting the nails across the line and see that they were well guarded. Jug actually seemed to enjoy conquering the pass. It would put him back into shape, he insisted.

The return route was tough, the Skagway river more dangerous downhill than up. If you got to going too fast, the ice opened up, a hole vaporous with the breath of hell. It smelled ominously of trapped man and beast. It was half a day's walk to Dyea, and thence to Skagway.

When he arrived in Skagway, Kelly needed a shave and a bath. He chose the same barbershop where he had cached his Castile soap. The same Chinaman again laundered and dried his silk underwear.

Once he got to the hotel, his key was gone. The clerk pretended not to know what had happened to it. Kelly went upstairs and opened the door. The gas was burning inside the globe, but had not been for long — he caught the scent of acetylene, indicating it had not burned long enough to get hot, and hence some of the gas escaped. Kelly knew enough when entering a room always to test the smell, especially at night, *then* to light the lamp. He let the door swing open and stood for a fraction of time. He could smell more than the gas. He could smell Blackmore.

"Well!" cried Kelly with a false cheer. "So you got here! That's a bit of all right. By God, Major, am I glad to see you. Welcome to Skagway!"

"Come in, damn you!" Blackmore didn't sound angry — surprised perhaps, but not angry. He was standing with his hand out in greeting. So Kelly went on and closed the door. That was a mistake. However, the door was closed, and he left it closed.

113

"Kelly, I came for my money."

"Money?"

"Insurance money for the horses."

The money wouldn't have had time to get there. It took weeks to get a claim settled, even if you were not half-way to the North Pole. Kelly decided to let him have it point-blank.

"Sorry. No insurance! The underwriters absolutely refused to even visit the ship! Dead loss. I mean *dead*. Sunk. Wrecked. Act of God. Hidden reef. Only a miracle I was able to save myself."

"All right, then, you owe me that money!" Blackmore waited, then: "Pay up! The Sheridan money! You must have half of it left. Fork over the money."

"I can't do that!"

"Don't tell me you spent it, or lost it playing poker?"

"No, I'll tell you what I did. I had this great opportunity to buy square copper boat nails. Russian. Absolutely a must to hold boats together up on the lakes. Ten-inch and five-inch, framing and planking, and here's the good news. I have them at the top of the pass! Ready and waiting. Russian, square-shank, pure copper boat nails. They're worth double the horses."

"You damned fool!"

Kelly pretended to be outraged. "Call me that after all I sacrificed! I went down with that ship. I suffered and almost died. I would have, but for two Scandinavians that hauled me home and dried me out by the fire. They're the ones who put me on the track of the copper nails. The Chilkoots found this Russian cache and were making jewelry of them. Jewelry! That should tell you what they're worth here in the North."

"All right, how much do you have left?"

Kelly was stubborn. He was not going to be left broke and adrift. "No, under the laws of Oregon, by which Alaska operates. . . ."

"To hell with that. Don't start quoting law to me."

Blackmore had obviously vowed to keep his temper but when he heard Kelly, that tall cowboy in his sourdough pants and Siwash leggings and parka hood, reeling off the law, he assumed a crouch, weaved and sprang, trying to seize Kelly in a wrestler's hold. Kelly shifted, and caught Blackmore with a left fist, overhand and downward. The blow failed to land on the back of the neck where directed. Blackmore shifted and took it between spine and shoulder. Still, Kelly had a tall man's advantage, and down went Blackmore. Blackmore, however, was a wrestler and, as such, he did his best work on the floor. He caught his weight on two hands and, from that horizontal position, swung both legs trying to catch Kelly behind the knees, and rolling, slam him to the floor. He would then have Kelly at his mercy, face down. This was how he intended to win the argument.

Kelly snaked forward and escaped under the bed. He rolled over and glimpsed in Blackmore's grasp what he thought was a pistol, a very black, snub-nosed pistol. Actually it was a sap of black leather, a shot-filled bag on a thong which fitted around the wrist. Blackmore must have had it concealed in a sleeve pocket. But Kelly didn't know this. At that instant, he thought it was a pistol. He kept going under the bed. A mattress will stop bullets. Of course there was his .32, but Kelly didn't want to shoot Blackmore. It was just that he didn't want Blackmore to shoot him.

"You son-of-a-bitch! Come out of there!"

"You bastard! Put the gun away!"

Kelly, on his back, looked at the bed slats inches away, the springs, the grayish mattress. He bumped against something that sloshed. It was a heavy china chamber pot. The maid scoured it daily, and left it a quarter filled with soapy water. Kelly had never used it. He had preferred to urinate out the window, which faced the back, with a shed roof below. The shed roof was washed

115

daily by the Skagway rain and mist. He grabbed the chamber pot. The bale was a solid one, ringed to the china. Holding it as a weapon, he managed to get his legs doubled, then on his back, he thrust upward. The bed springs and mattress were lifted with a crash from the slats against the metal-framed springs and pinned Blackmore against the wall. When Blackmore tried to get free, he tipped the dresser over and, falling, it shattered the mirror. In the confusion, Kelly had the impression that a gun had gone off. He freed the chamber pot. He saw what he still thought to be a short, black pistol in Blackmore's grasp. The springs fell, half skidding, tangled with dresser and a chair. The room was very crowded. He had a tall man's view of Blackmore and his weapon. More with the intention of spoiling his aim than doing damage to his skull, Kelly flung the chamber pot. He did not actually throw it: he swung it by the bale. One end came loose, so he still had it, but the bale straightened and Blackmore was saved the danger of getting heavy crockery on the side of the head, but its contents, soapy and perfumed, sloshed Blackmore and the wall. Staggered and shocked as he was, Blackmore showed revulsion, trying to dry his face and hair.

"You foul son-of-a-bitch!" he yelled. "You foul, dirty son-of-a-bitch!"

"It was a goddam accident! Just soapsuds!"

Blackmore would not listen to reason, that it was only a soapy, perfumed water, and Kelly had never used the chamber pot. He kept cursing Kelly.

Rising, Kelly hunted the door. With springs and mattress in the way and broken mirror underfoot, the mukluks and his height were a great advantage, and he got the door open. It took all his strength because of the dresser.

There were people coming up the stairs. They stopped when they saw him. He still could not get the image of the gun from his mind. He moved along the hall. Men stopped to stare at him.

"A man attacked me in my room," he announced. Most of them knew he was a federal marshal. He knew it would win him a proper hearing and respect; they would make way. He could get down the stairs, and their crowded presence would deter Blackmore from shooting. "A man pounced on me in my room. He was waiting for me."

The clerk, too, was coming up the stairs. He tried to explain: "He claimed to be your partner."

"It's all right," said Kelly. "I don't hold you responsible. He's the one who originally reserved the room for me. He had arranged to buy the horses lost in the shipwreck." He allowed himself a bitter laugh. "The poor man was overwhelmed by disappointment. He was in Juneau at the time, trying to get it greater recognition. He was promoting a railroad which would bypass Skagway, a shortcut via Inkun and some hot springs on Taku." He had their attention now. "He has a right to be a Juneau booster! He made no secret of it. The whole thing was on page one. And I? Well, I lost my temper. What was he doing to Skagway, and our sister camp, Dyea? And the White Pass railroad? Understand, he's British and American, dual citizenship, so it's his right to stand up for the Juneau-British Columbia route! I'll admit to being tired out, just got back from Chilkat. So, I make no apologies. I'm not one bit apologetic for hitting him with the chamber pot. I considered it a blow for the good old U. S. A.!"

The clerk accompanied him downstairs to the lobby.

"I've been too long at the fair," Kelly said, settling his bill at the reception desk. He didn't mention the damaged furniture, and the clerk hadn't been up to the room yet to see the damage.

117

Chapter Thirteen

At an old sourdough's suggestion, Kelly purchased a tarp large enough to bed under the snow, and fell in with the steady movement up Skagway Canyon. He had decided to make a leisurely trip of it, having just come and gone this way twice. The scatter of camps at the foot of the pass remained, some leaving, others taking their places. The smoke from chimneys in Sheep Camp spread close to the ground and smelled as if excrement was being used as fuel. Mazie, disgusted, said she was looking for a buyer. She intended to go over the pass with the two new girls she had hired. Jug had finished carrying all the nails over and was camped at the summit.

"Water on his wheel!" Mazie said. "You know he came in here and did the damndest thing! He took a step and fell flat on his face. You see, he'd become used to the pass."

She showed Kelly a quantity of gold, coarse colors and nuggets, a buckskin poke, spilled across the bar. Gold! The shine of it!

"They come over every day, headed for the States. I've seen, I'll wager, a hundred pounds of this. Gold! The real stuff. It does something to you. The devil's own metal. Something to that! The Yukon Trail. Still heavy snow inside. They pass White Horse to the west and still travel by sled up Lake Laberge, the Carmacks-Braeburn trail, if that means anything to you. It doesn't to me, except it's a shortcut. The Klondikers sell their dogs at the top. Of course dogs are useless here. But gold! Oh, they bring that! It's the real thing, Kelly." She had about ten ounces. It looked like that from Bear Creek in Montana, oatmeal size and small nuggets, good dark yellow. "The biggest nugget so far weighed ninety-one ounces, troy. A little under sixteen hundred dollars."

She had picked up a lot of news at the bar. There was a mail route from Skagway to Dawson. It cost a dollar to send a letter. "I understand your partner has that Indian bookkeeper."

"The Kid? Yes, I put Blackmore onto that. The man's a godsend, but do you think I got any gratitude? No! He ambushed me at the hotel."

"I heard something about that."

Kelly was willing to change the subject, though he was always glad to talk about the Piegan Kid. After all, it was Kelly who had left the jail door unlatched. Unlike Blackmore, the Kid was not without gratitude. He'd keep Kelly informed if Blackmore intended to do him any more dirt.

"He'll be glad enough to deal with me when he finds out he needs those copper nails," Kelly said. "Better than lag screws. Better than hanger bolts. There's nothing, absolutely nothing, to take the place of square copper nails when it comes to binding a boat together. Two sizes, framing and planking. The two *vershook* and the half-*arshine*."

Mazie laughed. "That sounds vulgar, Kelly."

"It's Russian! The half-*arshine* is a king spike, ten inches long, square shank, bent head. It can be inset by driving and never works loose. Best sluice nails ever devised."

Jug came in, beaten into exhaustion by the pass. "Oh, you're here, Kelly."

Kelly knew something was amiss. He stood while Jug took off his boots and padded around in his wool socks. The wool socks grabbed splinters from the wood floor. Gad, he was slow, but Kelly knew better than to ask why. It was well to let Jug take his time.

"Blackmore's been up here," he said finally.

Kelly waited. It had been a mistake to have taken his time on the way back from Skagway.

"Aren't you going to ask why?"

"Why?" said Kelly pensively.

"That's just the point! I don't know. He has something going with the police, though, that Corporal Burke. Burke came out and snooped around, but our stuff is still on the Alaska side, at least what I think is the Alaska side."

"How do you mean, he snooped?"

"Well, he kept looking at it."

"Did he say anything?"

"No, he just snooped."

"Well, it's a very small outfit. He's probably used to looking at flour and potatoes. He probably was wondering, nails, what the hell?"

"And I wonder, too! I think Blackmore's set him against us."

Kelly was in time to help carry odds and ends and their camp rolls. The creeping mass of the pass was thicker and slower since the last time Kelly climbed.

"Oh, Mister Kelly!" Corporal Burke called when they came to the police house. "Are you intending to take this cargo over the boundary?"

"That was the idea."

Burke thought about it. He evidently had a problem. He didn't know whether to stop Kelly there, or cry halt when he made his first step into the Queen's domain. He chose the former.

"Will you come inside, please?"

"I'll stay here," said Jug.

"You can come too, if you like," said the corporal.

"No, I'll stay here."

"There's gold in those sacks!" said Kelly.

The corporal did not smile. Inside, Kelly had a strong feeling of Blackmore's presence, a smell. Perhaps he was in some other room. There was a stand-up counter, a desk, and some shelves, and there was a bottle of Blackmore's company Scotch, S & M pure malt Scotch whiskey. It was about the only Scotch whiskey Spottswoode & More handled that did not hail from Spain, with dates on the label such as 1492.

"Oh, Spottswoode and More!" Kelly said, as if just noticing the Scotch. "My old boss, Mister Warren, used to be the distributor."

Instead of offering Kelly a drink, the corporal handed him a document. It was stiff, like a parchment, yellowed at the edges, perhaps rained on.

SUMMONS

The whole summons and complaint was written in that old English script, as such documents had not been for years in the States. Under the word SUMMONS, someone had written in blunt pen, with affectations of a legal secretary's hand, "*Writ of Attachment.*" Then in a more hurried manner, but still with flourishes, and widenings of the pen point, "*At issuance in coupled jurisdiction, to wit, the Territory of Yukon, Dominion of Canada, at the direction of Studdsworth. P. Blackmore, Esq., British and American citizenship. . . .*"

Kelly had to laugh. He couldn't help it. By God, this dual citizenship was serving him well. Kelly rapidly scanned the document, which was actually a claim of ownership comprising "*diverse stock of square copper nails, designated as security against debts certified and due as of the 21st inst., in Butte City, Montana, U. S. A.*" and bearing the signature of T. S. Donahue, United States Commissioner, Skagway, Alaska Territory, (which it wasn't: it was a federal possession) and the date. "*My commission expires. . . .*"

121

Kelly held it at a distance. He held it to the light which came from the eastern window, and regarded it from several angles. He held it to a ray of sunlight to see if it had any of the silken threads that distinguished U. S. paper money. Kelly then made what he considered an amusing remark.

"Genuine parchment, like our own Declaration of Independence."

"You seem to think this is amusing, Mr. Kelly." Burke was far from happy with his task.

"*Marshal* Kelly."

The corporal jumped on it. "Not on this side of the line!"

"As a strict constructionist," said Kelly, "I would say that if my authority terminates at the boundary, so also does that of the United States Commissioner. Point of equity, corporal."

"That may be, but I am sure I have the authority to stop any merchandise, or any individual, upon reasonable cause or suspicion."

"Suspicion of what?"

"Illegal removal. In short, theft. You have no proof of title and you lack sufficient comestibles to prevent starvation. We are given a very broad latitude of interpretation." He came to a stop. It was abrupt, apparently in response to a sound. Someone had entered another door. Kelly turned and saw a red-coated and gold-braided man who had just shed his overcoat.

"Inspector!" said Corporal Burke. "Inspector MacIvers!" In quick retreat, he saluted and came to attention. The inspector had been outside and cold was part of the strength of his hand.

The inspector looked at the Summons and the Writ of Attachment. "Oh, for God's sake!" He did not go so far as to wad the paper and cast it in the stove, but he did toss it aside like trash. "Your U. S. Magistrate seems to be enlarging his jurisdiction."

Kelly said with great toleration, "I suppose he wanted to collect

122

the five-dollar fee."

"Headed for the Klondike, Mister Kelly?"

"U. S. Marshal Kelly, sir." Kelly flashed his badge.

"Ah, so it is. Corporal, give the marshal a set of those new maps." He smiled at Kelly. "So, you're Ho! for the Klondike! I may be, too. We seem to be moving headquarters, or creating a new district of Dawson. I hope the latter. White Horse is the old traditional key point in the Northwest, you know. I'd hate to see it downgraded. It looks like plenty of business for both. I wish I could sign you on. Oh, we take foreigners, Marshal Kelly, but not in positions above private. Corporal, will you have your Dogribs furnish the marshal a good sled and good huskies? They have the best dogs here and they won't try and rob you. There are some hills, then a gentle passage to Lindeman. That's the first lake. All ice. You will be able to see Bennett if you climb a tree . . . if any are left! You'll be able to smell the fresh sawdust a mile or two before you're there. Green timber for greenhorns. I hope none gets drowned. Drowning is our chief worry. We were very fortunate last year. But, of course, it was a much smaller rush then."

"I heard they sank and had to burn their boats for the nails."

"That's what I heard, too, though I didn't see it. I was still at Division M. Dawson will be Division B. We're switching old Division B up here. That was Fort McCloud. There'll be a great shuffling around, what with the road they're talking about from Edmonton and Peace River. One road is supposed to come up the old railroad survey through Sifton Pass. Great things are happening, Marshal. Even if the Klondike doesn't live up to expectations."

The inspector was in a bit of a rush. There were more police posts to visit, a trip by dog sled to distant White Horse City, and from there to Dawson. He gave the corporal very explicit instructions as to the drivers and teams to be provided the marshal and his friend, and then he left. Kelly found himself feeling genuinely sorry for Corporal Burke.

The Indians were Takanis. Their dogs seemed excessive for the cargo, but the cargo proved heavy for its bulk. "Ho! Carry gold to Yukon?" one of the Takanis asked. Who said Indians had no sense of humor?

They set out on a surface of greenish ice that rang under the runners. There was a slight grade of less than a half percent to a barrier of hills. The hills eventually opened to a winding trail, and level lake ice could be seen — lakes, and the smokes of woodcutters' camps, and boat builders. There seemed to be no true horizon, only false horizons with more mountains. Kelly would ask, "Bennett?" or the name of some camp he had heard of, but it would turn out to be some place else. The air stayed blue from a thousand fires. You could smell the sawed wood.

Partners built platforms. One man sawed on top and the other beneath. The logs were sawed, using long, two-handled rip saws called "Swede fiddles". The sound was a deep note in clear wood, with sudden screeching where the knots were encountered. The sawdust fell, gummy with sap. Each position was difficult — the upper sawyer had to do the lift, and the one below, who furnished the downward power, received the sawdust, turning his face into something that resembled a groundhog, only larger and woolier. Because the timber was so swollen with sap, there was need for copper nails which would never rust and would hold their "drive," rather than iron nails which pulled loose from wood that failed to swell more.

They came to a town of log and canvas where the improvements consisted of plank and pole walks, a two-story building, and a police tent with a flag. Bennett City. There were actually several Bennetts. The Indians had taken them on to the top of White Pass and this was the White Pass Bennett.

Kelly took time to study the new maps they had been given.

124

Apparently the lakes changed yearly.

"Two hunder dollar!" the Takanis were shouting. They had finished their task, and were unloading the cargo.

"To hell with that! Fifty dollars!"

Ultimately, they were pleased to get one hundred dollars, much of it in silver coin. Kelly was becoming expert in dealing with Indians: coin, the more coin, the better.

Bennett consisted of shacks, tents, pole walks that splashed mud, and smells: fires of rotten wood, liquor, frying meat, stenches of backhouses. There were also barbershops and the sounds of strange languages and accents. Kelly visited the police shack first to register his revolver. It wasn't required, but the young constable wrote it all down, the serial number, caliber, Kelly's name, and was duly impressed with his badge. He asked, did Kelly have extradition papers for some fugitive?

"No, just a furlough assignment. We want to see how our Yanks disport themselves."

"We have a lot of them," said the constable.

"My partner may have a camp here, a Mister Blackmore?"

"Oh, he's the English national who's building the barges. You'll find his camp beyond the railroad grade, some miles over on South Arm."

They waited in line to buy supper at a tent restaurant, The Elite, serving moose-rib stew, biscuits, dried-apple pie, and coffee at a dollar a throw.

"Mazie had the right idea," Jug concluded. "Start a joint in South White Horse where they stack up, waiting to shoot the rapids. Get dollars going, and gold coming!"

A clothes merchant with nothing left but a few pairs of pants and some empty shelves said they could move in if they paid him his unused rent — fifty dollars. They decided to take it. The store was large enough for a counter and about four men. They had signs painted on new white cheesecloth. Cheesecloth, not wool, was the premier fabric of the stampede.

"Some fellow packed over with fifty bolts of this and is making a fortune," the clothes merchant told them.

MACURE AND KELLY
SQUARE COPPER NAILS
4 inch or 10 inch
Never Rust — Never Come Loose
SELL FOR SLUICE NAILS IN DAWSON

"We won't put the price on," said Kelly.

"What is the price?"

"Twenty-five cents per inch."

"They'll never pay it!"

"Of course they won't. That's just the point! We don't want to sell the nails. We want to wait for the ice to break and the boats to fall apart. Then we'll sell the nails at advanced prices."

As expected, quite a number came in to look, but nobody bought. There was a perpetual tread, a slosh on the plank and pole walks. Kelly decided to go get a shave. Their store was two doors down from a one-chair, home-made barbershop. When he entered, a large, long-haired, yellow dog got up from his rest and smelled Kelly's mukluks. He lapped the sides, experimentally.

"Go away," said Kelly.

"Thinks you need a shoe shine," said the barber, "or maybe he's hungry. Those Tlingit dogs eat all the old clothes. Nothing goes to waste in the North."

The dog left and lay sulking, with his head on his paws.

"Be careful of that mustache," said Kelly, lying in the rather ingenious barber chair, carpenter-made to straighten and let down, by lever. The lever was a pole that landed on the wall and was each time fit in a socket to be operated by a single long pull. The chair had no swivel, however, and so the barber had to move himself around. A shave that was twenty-five cents in Skagway, fifteen in Seattle, a dime in St. Paul, was fifty cents in Bennett. What would it be in White Horse or in Dawson, where they would pay in gold? Kelly had heard that nothing bought with gold was less than a dollar in Dawson. Nobody could weigh less than a gram of raw gold. There were only gold scales in Dawson, no cash registers.

Outside a peculiar light had filled the sky. A shifting glow, like heat-lightning, appeared and disappeared along the northeast horizon, dead purplish gray in the south. Kelly could feel the electric energy in his hair. The barber was going to close up. Kelly decided they should do the same. There was no lock on their store, but the police said they'd keep an eye on the nails. There was almost no theft in the North on the Canadian side, north of the boundary, north of the Sixtieth, or to be exact, fifty-nine degrees forty-five minutes. Or, almost exact. With the glacial earth ever shifting, nobody was ever sure where anything was exactly, but the police would keep watch. The copper nails were like gold — the gold of the boat-building south.

They hailed a dray to haul their outfits, actually a home-fashioned bobsled, pulled by woolly, undersize horses, woollier and smaller than those that had carried the nails to Chilkoot. These consisted now of little but themselves and their dunnage, with tarps and bedrolls. There was a campgrounds, much advertised by cheesecloth signboards with red and black letters on uprights. The signs rippled in the vagrant winds.

GIBSON'S CAMP
Safe — Secure
Full Drainage   24 Hour Watchman
TENTS FOR RENT — 2$ PER NIGHT
Agent for the Grand Union Hotel, Tagish City

127

The camp was surrounded by a rail fence. The owner helped them unload.

"Where's Blackmore's camp?" Kelly asked. "You know, the barge builder?"

"You're almost there. He came up the railroad grade. This will be a railroad town some day. I staked this ground under the mineral act, before the town site."

"It will make you a rich man," Kelly predicted.

"Yes. I can subdivide."

"What's it called . . . the town? Bennett Lake or Tagish City?"

"We generally call it Bennett from the north and Tagish from the south."

They decided to see what the town had to offer. There were several tent theatres, in fact, a theatre section. **Sleeveless George and his Delmonico Girls. The Rialto. News of the World, T.S. Sullivan, Readings Hourly — Chicago, Seattle and San Francisco Newspapers.** Through one canvas they could hear the music of a small band. A sign read **Rastus and his Original Cotton Blossom Minstrels.** The band stopped and after a time laughter was heard. Apparently the minstrels were seated and the end man had taken over.

They walked on, watching the strange lightning. No thunder — just a crackling of electricity. Things magnetized. Gas pressure lamps shone on a lecturer speaking to a crowd of fifty or more. According to a sign, he was selling his book, **The Cardinal Principals of Gold Prospecting by Dr. J. D. Stephens, Ph.D. $2.00 per copy.** Apparently it was Dr. Stephens himself speaking. His audience forced people off the sidewalk into the slosh.

"He's a fake," said Jug, who was a better speller than Kelly. "He spelled 'principles' wrong. I'll bet he spelled it wrong on the book, too."

However, the book which Dr. Stephens was holding aloft had *Gold — Cardinal Principles* on the cover. They paused to listen.

Actually, he was pretty good. He'd probably given that speech five hundred times. His subject was Gold: Mother Lode to Bedrock. Several bought books. Then he started a demonstration of his "gold compass" by offering to let any man in the audience conceal his gold watch. He'd pay ten dollars if he could not locate it.

A peculiar glow had spread along the horizon. It couldn't be the Northern Lights. The glow was south and west. Wind rose in a sudden gust, flapping the canvas and putting a stop to the professor's demonstration. Rain came, fine as a frozen mist. Then it quieted and the south became purplish dark.

"Feels like an old-fashioned Montana Chinook," said Kelly.

Electricity glowed on the poles of the show tents, but the people inside were unaware and the music continued. Balls of light, as from giant Roman candles, bounded along the street.

"Let's get the hell out of here, Jug!" Kelly said. "It's a polar storm!"

They ran until they reached their tent.

"Kelly, look at you!" Jug exclaimed. "There's a glow all around your parka! Right off the tips of those damn wolverine hairs. Kelly! It's a halo, a nimbus! Oh, Jesus protect us!"

He actually crossed himself.

Kelly laughed. "After forty days, I have arisen!" he cried.

"Don't challenge the Deity," Jug commanded. "Not at a time like this!"

Kelly held out his hands. He could see every finger. He could see the seams in the tent. Not against the sky, but from inside.

"Get your wits about you, Jug. If Jesus decided to come back, it wouldn't be in me!" It frightened him a little, but it was funny, too. "Do something religious, Jug. Cross yourself again."

"It's not funny!"

"*Domini, domini, sanctus . . . ,*" chanted Kelly.

"Stop that! I mean *stop* it!"

He stopped. "Sorry!"

The nimbus faded from his head, from his fingers, from the tent. They entered the dark interior of the tent and got ready for bed. Kelly removed his mukluks, climbed in, and rammed his feet against something hairy, wet, cold, and trembling.

"It's that damned dog!"

"What damned dog?" Jug asked.

Kelly found a match. He didn't need it. The dog gave off a glow from his yellow hair. It was that big dog of the barber's. He'd followed him and beaten him under the covers.

"Hey, get out of here! Get out!"

But the poor animal only showed his wide, terrified eyes and, whining, tried the more desperately to find protection deep in the sleeping robes. Kelly lay with his knees under his chin.

"Let him stay," Jug suggested. "The poor animal, he's scared."

Since there was no easy way to drag him out, they got warm as best they could. Kelly took off the parka, but its wet had chilled the entire top of the bed. It became lighter outside than in. The sun came out. One could see the seams of the canvas as dark strips against the sky. Kelly managed to move the dog over to Jug's side where there was more room.

"Kelly?"

He pretended not to hear him.

"Kelly?"

"Go to sleep, Jug. The dog's all right. He feels sort of warm, now. Poor animal."

"Kelly?"

But Kelly started snoring, feigning sleep. And he did sleep. When he awoke, the dog was gone and the sun was still shining. He slept again. He never did learn what Jug had wanted.

Chapter Fourteen

It was a very slow time for copper nails. Everyone seemed to be building a boat, but had brought their own nails. Iron nails that would only rust out, but they wouldn't listen. And wouldn't you know it? There stood Blackmore.

"How's business?" he asked, smug about it. He had no bruises from their fight, no scars from the flung chamber pot.

"We're thinking of raising the price," said Kelly.

"By rights, those are my nails," Blackmore said, "but I don't want trouble. I decided to let you break your backs, carrying them. I came because we'll probably get to the Klondike together, Kelly, or not at all. Frank Woodward says we can use the square nails to anchor the keel timbers."

"Did Diamond Jack's boat get through?"

"Not so far," Blackmore conceded. "Diamond Jack had the *Olympia* rebuilt at Skagway and renamed *Faro's Daughter*. Talk about your brainless schemes. This time he may have pushed his luck too far. Take that hulk over the White Horse Pass? You didn't get a look at that place, Kelly. A thousand foot declivity! Diamond Jack used skids and a steam winch and through she came to Skagway, but he'll never shoot the White Horse without lightering. He'll have to do it empty, so the old pilots all say. But Diamond Jack knows boats. He's a New Orleans gambler, a riverboat barracuda. He killed a man one time, in cold blood, mid-river between Arkansas and Mississippi and

131

walked free while they argued over jurisdiction. But stay away from that girl, Lyla, the one they call the 'Maid with the Flaxen Hair.' There's something evil in their relationship. When the time is right, Jack won't give you a chance. He'll do it without a word. Beware when he goes pale around the mouth! He has that double Derringer around his neck on a green silk cord, barrel in a vest pocket, right side. A pull of the green cord and it's in his hand. You'll just think he's reaching for a card, Kelly. In this country you'll be lucky to have a grave three feet deep."

He cared not a damn about Kelly or the copper nails. What worried Blackmore was not having Sheridan's bank. If the bank is big enough, the house doesn't matter. A tent with a quarter million dollar bank is better than the Taj Mahal with fifty thousand.

"How about those copper nails?" Blackmore inquired.

"I bought them to make up for the horses," said Kelly, a concession. *At least,* he thought, *I've made him come around and ask.*

"How many . . . f'God's sake . . . nails have you got here?" Blackmore asked. "They must weigh twice as much as iron."

"No, they weigh the same." Nobody ever believed that iron, copper, and lead all weighed about the same.

"How many?" Blackmore asked again.

"Twenty *pood.* Actually, it totals to just about half a ton, American."

"Kelly, you hauled them all this way, and I get them after all!"

"*We* have them! You, and me, and Sheridan. The Three Musketeers!" Then Kelly gave him a lecture on the subject of copper nails — weight, tensile strength, hardness on the Mohs scale, friction of removal, resistance to corrosion in fresh and sea water, and elasticity.

Blackmore said: "You think you're educated, Kelly? Actually, you don't know a damned thing about metals, acids, melting

132

points, and horse manure without pulling out that old book the engineer threw away."

"That's the secret of being a lawyer, too," Kelly assured him. "Knowing where to look things up."

Blackmore had heard it all before. He quieted Kelly and listened to the lake. Every once in a while one heard a booming sound. It was the ice. Lake-wide ice would rise as it warmed, give way, and settle again. Kelly had looked at the maps the inspector had given him. The lakes were different on every map he saw. They started in British Columbia. In fact, they themselves were probably in British Columbia right now, and had been since the Chilkoot — Yukon territory was entered on the way to Caribou Crossing — and there were lakes on lakes. Far inland as one could see, the country was a plateau about 2,500 feet high, with mountains from two to three thousand feet higher spread without apparent system.

"That's Mount Montana," said Blackmore, pointing to a mountain peak, unusually cheerful. Things had been going rather well for him, making up somewhat for loss of the horses. The railroad had two large barge bottoms used to transport steel, which had sunk away in the muck somewhere, and he was able to buy them for a trifling amount and use their boat yards free. Woodward, his shipwright, had some of the job done for him, although it was still necessary to build cabins and storage for liquors. One more barge was being built and the last, a fourth, was on its way over the White Pass, chiefly in the form of pre-built sections which could be hauled like large sledges right over the spring holes and the dead horses.

"God! The stink there'll be when the hot weather comes," said Blackmore, cheerfully. "And, by the way, thanks for hauling the nails. I was willing to do it, but you're long on muscle."

"Glad to oblige," Kelly said.

"Yah," said Jug Macure.

The headquarters barge, when finished, would have a large cabin-office, tiny bedrooms, a pilot house, and a flagpole flaunting a big B, black on orange, for Blackmore.

"Office, galley, sleeping quarters," Blackmore said. "You really hit it lucky, Kelly."

"So did you," said Kelly. "Don't forget I put you onto hiring the Piegan Kid. Square Cree. Your own private set of books. One for you, and one for the others."

"Kelly, that was uncalled for."

"Just a joke. Shot in the dark . . . sort of."

They were crossing the ice. Hay had been laid to make a wagon way.

"But you're right, of course," Blackmore conceded. "Indian writing if needed. Anyhow, he's your friend, Kelly. And there can be no secrets between partners. We'll have to lighten cargo by using pirogues. That's another way the Kid will help. French-breed *bateaux* men. At one ton each, that's a lot of lightering. There's said to be up to a hundred of those pirogues on their way from the Inside."

"The Inside?" Jug interrupted.

"What old-time Northerners call all those vast lands of the Athabasca, the Slave and the Liard," Blackmore explained, and then looked again at Kelly. He paused for a moment, then continued with another thought. "I pray to God we don't have Diamond Jack on hand to enter the bidding . . . for his own good, if that picnic boat ends up here at the lake. I'm going to need that money, by the way."

"I'll pay my share," Kelly said, annoyed. "I've written Sheridan."

He hadn't, but he intended to, as soon as he saw how the ground — and rapids — lay. He wanted to reach White Horse, R. C. M. P. headquarters, to find out about the telegraph. He knew they had a telegraph, of sorts — wire, boat, and foot,

134

down to Prince Albert in Saskatchewan. It all depended on how much of the line had fallen victim to the porcupines, hunting fresh sap. It was something that happened every spring, shorting out the forest insulators. If Inspector McIvers was there, or could be contacted, Kelly was sure he would favor him by sending a message to Butte, via Deare Lake, Fort Nelson, and Regina. And who could tell, perhaps Sheridan could get money credits paid over in White Horse. Never underestimate the power of money!

"Ah, M'shu Kelly!" The Kid had seen them coming.

"B'jou, M'shu!" answered Kelly in his best Coyotie French, and went on, *"in nomini Patri . . . mea culpa, mea maxima culpa!"*

"No, Kelly. You don' know what you say!" the Kid answered. "You say you guilty man. You no guilty man, Kelly. You do many brave thing for poor-devil Indian in *le gran' court, cour-de-appel! La marquer d'or!* You leave ol' stone jail door open for innocent *sauvage!* False charge!"

"I got this damn job for you, too," Kelly said out of the side of his mouth, "so you could help the big *tyee* keep a set of books nobody else could read." It occurred to him that the Kid's employer couldn't read them, either. He had delivered Blackmore into the Kid's hands, barring the distant possibility that he'd be able to locate some old Indian who was able to translate the Square Cree.

"How about you teach me to read Square Cree?" asked Kelly.

"Sure thing. Ver' simple. Much easier as Chinese. You know how long to learn to read Chinese?"

"Five years?"

"Ten year! You know how many Chinese character? Five thousand!"

Work on the barges progressed steadily. There was still cargo to come by sled and toboggan, but horse travel with heavy cargo was all but stopped by Diamond Jack McGowan's *Faro's Daughter* which required as many as twenty teams, although not all in use at a single time. There were stretches where rails and ties from the aborted White Pass and Yukon could be used. Kelly, being no boat builder, went down to watch the action.

He introduced himself to Diamond Jack McGowan. Lyla was also there, standing beside her father. There was a shine in Diamond Jack's eye Kelly didn't like at all, but how different were the eyes of the beautiful Lyla. They could turn from a merry, sparkling blue that seemed to laugh into his with a special, hidden meaning, and then quickly metamorphose to a serious gray that reminded him of a deep pool where he had caught trout as a boy. There was a tantalizing mystery about her that he yearned to solve. She stirred feelings in him that he had never felt before. He resolved to spend as much time in her company as possible in the future.

"Heard Blackmore was building barges," Diamond Jack said.

"Oh, we're still nailing things together," Kelly told them. "Blackmore'd be sunk without my copper nails."

"Very strange partners," said Jack, "you and Sheridan and Blackmore. What if your Alhambra doesn't get there? The Yukon is a long river."

"We're all gamblers," Kelly replied easily. "If it doesn't work out, we'll still have the biggest bank . . . Sheridan's . . . on the richest gulch in a log cabin."

He had barely returned to the home camp where the barges were going together with much use of copper nails — when here came the *Faro's Daughter*! It had found some track under the snow and, by God, the boat floated. There was some open water, and the police blasted for them, or stood by while others blasted. Blackmore was enraged, being a British subject, and the channel severed his own camp from the town. It made an extra quarter mile journey up to the creek and around, but there was nothing he could do. There was more blasting to bring it to a berth, about four hundred yards farther on. There Jack set up and started putting things together again, chiefly cabins, super-structure, no keel, and he moved what proved to be a small circus tent across to the theatre district, where he set up for business.

"The son-of-a-bitch must be broke," Blackmore declared. "Earning his way."

Diamond Jack had all the usual games and enough lumber for a partial floor. What was more, he had use of a Hudson's Bay Company steamboat, thawed and with white lead cleaned from its sliding surfaces, black pitch smoke pouring from the chimney, while Blackmore had been told it wouldn't be ready for another two weeks.

"By God, I had a contract for that boat!" Blackmore cried.

Kelly asked to see the contract.

"Who do you think you are, a lawyer? Where'd you learn law? Hanging around with Forbes and Carlyle? Those damned atheists!"

The agreement, not a contract, was inside in the Kid's lock box and Kelly saw it was only for the big Yukon Lakes, Laberge and Marsh.

"Well, we're not going anywhere very soon," Kelly told Black-more. "We still have a lot of boat to build. And you should be happy if Jack needs the money."

"I'm not happy. It's the principle of the thing!"

Blackmore then took to standing long minutes in the pilot house watching through field glasses, seeing the tent go up, watching the superstructure go back on the *Faro's Daughter*. And the flags. Diamond Jack had raised the Union Jack, the Stars and Stripes, and the Irish Shamrock.

"This is Canada!" Blackmore told Kelly. "Are they going to let him get away with that?"

"Why not?" said Kelly, sick by now of listening to him. "What should he do, consult you first? You're flying your own flag."

"Don't push me, Kelly. My insignia is registered!"

"Just a joke. You have to keep your sense of humor."

There was really not a thing for Kelly to do. He could talk to the Kid about old times in Montana, or do odd jobs for the boat builders which were demeaning. He was just no good with tools. A pontoon bridge, charging a twenty-five cent toll, had been built where the *Faro's Daughter* had passed. Kelly paid it. It seemed cheap for anything in this country. Besides, he wanted to visit Diamond Jack's circus tent.

When he entered and found the gaming tables, Lyla was dealing faro and watching her was a delight, total purity of motion. She caressed the cards. And how they slipped from the box, soundlessly, as if by their own volition! She didn't wear diamonds or rings. Her fingers were incredibly smooth and white. Even her fingernails were white as ivory. No pink color. The nails were exactly the shape of her finger ends, to feel the touch of the cards.

There were a number of very nice touches in the circus. One was the chips, used in bank games, faro and roulette. They were white, red, blue and yellow. They were all inlaid J. M. for Jack McGowan, but the yellows were special, somewhat oversize and thicker. They bore a cameo profile of ivory against the cream yellow. Yes, ivory!

Kelly had moved up to the faro table and examined one.

"Your mother?" he asked Lyla softly.

She flashed him a radiant smile. "Papa had them made from a locket painting after Mama died."

"You must miss her. She looks like such a lovely woman. You favor her strongly."

That pensive look came into her eyes. "I was very young when she died, but . . . yes, I miss her. I often think that our lives,

father's and mine, would have been very different had she lived."
She dropped her gaze to the cards again, and he realized that
he should not distract her further. It was not a time for private
conversation.

When Kelly got back, Blackmore accused him of sticking his
neck in a guillotine. "You stay away from that girl, Kelly," he
warned. "If nothing else, Diamond Jack'll take you for a spy.
You'll end up getting yourself shot."

The only reason Blackmore cared a damn about Kelly's getting
shot, of course, was Sheridan and what would happen to the
bank with Kelly gone. What he did was launch forth on Jack
McGowan, how he'd gone with the Union Army to New Orleans,
returned to be mustered out in Ohio, and went straight back
and joined the Confederate Guards. It was the act of a traitor
to his own Union Army. After the war he became a riverboat
gambler. He had married a girl of prominent family. He had
a son who died and then his wife died in a yellow fever epidemic.
Lyla was only a child at the time, a girl of eight or ten, appearing
on stage on showboats.

"Tell me about Lyla," Kelly said.

"Oh, she traveled with him, performed on the stage on those
steamboat showboats. She was on the boat when he shot that
young planter under steam in the channel. There was a big argument about jurisdiction. The boat was between Arkansas and
Mississippi. He was closer to Mississippi when the shots were
fired, but closer to the Arkansas shore when the man died. Place
called Big Ox-Bow Lake. They took the body ashore in Memphis,
Tennessee! Jack stayed put. So there was a big ruckus over jurisdiction, Arkansas and Mississippi . . . even Tennessee where
they had the body. Jack thought it was funny. He had a stage
act and would make jokes about it. It seems like Mississippi won
out to try the case, but the judge had been a colonel on the
rebel side, and a federal judge in Ohio interceded. Jack was with

the tenth Ohio, a home boy. There's something evil in that man . . . his relationship with his daughter."

"Don't start that again!" Kelly protested. "I don't believe you. It's a damned lie."

"I mean nothing against her," Blackmore assured him. "Did you know he has a picture of her on his chips? The big hundred-dollar yellows?"

"No, that's her mother. She told me so herself."

"Oh, well, that's as bad. A fine way to honor your dead. Putting your dead wife's cameo on a chip! Some respect! But we'll have the Alhambra. Match that with any damned cameo poker chips! I wish you'd stay away from there. I don't want to lose you."

Blackmore would, at least once daily, wish Kelly would drown under the ice but, on the other hand, he was not certain of the Sheridan bank without him.

"What's the French word for predicament?" Kelly asked the Kid when he saw him.

"Predicament? We lak say, hell if you do, also hell if you don'?"

Kelly had hoped there was something like predic-a-maw with the accent on the last syllable. How it annoyed Blackmore when he said something in French!

"Sure," said the Kid. "Predicamau."

Kelly would come in smelling of the barbershop and Blackmore would ask where he had been, and Kelly would say, "At Jack's Circus," just to annoy him.

"You get to mooning over that girl and one of these days. . . ."

"That's why I wear the parka. The canvas will catch the bullet and carry it wide. The marshals in the tough towns always wore those old wolf-skin overcoats. They'd catch the lead bullet and swing wide. Weight always travels from the place of greatest density to that of the lesser. Principle of physics." Then to rile him still more, he said: "You know, the first real civilization I was ever exposed to was at the Alhambra?"

And Blackmore conceded: "Maybe you're not absolutely hopeless, after all."

Chapter Fifteen

The steady rock of the barge was restful and Kelly lay half asleep. He woke suddenly. The Piegan Kid was standing there.

"Hello, Kid."

"You know what, Kelly? Big rise come. Diamond Jack, he pull down heem tent. Get her across to big boat. Gone! You want me tell big boss?"

Did he, or didn't he? Kelly got a perverse pleasure in carrying distressing news to Blackmore himself.

"My duty," he said.

He got up and went on the deck. The lake, rising, was afloat with broken slabs of ice. He had a new view where the tent had been. He decided to bathe and get dressed. Then he looked to his medicine bundle, and to his revolver, as he did every morning.

"Major!" he finally called, rapping on Blackmore's door.

Blackmore liked being called that, and Kelly favored him. Little things counted for much and cost nothing. It was one of Kelly's charities.

"Yes?"

"The bird has taken wing."

"What do you mean?" It was Blackmore's surly, waking voice.

"Diamond Jack. He has done the A-rab."

"Damn it, say what you mean!"

"Why, Jack . . . he pulled up his tent like the A-rab and

as silently stole away in the dark."

"It never gets dark! How could he steal away?"

Kelly could feel the tremble of Blackmore's rising, then heard his barefoot, Sepoy-marching step as he went for his splash bath, then the Empire Lotion he rubbed under his arms and around his private parts.

Then out he came, flexing those shoulders. He was strong like an African ape, only hairless. He had a pair of field glasses.

"I can't make out a thing through all the mist." He wiped the lenses.

"Oh, he's gone," Kelly assured. "He must have hired the steam tug."

There was float ice and boats everywhere — small, whipsawed craft, many already in trouble, with men bailing to stay afloat. Served them right. They had walked right past and never tried to buy a single copper nail!

"We can't just stay here!" Blackmore insisted. "They promised me I'd be first with the steam tug. It's that daughter of Jack's. She makes goo-goo eyes at the police."

It sounded so damn funny, Blackmore using that term "goo-goo eyes," that Kelly laughed aloud.

"Laugh your head off. I paid over hard money in Juneau!"

"And you have dual citizenship, too," said Kelly, sounding as stupid as possible.

"Don't push me, Kelly. I've taken all from you I intend to! You were over there yesterday. Haven't we got a watchman on this outfit?" They did, but it was Celden Harris, his pilot, whom he didn't dare curse out. So Kelly had to take the blast. "You must have seen something. It took them time to strike that tent and fly all that equipment. All you ever see is that girl. Jack will teach you a lesson, mooning around. I still say, there's something evil there." Then he went into his tirade about Jack's war record, and ended up with: "And that's who you're dealing with, Kelly!"

To get away from him, Kelly took a folding carpenter's rule to measure the ice. He measured the exposed part of each slab. Since there were waves, they joggled, so it took a while. Then he went back in and, while Blackmore watched — in fact, because he watched, Kelly computed the totals.

"Sixty-inch ice, give or take half an inch. Waves."

"How can you be so damn sure how thick it is?" asked Blackmore.

"Ice. Specific gravity, point-nine. Six inches of water. Nine times six is . . . ," he squinted as if having a hard time getting the exact figure.

"Fifty-four!" snapped Blackmore.

"Yes. Right you are! More than four feet. That is heavy ice."

"What are all those rowboats doing out there?" Blackmore sounded as though it were Kelly's fault.

"They got caught in the backup. There's a big swirl where the river beds meet. The steamboats have rescued dozens. Mainly just the people. They let the boats go. Some of the boats came apart, almost board for board. They'll be picking up boards for a week." Sadly, he added: "See what happens when they don't use copper nails?"

"You think it's funny!"

"No, just how lucky it was I bought you the copper nails."

"We used seasoned cedar! I made a special trip to get that cedar!"

They sat in the galley with Celden Harris, drinking tea with a drop of rum added for energy. There were some glasses sitting on a shelf. One heard a tinkle, vibration, and seconds later a dull boom, like distant thunder.

"Dynamiting the ice jam," said Kelly, "at Caribou Crossing or Tagish. There are jams at the outlets." He examined the maps. "Twenty-one miles to Caribou Crossing. Forty-two to Tagish."

144

"There should be mist or smoke," said Blackmore.

"Too many hills. The lakes make a big quarter and a half turn east." Kelly laid out his railroad watch. "Sound travels how fast?" He pretended to forget. He checked his black book. "Speed of sound in air? Speed in water? In ice? What we're concerned with is the speed through air as against the speed though the earth, not this thin layer of water. Basalt. Thousands of feet deep. Igneous rock."

Blackmore was annoyed at paying this damned cowboy the heed he would a real expert, but he didn't let on because Harris was there.

"Now, the glasses tinkle at the vibration though the frozen ground and the basalt. But the boom comes through air. We can ignore the lake. Miles of air, miles of basalt, and a thin skiff of water. Right? Right, Major?" Blackmore pretended to show interest. "So the glasses tinkle at the earth's vibration, and we hear the boom through air. Dry air, zero degrees temperature, centigrade, eleven hundred and fifty feet per second . . . this raggedy book! But basalt, twelve-thousand-nine-fifty. That's more than ten times as fast! Twenty miles to Caribou Crossing. Let me run this off on the old slide rule. And I mean old. You remember Jack Ridgeway, geologist for the Northern Pacific? He gave it to me. Got stepped on and we glued it back together. It works a little rough, but I'm a rough operator. Ha-ha! Not bad for a cowboy. That's what he said. For all practical purposes, you subtract ten percent from the difference, tinkle from boom. You get twenty-two miles. So they're dynamiting at Caribou Crossing. That tinkle. The glasses respond to the vibration through basalt. How does sound diminish? By geometric ratio? I think the surface of the earth, being a skin, has a tintinnabulary effect. I'd have to consult the authorities."

"Didn't get around to teaching you that at good old Burlington?" asked Blackmore.

"No, they didn't. Science and Latin school. I never had the funds. I'm self-taught, like Lincoln. I had to learn it the hard way, tagging after men like Ridgeway, listening. Engineering is like law." He waved the limp, black book. "Four hundred pages, thin paper, and print you have to read close up, or magnified. For a fellow who never got through the fourth reader in school. . . ."

"All right, Kelly! I don't want to hear about how you peeked in at grade four and saw how you'd have to sit like a grasshopper with the desk in your lap!"

"By God, I'd like to hear that!" said Harris.

So Kelly told about his visit to the Billings graded school where he'd gone sneaking out, never to return, and about Burlington.

Eventually they got started. The shore lines were loosened. Men with pikes rocked the barges and slowly, very slowly, they found current. All seemed still, but the shore moved. The main task was keeping them in line, because the rear barges felt the moving ice more strongly.

The business section slid away. An empty space marked the spot where Jack's circus tent had stood. The yellow and white boat was gone. It could not be seen, even high up in the pilot's enclosure.

"He got the start on us," ruminated Blackmore darkly.

"Maybe he'll get wrecked," said Kelly to cheer him.

"God damn it, I don't want anybody to get wrecked!"

"You're a hard man to please."

Only the mountains changed — Stony Mountain, Mount Montana, Lime Mountain, Woody Peak, Jubilee. One could measure their changing angles on the maps and know their own exact position.

"Triangulation," said Kelly.

A police boat hailed them, a corporal and an Indian boatman with two derelict passengers wrapped in a single tarp. The Indian

146

stood holding a steel-shod pike. Oars were almost useless in the big ice.

"Is this the Alhambra outfit?" asked the policeman.

He was told, yes. They tied fast and came aboard, the policeman and the two cold, wet, derelict men in their tarp, and the Indian who hesitated.

"That fire feels good!" said the policeman. The Indian stood apart, not knowing if he were welcome.

"Come on, get warm," said Kelly. "How about some coffee? Tea? Something stronger?"

Blackmore looked mean, not liking the looks of this, bringing two shipwrecked men aboard. He stirred himself, however, and told the cook to make coffee and look sharp about it. "A little brandy wouldn't hurt," he added.

"For the Indian, too?" Kelly asked.

The Indian shook his head, no.

The policeman was Corporal Gibbons and the two shipwrecked men were Skip McGuire and his partner, Bob Nelson. "Good men," he said.

"We can use two more men," said Celden Harris. "A dollar a day and keep?" He looked at Blackmore, "At least far as White Horse."

Blackmore looked dark as his name, but Harris was the pilot. Pilots were hard to find and they both knew it.

"How's Diamond Jack making it with his keel?" asked Kelly.

"Oh, that!" responded Corporal Gibbons. "He took that off back at White Pass. He said he'd put it back on when he dry-docks in Dawson. He'll have a bad enough time in the rapids without a keel."

"We heard you shooting."

"Shooting? Oh, the dynamite! That was the new gelatin powder. The ice jam at Caribou Crossing."

"How far do you call that?"

"Twenty miles."

"Damn," said Kelly, "I had it twenty-four! But we've been moving. I might have had it on the nose."

Blackmore looked disgusted. "You blasteth the ice jam and my partner tooteth his horn!"

The policeman saw to it his shipwrecked charges were served, and save for the Indian, they all sipped brandy-laced coffee.

"Will there be fast water?" asked Woodward who had come up from his stern watch.

"We don't expect it, but you can't tell one season to next," said the corporal. "You'll have the day's swing to Tagish and a chute into Marsh Lake. Strung out, these boats will take it, but I don't know about being tied stem and stern. Ask the police there. But right now there must be thirty feet of ice stacked up, so you'll hear more blasting."

"How do you get dynamite under the ice?" asked Kelly.

"Don't. The concussion makes it go. All that weight, pressure. Well, I'll have to be toddling."

"Toddling?" said Blackmore, still annoyed at being stuck with two deadheads and a dollar a day, besides.

The day passed. They had a noon dinner. The Chinese cook was sent back to his charcoal stove for extra portions. Appetites had increased, and now there were two more hands on board. There were more distant explosions. One could feel them in his body and later the rumble deep, like thunder.

"Tagish," said Kelly. "At one mile per hour, we'll be a day and a half."

Small settlements kept creeping in sight. One never realized the extent of the stampede. You could close your eyes and know by the scent of fresh sawdust when the boat camps passed. Harris marked position by the mountains, with maps tacked to the wall, triangle and protractor handy. "That puts us right here," he would say, marking an "x."

148

Again explosions — one felt the tremble through the water, and the thunder long afterward.

"They're opening Tagish now," said Harris. "I'd better go above."

Kelly went along. The pilot house had a fine view. The ice seemed to gather mist, and high up one saw over it. There were buildings on a summit. A red flag seemed to be mounted, but it was hard to be certain. The smokes of stampeders' camps had cleared, but an icy mist remained. The far sky was streaked with red, a remnant of sunset, and against it the flag seemed to have gathered light, a red of its own.

The pilot lowered his spy glass. "You know, there's a damn boat on fire! I wonder how they managed that?"

"Carbide?"

"Yes, you're probably right. Fifty pound cans of that stuff, a little water, and whoof!"

Kelly told him about the pitch balls, pitch and compacted pine needles. "I had a chance to go partners. The big fortunes in gold camps aren't mining fortunes. They're in supplies. That was true in the States, too. California, for all its Mother Lode . . . it was Stanford and his railroad bunch who came out with the fortunes."

There were chutes at the lake exit where the ice jams had been blasted. The boats had to be uncoupled and maneuvered to make the run one at a time. They made a mighty splash, but all was well. They rode with their square prows high. Woodward, who had been at work since planning and buying cedar the autumn before, knew his business.

It was one hell of a run down Tagish River, four miles into Lake Marsh, the source of the Yukon. Afterward, hours of poling and paddling were required to bring the boats back in line, strung out in the very slight current.

"Due north," said Kelly, closing the transit. "Do you realize we have a declination here of thirty-one degrees?"

One counted the time, like Indians, by sleeps. It was two sleeps down the length of Lake Marsh, where there should have been a tow from steam tugs, but there wasn't.

"I paid over hard cash for steam towage on those boats!" Blackmore fumed. "And by the holy hell, I'm going to get a refund!"

"Have the Kid write them in Square Cree," said Kelly. "Tell them it's an Eastern Constantinopolitan Catholic curse."

Blackmore decided to laugh at that because he claimed to be a Constantinopolitan Catholic, not Greek Orthodox, but one of perhaps only four thousand descended from the original Constantine the Great.

New shores and new mountains. From the pilot house one saw a hundred camp smokes. Deeper and wider had gone the stampede and the boats on the water. From the pilot house, using the spy glass, Kelly thought he saw a glint of yellow in gray ice, through icy vapor — Diamond Jack's boat. Down in Skagway they had said he'd never get it over the White Pass. Now they were saying he'd wreck it in the White Horse rapids. New shores and new mountains, but less interesting summits. The timber here was uncut; stands of jackpine, fir, and leafless white-bark aspens or birch whose buds, sensing spring, had started to swell. And here and there a fragrance carried on the breeze, a balsam-poplar odor. Kelly had read of the northern summer — a paradise of flowers and a scourge of black flies and mosquitoes.

Two more sleeps down Lake Marsh, and one finally sensed a current, the deep power of the Yukon. They passed settlements, some large enough to boast a street, and one had a police shack with the flag up. Many boats were upended, in the process of being caulked or having new boards fitted. There were Indians selling fresh and smoked fish. Some had been taken from the lake ice, a fish bonanza. There was a sign reading: **Saloon.**

150

"Ah, civilization!" said Kelly.

"Next stop, South White Horse," said Harris. "I hope to God we find a place to berth."

"We better," Blackmore said. "I paid over enough money."

"By the great horned spoon, I'd sue!" said Kelly. "Is it down on paper?"

Blackmore did not answer.

"Which shore?"

"Port," said Blackmore.

"If we have papers, the police will enforce it," said the pilot. "Those red coats are next unto God, or the forces of Lucifer in this country."

Kelly liked that "the forces of Lucifer." "Fallen Angels?" he asked.

"I didn't mean it that way. I'm not much on the Bible. But they rule the ground here, *and* the waves."

It amused Harris to see Kelly take readings on his transit. "What direction should I steer, Marshal?" he would ask. "Up river, or down?"

"I'd advise down, but in this country the declinations are all wrong. As for the North Star, forget it. It's nearly straight up. Magnetic north should be north-northeast, but compasses go crazy. Right now, by the map, we're heading almost due north."

"North to the land of gold," said Harris. "Once we run the White Horse, right side up, all hell can't stop us. They'll have a channel open on Laberge, with steam power to give us a tow. If the money holds out . . . but that's your department."

"Money never interested me much," said Kelly. "It's the game that counts. *Le game! Toujours le game!*"

"*Le jeu,* Kelly, but you speak pretty dam' good Coyotie French most tam," the Kid said, having come up and overheard. "*Maintenant, français des petits signes!* You savvy? You don' use hands 'nough. Use much sign language, Coyotie French. More hand even as French . . . Montreal French."

What Kelly wanted to learn was that Square Cree. Then, if Blackmore burned the one set of books, he could read the other. Yet, when it came down to the payoff, right down to the case cards, Kelly didn't completely trust the Kid, either. He wasn't suspicious. It was just a matter of policy.

They were entering an area far more thickly settled, judging by the placards and advertisements. **Garfield Real Estate — Choice Lots for Sale. The Easy Hour Saloon — Last First Class Bar Before South White Horse. Lumber — Some Choice Seasoned Pine — Close-Out Prices.** And, at last:

ENTERING SOUTH WHITE HORSE
Notice
No anchorages on Left Bank of River
C. N. W. M. P.

One could hear the dull roar of icy rapids, the sound held in by the rocky, sheer basaltic cliffs, and see the rise of mist, which seemed to be a minutely-pulverized ice. Many boats were at anchorage, some on the left bank, which appeared to violate the proscription. But these played out and there loomed what appeared to be a cable, blocking further passage.

"Sons-of-bitches!" yelled the pilot. "They left us no clearance!"

It proved to be a ferry cable. There was a great stir on shore as men tried to get the block and tackle arrangements loose, so a mast could be raised to lift the cable and give the pilot house clearance. The sides of barges rubbed shore. There was much shouting through a megaphone.

"I see Jack's boat made it and, if he made it, we can," said Harris.

The pilot scow passed beneath the cable with inches to spare. Anchorage was reserved on the port shore. A crowd of at least

152

two hundred, most of them on the north shore, the town side, were on hand to watch and to shout advice, much of it humorous.

"Those bastards want to see us get hung up," Kelly said.

The barges came in, one after another, and tied to mooring posts set in rock. The shouting died with the arrival of a policeman. Blackmore, after an angry minute or two, was happy enough to ask Kelly, "Don't you wish you could command that kind of respect? You and your golden badge!"

"The Queen's best," assured Kelly. "I naught begrudge."

Steeply uphill were remnants of streets and buildings, but all had been moved, apparently, across the river. One couldn't begin to guess the population, three or four thousand perhaps. But, of course, there were the camps already passed, and one saw the smokes miles away, downcanyon of White Horse proper — one of the great "cities" of the North. The right bank had an extensive Indian camp, with a mass of skin boats and canoes on shore, upended, many being mended. You could smell the hot pitch and asphalt tar. They were getting ready to collect a high fee to lighten the cargoes — Blackmore's and Diamond Jack's being perhaps the largest. Most of those who came with large outfits had a number of boats, built upriver or purchased and hauled over from Skagway. They had already passed a mile or more of such outfits, boats upended on the bank, receiving further attention.

"We'll be the biggest here!" said Blackmore, not hiding his satisfaction. "We'll have double the cargo of Jack McGowan."

Chapter Sixteen

The ferry held a maximum of six, with "Charon," the name Kelly had dubbed the operator.

"One dollar," said "Charon," but Kelly showed his badge, looking him dead in the eye. He did not begrudge the dollar fare, but he resolved to set off on the right foot.

"Has the inspector been across today?"

"Why . . . no," the operator said, surprised.

Kelly made no comment. The ferry was powered by the current, with twin blocks fore and aft, and there should have been two men running it because the ferryman had repeatedly to grab a long, steel-shod pole and fend off ice chunks that bore down on them.

"Been all season at this and ain't drowned yet!" said "Charon."

Kelly took his time to saunter the street, River Boulevard. He could see what looked like a cemetery on a rise of ground to the west. He walked past a clutter of sheds, what seemed to be one- or two-room residences, and some stacks of lumber — second-hand by the looks of it, a vacant lot with a **For Sale** sign, and at last pole walks and a substantial, painted building with a gas light and reflector. The gas burned inside a mantle; there was a thick glass chimney to protect it from the weather. The gas came from acetylene pressure, produced by a generator of some size apparently, since the building was large and light streamed from large front windows. **GOLD PAN SALOON, J. R.**

Finch, Prop. read the sign. No curtains and no brand signs for the liquors sold. One could see the bar and a couple Rocky Mountain or Blackjack games, men in a clot, customers.

Kelly went in. It smelled of liquor, of men, and of business. Finch himself was behind the bar. A person could generally tell who was the proprietor. He spoke to Kelly and Kelly spoke back. Finch had a good eye for judging a stranger; he could sort a drinker from a gambler, or from just someone who liked to moose around. It was plain that Kelly, in parka and high-heeled mukluks, fit another mold.

"Mister Finch?" said Kelly, "Kelly here." They shook hands. "Deputy U. S. Marshal." Although he was not a drinking man, he decided to have a short one. He could tell by the decorative decanters what the specialty was. "The Old Barbee, a short one. And would you have one yourself?"

"My pleasure," said J. R. Finch.

They drank. "Will you have one on me, Marshal?"

"Just a drop," said Kelly, although it was one of those better places where the customer poured his own.

"Montana?" asked J. R. Finch. In the Yukon everybody, except maybe the Indians, was from somewhere else.

"Wyoming, by way of Montana, and the city by the bay."

"Spokane Falls," said Finch.

"Just came from there! I had to sleep on a depot baggage wagon. No room at the inn."

"Oh?"

Business was good and the proprietor was called elsewhere. Kelly had allowed him an accidental glimpse of his golden badge. He paused briefly at the-man-in-the-slot games and went on to the rear room, which was larger but more crowded — poker, stud, and draw. All card rooms sounded the same and smelled the same. Each table had its own banker, behind pillars of chips. Each carefully tended the pots, keeping things nice and neat.

When somebody was tapped out, that pot was put aside, but the deal and betting went on. There was very little talking until the pot was won. Kelly's eyes and those of the house man met. Kelly nodded hello, and the house man acknowledged.

The tables were frequented by the usual types. The nervous newcomers whom you could identify by their eyes, the straight gamblers who played an intent but casual game, and the hustlers who were inclined to be loquacious and friendly to all and who marked the cards as the deal went along, certain cards, not necessarily aces, using thumbnail creases, reverse bendings, or most adroitly a pressing of the thumb's oily essence which broke the reflection and yet couldn't be seen — just a break in the shine from the bright gas light. Decks were continually changed, as straight gamblers requested. The decks came from boxes but were not necessarily brand new. Cards, Kelly supposed, were hard to buy in a stampede. So decks were changed as requested, quickly flipped, shuffled, and passed on. A slightly-used deck would be wiped card by card with clean cambric, thumbnail marks smoothed, oily essence removed, bent and rebent, shuffled, and placed several decks at a time in a wooden carpenter's vise to be pressed into an apparently pristine condition. This all took approximately a day or two, and then each deck was reboxed, and sometimes even a new seal was pressed on. Older decks were often passed on to the pan joints, where they became one among hundreds. Nobody ever marked a pan deck. They just wore out, and the bad ones were cast aside, often to pave the street, to judge by many cow-camp and mining-camp thoroughfares. In all but treeless Wyoming, in autumn one was likely to see more cards than leaves.

He went on from there, looking around, then sampled a side street and found police headquarters. He went inside.

"Not Kelly again!" It was Constable McKay.

Kelly thought he'd better have his revolver checked once more.

156

The mounted police were very tough on guns. He had heard Dawson was an unarmed town. An unarmed gold town? It was hard to believe.

The constable took down the number, smelled the barrel, rolled the cylinder, noted the oil, and wrote down the facts. He handed it back.

"You seem to have had a peaceful voyage, Marshal."

"I hope it will be as peaceful for the next four miles," Kelly said, a reference to the published length of the rapids ahead, most feared in all the North.

"You'll wait a while for that. The big ice isn't here from far away Taku." He smiled.

Kelly wanted to know how they knew the source of the ice and learned it had a look based on the species of fish frozen in it or weeds from the summer lake bottoms. The fish flopped around when freed by the thaw. The Indians and their huskies had a time of it. They were salted and sold smoked. The huskies gobbled them still frozen.

Kelly ambled back the way he had come, toward the river. This time he heard singing. It came from the *bateaux* men across the river. Due to a trick in sound, it seemed very close. Then something went wrong. The singing stopped. Wood had been tossed in the fire. Sparks rose. Now he heard the tone of Blackmore's voice. He was over there, getting acquainted, feeling the Indians out about barges. But French-Indians didn't like to do things right away. They preferred to dicker. It was the fun part of the game. They liked to receive gifts. If Blackmore hadn't known that, then the Kid would inform him.

Looking down another side street, he saw a sign — **Mazie's**! She had made it. She had crossed over the pass and, damn if she hadn't brought her mechanical piano, that quarter in the slot melodeon. It ran by bellows, a paper roll with slots cut in it, and a wind-up crank. A Primrose and West minstrel tune was playing, and it sounded great. Kelly headed that way at once.

When he was outside, he saw a couple of fellows working a machine that spun five wheels, each with the picture of a playing card. Through the polished window Kelly could read the signs: **Any Four of a Kind $200. Any Straight Flush $150.**

A pretty girl ran the poker machine. Mazie was there, smoking an English cigarette. Upon entering, Kelly could see the cigarette was cork-tipped. Mazie had real class. He would have to tell Jug what he had missed by staying back with the boats.

"Kelly!" Mazie exclaimed, recognizing him. "So you made it. I saw the barges. I thought maybe that Blackmore fellow had had you drowned." Once he came closer to her, she wriggled up her nose. "Kelly, you need a bath!"

He'd been taking sponge baths, but hadn't had a hot bath or a change of clothes since leaving Bennett, so he used the bath house which Mazie had installed — no Castile soap, only something in a clear, transparent pink bar called Jap Rose, and it was perfumed.

He sat for a long time in the brass tub, of necessity, because he had sent his clothes to a Chinaman for laundering, by coincidence the same one who had done his laundry in Skagway. Everyone certainly was on the move in the Yukon!

His clothes came back hot and only a little damp. He felt (and also smelled) like a new man and all at a total cost of twelve dollars. Everything was twice the price of Skagway which maybe explained in part why everyone was on the move. He asked Mazie about a barber and then left to get a shave. It wasn't the same barber as he had had in Skagway.

"Yes, that's a moustache!" Kelly told the barber. "It starts here, and ends about there. The longer I'm in this country, the closer my skin and hair get to being the same color. And I'm from Montana! We have sunshine there. More than here. Somebody please explain why you get so brown in the North?"

"It's reflection from the snow," said a man who had just come in and was sitting in a chair, waiting.

"I've been on the river," Kelly stated.

"No matter," said the man who was waiting. "This is the biggest ice we've had since 'Ninety-Four."

"I hope you have the right change," said the barber. "I sent up to the bank for change and a fellow had been there and took all they had. He traded paper for it. He paid a premium."

Kelly felt in a pocket. He had the change. "Who was this fellow?"

"I don't know," the barber said.

But the man who was waiting did. "Blackstone, or something like that."

"Blackmore?"

"Yes, that's it, Blackmore. He walked off with about twenty pounds of dollars, halves, quarters, they say. Quarters is the smallest the bank had, but he took them all." He saw Kelly's startled expression. "Do you know him?"

"We're acquainted."

Kelly left with a bad feeling in his gut. He was responsible. He'd told Blackmore about the Indians, and how they would trade off horses for quarters, halves, silver dollars, even old-time pennies or brass trade checks from saloons. What Blackmore intended with all that coin was obviously to lease *bateaux*. No doubt about it, Indian or no Indian, French-Canadian or not, used to money or not, there's something about money you can heft! The frontier had never been cordial to paper money. The pioneers had cut silver dollars in eighths, two of which was a quarter, or two-bits. Everyone knew the story. Greenbacks were called shinplasters. In fact, some of the old-time fifty-cent shinplasters were still floating around and Indians were likely to end up with them, led to believe they were fifty-dollar bills. Even dollar bills were looked down on in Wyoming, and called saddleblankets.

In Billings the bartenders didn't like nickels and dimes, although they were kept, while pennies were tossed scornfully in the coal scuttle. "This is for you," Mr. Gerrigan used to say, giving Kelly a nickel, but he'd never dream of giving a customer two dimes and a nickel for two-bits change.

After hearing what Blackmore was up to, Kelly decided to pay a visit to Diamond Jack's tent to see how he was faring. Of course, it might be that Jack himself was likewise in negotiations for *bateaux*. That didn't matter so much as feasting his eyes again on the beautiful Lyla.

Business was booming. The faro game was crowded with customers. Lyla was dealing. Eddie "Slim" Chance was at the cases. Jack's outfit seemed mainly run by old friends, who lent a hand where needed. No chips were being used, not even the big yellow chips with the ivory cameo, only silver dollars, American or Canadian, halves, gold pieces. Kelly bet silver dollars. He watched Lyla's fingers, so slim, so swift, so sure. He wondered again if her nails were tipped with thin ivory, the thinnest of the thin, protecting the tips of the nails. Faro dealers were always proud of their hands. Many wore kid gloves when not at work dealing, even when dining or at the bar having a short one. A good faro dealer was always thought to know the next card by the touch. There were various ways of coding the edges, sand-touch, point touch, a dot and dash system, but there was really no way to fix a faro game. You couldn't draw two at a time, or deal seconds. You could slip in a stacked deck on some big bettor who was playing the same cards ever and anon but, if he got a hunch, why all he'd have to do was to start coppering or uncoppering his bets and break the house.

There was nobody in Jack's lookout chair so, after losing all his silver dollars, Kelly mounted to the throne, rolled a cigarette of the brown paper and the ever-damp tobacco of the North, and finding it warm in the tent took off his parka. He shifted his .32 to a higher, more comfortable position. He let just the top of his golden badge show above the pocket of his shirt.

"Part of my lookout costume," he said, grinning down at Lyla.

"The gun?" she asked, not raising her head.

"Oh, yes, that too, but I meant the badge."

"Let me see it." She looked up at him.

He took it off and handed it to her. They were not ivory tabs. Of course the nails weren't so important; it was the very sensitive ends of the fingers. She handed it back and Kelly sensed by a slight twitch in her composure that Jack had entered. She was probably uncertain as to his response, with Kelly perched in the high chair.

"I hope you don't expect to be paid for this," Jack said, not unpleasantly, as he came over to Kelly.

"No, just a courtesy call. Did it ever occur to you that we might be making a mistake heading for Dawson? The funnel for that gold is right here!"

"Funnels work both ways. This season we're at the big end, but at season's end the small one."

"Yes, there may be some truth to that," Kelly conceded.

Jack reminisced about his steamboat days and Kelly about when he was a detective on the mail trains, riding the tender, back side, where the cinders and water hit him.

"Catch anything?" Jack asked.

"Just pneumonia. Twenty below zero, got in the blind baggage, and froze solid. The yard bulls mistook me for a tramp. They yanked me out and I left the back of my mackinaw."

"Thought you were a cowboy. Chaps, peso-spurs with which you laid down the perfect calculus curve."

"That's what some professor called it who got his picture in the paper."

"How'd you get to be a U. S. Marshal?"

Kelly told the truth without flourishes, about the Bank Saloon,

161

Blackmore, and Warren who once had been Sheridan's partner in Deadwood and had hired Wild Bill Hickok and fired him.

"That might have been an interesting night," Jack said.

"No, Hickok just took his wages and left."

"But that's how you made the Sheridan connection?"

"Yes, and now you have my business history, my rise to fame. I got acquainted with the Appellate Court when they fobbed off the Indian land and water cases on me. Every knock is a boost."

"What do the mounted police think of you wearing your badge in Canada?"

"Couldn't be happier. Every day I'm afraid they'll shove some Missouri bank robber at me and say take him away!"

"Would it be legal? You have no jurisdiction."

"I asked that at the Appellate in San Francisco. They said it would be up to Canada whether to provide extradition. The way it's generally done, they take him to the boundary. You stand on the Alaska side, and they give him a shove. You grab him. Saves a lot of book work."

Lyla smiled as they talked, but he could see Jack was growing annoyed. He was the showman, not Kelly, and Kelly told him as much.

"Don't flatter me, Marshal. My daughter is the star in this family. I only furnish the setting."

"Oh, Papa!"

It was starting to go better than Kelly had any right to expect. Then he saw Jug Macure standing near the entrance, looking at him.

"Do you really expect those scows to make it through the rapids?" Jack asked.

Kelly chose not to answer. Instead he said, "If it was me, I'd send one empty, and see whether that big river thought it was another block of ice . . . or crushed it to splinters."

162

"The float ice is three or four feet thick. It would crack it like a walnut. You'll have to wait for the ice to clear. We'll be bidding against each other for those pirogues."

"We don't have to," said Kelly. "Those French-Indians get together and agree. There's no reason the shippers can't do the same."

"Have I your word on that?"

"You have my word, for what it's worth. I'll tell Blackmore what you said." He looked again toward Jug at the entrance, waiting. . . .

Chapter Seventeen

"What is it?" asked Kelly as soon as they were outside.

Jug cried, "Blackmore! He didn't waste a minute. As soon as you were out of the way, he took every piece of currency he had and headed across to change it for coin. The Kid said so. He said, 'Where's Kelly?' and of course Kelly was gone." Jug was truly disgusted. "Offering to buy the ferry!"

"What did you tell him?" asked Kelly, amused.

"I didn't tell him one way or the other. One thing about me, I don't talk too much."

Kelly burst out, "All right, I found out what Blackmore was doing. How could I stop him? He's the boss. The big *tyee!* Don't forget, we're partners. I'm in for a controlling ten percent."

"You're in for ten percent control when and if . . . ! You headed straight for Jack's. Jack will now assume you're a spy. Especially when he hears Blackmore is stripping this camp of coin." Jug wasn't through. "And you smell like a damn whore house."

"I needed a bath. All they had was that Jap Rose soap. Anyhow, Jug, you're a specialist in trouble from the Barbary Coast."

"All right. I was a bouncer on the Coast. But I know better than to go and get perfumed and shaved and powdered and then move in on a man like McGowan, making up to his daughter. She's the apple of that man's eye! I agree with Blackmore. There's something not right about the way he looks at her. There is, Kelly! I'm saying nothing against her. She does her best. He'd be dead, or broke, long ago but for her. She's his balance wheel."

"You have been listening to Blackmore."

"Blackmore has nothing to do with it. McGowan'd be nothing without her. *Nothing!*"

"Well, he has her. She's in there dealing and the money's rolling in. According to you, I was stinking them out with my soap. Anyway, there's no rush about bidding for the pirogues. That river would crush them like hot-roasted peanuts. French-Indians love to dicker. There's no damned hurry, not judging by the water."

The river would jam somewhere down in the canyon. The water would creep back, lifting the barges, then boom like distant thunder the jam would go out. Water might back up till it touched the sidewalks, then recede, leaving blocks of float ice on the shore. The walks would get sodden, though only a few of the low-lying establishments would actually suffer and have to hustle things out of the water's way.

"Biggest ice year since 'Ninety-Four," the fellow in the barber shop had said, and Kelly repeated it: "They never should have blasted. Those lakes around Bennett should have come at their own time. Mother Nature knows best."

They stopped with a good view of the main barge. The Kid's light ever burned. You could see his shadow moving about. Kelly, just to try his arm, picked up an egg-size rock and threw it. He couldn't tell where it landed. He tried again, then gave it up.

Beyond the town, the White Horse funneled down between canyon walls, not deeper, just speeded up. You could actually see the big ice make a dive a little way downstream from the last house. Twelve to fourteen foot slabs would get caught and stand on end.

The fire at the *bateaux* camp had received new wood. Sparks rose to considerable heights now, then burst like minute rockets, apparently when they met a strong current of air.

"He's rented those boats." Jug was like a bulldog with his teeth in a tramp's underwear. He'd get that dogged look and nothing could divert him.

"There'll be boats and boats. They haven't even started from the Taku."

"How do you know?"

"Because, damn it, the men who do know say this isn't Taku ice! It looks different. It has different plants and fish frozen in it."

"Optioned everything in sight!" muttered Jug, still on Blackmore.

"Optioned? What do you think we have here, the San Francisco Exchange?" Kelly asked. "Anyway, I didn't hand over near enough money."

"You have no idea how much he has cached away. All you know is about the vouchers you handed over to him. He might have a line of credit. He's a big customer." Jug had started and now he was getting it out, all the things he had stored up and wanted to say to Kelly. "You think you're smart with money. You never met a payroll in your life. And what about Diamond Jack? He's the key figure and he'll think he's been doodled."

"Doodled! Is that worse than diddled?"

"Doodled, diddled, he'll think you were there to keep watch while your partner tied up the *bateaux!*" The party over in the camp was growing livelier by the minute. Apparently they'd had some wine, or some of the major's brandy. They were rich. "I'll bet he dealt for every boat they got."

Kelly said, "Okay, let's go over and find out."

The ferry had been pulled up on the far shore and was on skids. The celebration went on. They couldn't just stand there. Kelly felt better walking. They went back to Jack's and walked in the door. Jack was sitting lookout. He saw Kelly was back,

166

but made no move. Kelly would have felt better if he had.

"Let's get out of here!" said Jug.

"Damn it, I'd like to have a word with him. He's cold sober now. I have this feeling that . . . if I could just lay the cards on the table. I always felt that damn' Blackmore had an ace in the hole. It all started when we were shipwrecked."

Jug kept urging Kelly to leave and he gave in. They walked back down to the river. Now the *bateaux* men were singing:

Ha-ha-ha! Frit a l'huile!

"Ha-ha! Fry in oil," said Kelly. "That'll be me."

**Mon père a fait bâtir maison
Ha! he! ha! frit a l'huile!**

It was no ordinary celebration! They were rich! Blackmore really must have scattered the money around.

**Fritaine, friton, pailon.
Frit a beurre a l'oignon!**

"Fry with the scales on! Fry with the hair on! Fry with butter and onion," Kelly translated for Jug. Both of them knew enough to recognize a song of celebration rather than one of drunkenness. They weren't full of wine yet. Their pokes were full of money.

"Fry in butter and onion! We're the ones that'll be fried, Jug!"

The ferry finally made a trip and Blackmore was aboard.

"Kelly!" he shouted when he could see the two standing on the shore. "We did it, Kelly! We tied up every damn boat they got!"

"For how long?" Kelly called back, trying to act pleased,

pleased but concerned.

"For as long as it takes!" Blackmore shouted as they were docking. "Oh, Jesus, will that flashy sport hit the New Orleans pokey now! We did it, Kelly. It wasn't cheap, but we did it!"

"Oh, that's fine," Kelly conceded as Blackmore hurried toward them. Yet Kelly couldn't take this as a defeat. After all, he was in for ten percent and that would be enough to make him rich.

"Don't worry about the girl, Kelly," Blackmore hastened to assure him. "Fair Lyla, the girl with the flaxen hair. They all love a winner. Ten percent . . . it will be a fortune. Sheridan, Blackmore and Kelly . . . the biggest bank in the Klondike."

"Of course I'm in for ten, but I don't want to get you shot . . . or me either."

"Worrying about Jack? There's room on the Klondike for Jack and us both. Let's not forget whose side we're on!"

"I'm not, but I say let's go slow."

The *bateaux* men were quieter now. They'd been mellowed by wine, a gift from Blackmore. He told them it was a fine old French *vin rouge*. They were singing a sad song.

Voici le printemps
Les amours se renouvellement.

They crossed back on the ferry. Kelly wanted a private word with the Kid, but Blackmore stayed close by, still blowing his pipes about how he had tied up the pirogues. He had, by God, left Diamond Jack on the beach. It had helped that the Kid knew their lingo.

"I have to hand you some credit there, Kelly," he confessed. "You were right to put me onto hiring the Kid. He talked to Flambeaux. The rest of them followed Flambeaux, to the man."

Jug kept up with them, but he remained silent. Back at the main barge, Kelly went into his cubby and flung himself face

168

down on the bunk. He was unable to sleep. His mind crawled with the events of the past hours. The timing! Blackmore had done it while he was at Jack's, in the lookout chair. Jug was right. Nobody would ever believe he hadn't been keeping watch while the dirty job was done.

He just couldn't rest. What a damned country — no north and no south, no night and no day. The Indians were still singing. Now it was a sad song about wolves:

Vous m'amuser toujours
J'ai trop gran' pour des loups . . .

Blackmore, still keyed up, wanted to talk. He pounded on Kelly's door and Kelly told him to come in. Blackmore entered and sniffed loudly.

"Kelly, where the hell have you been?" he blurted. "You smell like a whore house. I didn't notice it outside with the wind blowing. Have you been visiting Diamond Lil? I heard she'd come here and had set up a joint."

"No, I haven't been in any whore house. Mazie's. She has a ruby set in a tooth and is an old friend. She has a damn fine music and bath house. Best in town. And that smell is Jap Rose soap."

But Blackmore was on a new subject. There he stood, blowing to Kelly about what a skunk Diamond Jack was and implying things about Lyla, how he, Blackmore the Great, had left them on the beach. Kelly just wanted him to stop. Yes, Blackmore had brought it off. With the Piegan Kid's help he'd hired the *bateaux,* and now he was one of the Arctic brotherhood.

"I'll need more of the Sheridan money, by the way," Blackmore concluded.

"You'll get it, soon as I get it from Butte."

"At least half of what you have right now."

Kelly wrapped a pillow around his head. It was a straw-filled pillow and failed to shut out the sounds like feathers. He lied, "I saw the police. There's no telling about their so-called telegraph. Actually, they call it an express. Part by canoe and dog sled. I wrote, 'Send money and, if you can't send money, send cigars!' "

Chapter Eighteen

The *bateaux* camp was quiet after the all-night wassail. Kelly got up, dressed, spoke to the men on watch, and took the ferry to town. It was three-ten by his watch. In the afternoon? He wasn't sure. There was a rising gray cloud and rain. He stopped at the police shack. "Check your gun, Marshal?" the constable kidded him. They discussed the river and then he crossed to the Puget Sound Hotel. It was half canvas and half frame. The frame portion boasted a second story. A better than average saloon occupied a portion of the ground floor. The card rooms were off the saloon, with an entrance from the street, actually an alley which was called Second Street.

The Puget Sound was a hangout for professional gamblers. To Kelly, that made it seem almost like the Bank Saloon. Some old gamblers from Deadwood and White Sulphur knew Mr. Warren and hung around, waiting for the big action.

He saw Bob Selds, Charlie Mackey, a tall, stooped man named Slader and his Skagway friend, Billy-Behind-the-Deuce. All of them were poker players more than anything, but the camp did not as yet have enough Klondike money coming in. There were no really big games. They all retired to a private room, leaving the door open, and Kelly joined them in a game of hearts. When faro dealers, poker players, solo sharks and the like forgathered, they always seemed to play hearts. Kelly took a chair. Skip Shanks, a former harness driver with a crippled leg, came in.

The stakes were high, but Kelly decided to hang in as long as his cash lasted.

No chips were on the table, only coins — silver dollars and gold pieces, some currency, Canadian and American. There was talk of a Chinese who had started a fan-tan game and was doing a lot of business. Fan-tan had arrived in Alaska with the cannery workers, along The Passage. Sailors were crazy about fan-tan. It was played with beans and a bowl, or Chinese cash and a bowl. Slader remarked that fan-tan was a sucker's game, with too big a house percentage. The sailors liked it when everybody was jabbering in Chinese.

"They like the China girls and that damned dung they smoke in the pipe," Bob Selds said. "The China girls know how to please a man. It's a high art in China."

It seems they had this peculiar music, all dissonant strings and cymbals, and the girls would light their pipes and minister to them. Selds asked Kelly if he, as a marshal, could close them down?

"Not without an order from the court in San Francisco. Alaska is in a strange situation. It's not a territory, just a possession. When the U. S. bought it from Russia, the closest state was Oregon. So Oregon statutes are supposed to apply. I sometimes get the idea the chief resident authority is the Russian Orthodox Patriarch down in Sitka."

This got a laugh.

"How about that tough marshal in Juneau?" Charlie Mackey asked.

"It's an incorporated city. He's like the police chief in Seattle. The Alaska-Juneau Gold Mining Company is like an independent nation. They issue their own money. You've seen their gold vouchers? You could burn one and pan the ashes for a dollar ninety-five."

Skip Shanks said the Calumet & Hecla Company in northern

Michigan issued warehouse certificates against copper in storage and, when the lake was frozen, the Polish miners took it when they wouldn't take U. S. paper money.

"Well, they were burned by paper money back in the old country," Slader said.

The door opened and Diamond Jack came in. There was an instant silence. Kelly knew it was on account of him, because Jack would have learned of the *bateaux,* and it would be a kick in the teeth. But Kelly doubted that Jack would endanger his position in Canada by resorting to that brass Derringer on the green silk cord — not with the mounted police just down the street. His eyes looked a trifle bright. He'd had a drink or two, but appeared in perfect control. Kelly had taken off his parka. His six shooter was on the left side, pretty much out of view.

"Hello, Jack," he said. Speaking made him feel better.

Jack nodded. The others spoke or nodded. They went on doing what they had been doing, smoking, betting, waiting for their cards. They were playing straight hearts, no "rattlesnake" spade queen. Kelly waited for his cards and rolled a cigarette. He was grateful for the stiff brown papers and chopped burley tobacco, a trifle damp — no Bull Durham or Duke's Mixture, flakes that would reveal jumpy fingers. There was no tremble as he struck the match and lit. Jack sat down at the table.

"Damp climate," Kelly said, referring to the damp tobacco.

"Not like old Wyoming?" Bob Selds asked.

"You from Wyoming?" asked Jack. He was speaking to Kelly. "Ride for the Association?"

"As a matter of fact, I have."

"They're the bunch who hung the women, aren't they?"

"You find all sorts in the Association."

"Have anything to do with that?" It was a mean remark.

"Nope. Don't have many hangings in Wyoming. There aren't many trees. You'd have to dig a hole, twelve-fourteen feet deep,

173

to get a drop. On the other hand, you have a grave, real deep, all dug."

"Bury them standing up? Knees under the chin?" said Jack, not trying to be funny just mean.

"Well, you hear a lot of stories," Kelly said.

"Any mining down there?"

"Very little. We leave that to Butte."

"Sheridan? I know Sheridan." He obviously meant Sheridan in Butte, not the town of Sheridan, Wyoming. "He'd never put up the money for you if he didn't have control. Did he get you the job as marshal? Are you fronting for him?"

"Nope."

"Do you straighten all the crooked contracts on The Hill?"

"I doubt any one man could do that."

Jack went on, "Now Sheridan's Butte high-grade is here buying up *bateaux!* Clickety-clickety-click! That's how it works. Whenever I see anything go clickety-clickety-click, I know it's been put together like a watch. Like that railroad watch of yours. I want my share of those pirogues, Kelly. Sheridan bank or no Sheridan bank. Copper millions or no. I'm not going to be left on the beach."

"Jack, the season's early. The rapids aren't even cleared. I haven't closed for a single one of those lighters. Not a one."

It was technically true, but of course his partner had. Right now Kelly was playing for time, if not a day or two, at least an hour or two. He didn't like the pinpoint pupils of Diamond Jack's eyes.

Jack had been sitting with his left elbow on the table. He stood suddenly and Kelly almost reached for his gun. But he had learned his job as a railroad detective — never, never under any circumstances, fire the first shot.

Jack said, "Damned if I'll go over to talk to the *bateaux* men!"

He went out the door. All the men, who had pretended to

174

be otherwise occupied and had even played out a deal of the cards, breathed easier.

"He won't go, but he'll send the girl over," said Slader. "She'll talk them into anything."

"If you want my guess," said Kelly, "he'll go home and she'll go because they'll listen to her."

Billy-Behind-the-Deuce wanted to talk about how Lyla was the real boss, and Jack would listen to her, but you only had to watch out when the pupils of his eyes got small, which was when he was on the New Orleans pokey. The others started talking about McGowan, too.

Kelly left them at that point. He wandered from one place to another. Dark settled, such as it was. The river had gone down, leaving stranded slabs of ice. It was narrower now but swifter. You could hear the sounds of men, slamming doors, barking malamutes — South White Horse on the twenty-four hour prowl. The Canyon House was second only to the Puget Sound as a caravansary. There were private rooms for draw poker and the like. The main room reminded Kelly of Sheridan's, in a way, because the first thing one came to was a "pan" game. Men such as Diamond Jack or Kelly would no more play pan then suck eggs.

The pan game at the Canyon House was the biggest in town. At least fifteen men sat around a big table, drawing from a deck of a thousand cards, or less, held by a frame — the Dutch Shoe — tended by a dealer in a green eye shade while a house man walked around in carpenter's apron with chips and money, taking care of the customers. There was also a horse-race game, or Chinese lottery, except played with numbers one to a hundred, as at Sheridan's. Kelly thought of saying it should be called Sheridan's North, because there was even a tobacco counter, some great caribou horns, varnished, but there the comparison stopped.

Kelly left. He thought of getting a shave, but he didn't really need one, and men were waiting. Kelly liked to lie in a barber chair and have some fellow with smooth hands baby him with hot steam towels, and mother his moustache, then sit up and look at himself in the mirror. The barbershop window was all mist, but he could see into Mazie's window just fine. The mechanical melodeon was playing. Two men were playing the thumb-operated poker game. He went in.

Without turning, Mazie, who was writing something down, said, "Kelly? I knew you by the smell!"

"Your damn Jap Rose soap!"

"No. I'm used to that. You smell of the great alone. You and your parka. I saw Diamond Jack on the prowl, by the way."

"He's all right. I was just talking with him."

"Those damn *bateaux* men are at it again, drinking wine and singing. What's going on over there? You sure they're French-Indians? It's been wild as a Polish wedding."

"They came into some money. It's the Indians' turn to rob the white man."

He felt an unusual disquiet. He went back outside. A man who saw him stopped in his tracks. He just stood there, looking. It was unusual, as if he'd known Kelly somewhere, and the recollection alarmed him.

"Hey!" Kelly called.

The man turned and waited.

"Do I know you?" It was the only thing Kelly could think of saying.

"No, I'm. . . ." He decided not to say who he was.

"Wait a second. I'm Marshal Kelly." That turned it into a command. "What's the trouble?"

"It's no affair of mine. They said that fellow, Jack somebody. . . ."

"Jack McGowan? Diamond Jack?"

"Yes, Diamond Jack McGowan. They said he was looking for

you. I don't want to have anything to do with it."

"Why should you? I never saw you before. This is a private communication. Where is he?"

"I don't know. Down by the Caribou. It's that saloon. . . ."

"I know where the Caribou is. What else did they say?"

The man seemed unable to answer. Kelly thought he was going to turn and run. "That's all. Honest to God!"

"All right. You did your duty."

He damned near did take off at a run. He turned in among some shacks beyond the ferry landing. Kelly lifted his revolver and put it back. He considered going to the police shack, but he'd have to pass a third of the buildings on the street. And what was he to say? He found himself in front of the Gold Pan Saloon, the first place Kelly had visited in South White Horse. It seemed like days before, in a country that had hours, not days.

He saw a certain movement down the street, as if at some time or other, long ago, the man had taken a bullet in the hip. Kelly had noticed it when Jack had walked out of the private gambling room at the Puget Sound Hotel. It was a certain little stagger as Jack stood, or had to turn, using the hip as sort of a swivel, so he had to reach out an arm for balance. Unless one saw him rising or turning, he'd hardly notice it.

Kelly wished to God he was someplace else. But he didn't want to run. He wished he'd gone back to the barge. He could see it from where he stood. The office, deep inside and near windowless, was lit and he could see the Kid's shadow moving about. The river roared in the canyon, like the sound from a sea shell held to the ear. Kelly had a feeling, that strange contact of energy, which told him that Diamond Jack had seen him. Kelly was so damned tall with the two inches of mukluk heels and his sailcloth parka, hood up, his face circled by an aura of wolverine fur. It all made Kelly the most recognizable figure of anyone in South White Horse. He was still standing in front of the Gold Pan Saloon. He quickly stepped inside. He saw J. D. Finch, the proprietor, at work behind the bar.

"Hello, Jerry," he said.

"Why, hello Marshal!"

The place was heavy with the smell of damp clothes, men, tobacco, and damp, rotting wood. Everything in town seemed to be rotting away. Paint seemed useless that close to the river, on the driftward side. You painted, and it just fell off again. He walked through an arch into the rear room with its poker tables. A heavy smell of acetylene gas hung in the air. The lights were very bright under the pressure and mantle delivery. There were white-enameled reflectors over the tables.

He knew where the side door was located. Card tables blocked his way. Damned if he was going to run. He managed to seem casual. Men who stood, watching the games, moved to get out of his way. Poker players considered it bad luck if a spectator stood with a foot on the back rung of his chair. He took his time, walking through, and finally reached the side door.

The light burned overhead, hissing gas from its mantle, ash of cloth dipped in rare earths mined in South Dakota, a fluorescent light in a globe, clear glass under a white enamel reflector that spread its rays to cover a platform and a sidewalk that led back to the street, or was eaten up by the muck of the vacant lot, the one where a building had stood, now just dismembered boards, and the sign: **Lot For Sale.**

If Kelly followed the sidewalk, he would be right back in the street where he had started. So there was no alternative but the mucky yard. The mud was not of the sticky kind. It consisted of rotted wood and coarse basalt grit from the mountain. Everything shone from the fine, river mist. It had started sleeting now, hard enough to make a drumming sound on his already damp-stiffened parka. He could see the ferry and the lights inside the office barge. He was close enough to call, "Hey, Kid!" were it not for the grind of the river. He could actually smell the *bateaux* camp, feasting on smoked fish. He crossed the lot. Beyond the sheds, and a house or two, the flank of the mountain climbed and he could see grave markers. *Well, I'm walking in the right direction!* thought Kelly. He recalled the winter camps in Montana, silver camps now, a few gold camps, where ten percent died each winter, and there'd be no cemetery — not until it thawed and earth could be moved. The coffins were pulled on sleds by long lines of men, the pall bearers, and the photographer would always be out to take the pictures — the terrible black line against the snow, with the coffin on the sled following, men bending to pull the tump line. The photographer would display the grim photos in his studio window. There were sometimes ten or fifteen feet of snow and the rough boxes had to be stacked inside an enclosure to keep out the wolves.

Oh, God! how the wolves howled in winter! When men of means died, they made provision to be taken down to Helena, where graves had been dug by undertakers the autumn before, and where once — this was often told — a two-foot vein of high-grade quartz had been unearthed, throwing the whole cemetery into chaos.

The side door to the Gold Pan opened. Kelly seemed to smell rather than see the noisome interior. A man was silhouetted in the light. He closed the door. Kelly walked, knowing he was hard to see in the dull twilight. He turned and saw Jack standing, targeted like a duck in a shooting gallery. Kelly had his revolver drawn, hanging on a loose arm, covered by the parka.

"Here I am, Jack." It surprised Kelly to hear his own voice.

McGowan leaned forward and took a step down from the walk. Kelly could see the brass shine of the Derringer. The light was slightly at his back. It cast almost an aura around his head.

"Take your shot, Kelly!"

179

Kelly aimed and pulled the trigger. He shot out the light. He was not a great shot, and he might not have got the gas mantle, but he hit the glass protector. It flew in shards that rattled the wood and sang in the air. The light went out and on again. The mantle was gone, but the light remained, a white-yellow flame, long and irregular, a series of small explosions. Jack stepped down and peered to locate Kelly. He fired, but seemed at the same instant to lose balance. The shot was true enough but Kelly was three-times his size in the parka. He felt the nested bullet. It grabbed the rain-stiffened canvas and half tugged him around. "A projectile always tends to travel from the area of greater to the area of less density." It was like a voice saying it. When he heard a shot from an unknown quarter, he assumed it was an echo.

But Jack was hit and driven in a sidewise turn, knees buckling as he strove to take a second shot. The second Derringer charge tore the wet at Kelly's feet.

Jack had stumbled when firing. He was carried in a partial spin toward the river and went gunhand and side first into the freezing muck. With head down, he rolled over. He managed to get to hands and knees, and seemed to be groping for the Derringer, but his own weight dragged it by the silk cord. It was his final effort. The strength went out of him. He lay with his hat saving his face from the muck. Kelly never forgot seeing the flash of the diamond on his right hand, the one which dazzled like white lightning at the faro case.

Kelly still held his six-shooter. *I'm alive!* he thought. *Alive amid all that spreading, nested .44 caliber lead!* In his imagination he could still hear the tinkle of broken glass. The gas flame was about a foot long, threatening the building had the wood been dry.

Men came on the run from the sidewalk. There was always a crowd in South White Horse. And when all seemed safe, from the side door. Glass crunched underfoot, cutting muck-soaked boot soles. They saw Jack and they saw Kelly. Kelly still held the revolver in his hand, hanging long armed. He didn't want anyone to lose sight of it. It had been fired once and once only, and he could prove where that shot had gone.

"Get a doctor. Call the police." He called. He knew one of the men by name. "Jacobson, go get the police!"

Kelly didn't want anything touched until the police got there. The proprietor came out, saw the uncontrolled flame, and called in for the gas to be turned off. Nobody knew how. He cursed and bucked the tide to get inside.

"Finch, leave that light on!" yelled Kelly.

That stopped him. "The damn' place might burn."

"Then let it burn. I don't want anything disturbed."

The policeman, a young corporal named McKinnon, came on the run. He saw Kelly with the gun.

"Take this gun," Kelly said.

The corporal did so.

"This is Diamond Jack McGowan. John McGowan."

Kelly waited for the corporal to put the gun away and get out pencil and notebook — for him, jumpy-fingered, to write it down. He waited for him to write down that the revolver had been fired once. There was one empty chamber and one discharged cartridge. "Please write that," he said.

Jack had been hit from the side under the left armpit. When asked, Kelly said he had no idea where such a shot could have originated, but the elevated front platform steps were in that general area. He saw McKinnon's hand shake from the effort of writing it down, letter by letter.

"You keep the revolver," Kelly instructed the corporal. "Wrap it in your handkerchief." It was probably the first gunshot case he had ever handled and Kelly wanted it all written down.

Some men were carrying Jack inside.

"Not on my new table!" Finch cried. "That's brand new felt!"

"You'll put him where you're told," said a second policeman who had come in the front way.

He was a sergeant, but Kelly didn't know his name. It turned out to be Lockwood.

The doctor arrived at almost the same instant. Men made way for him and the body was put down again on the ground.

Kelly had to give Sergeant Lockwood his name again, "Kelly, Patrick, U. S. Deputy Marshal, Helena, Montana, U. S. A. By way of the Appellate in San Francisco. Alaska isn't a territory. The appellate has jurisdiction." He saw this written by the sergeant. "Watch the diamonds!" Kelly said, his voice low, but with force.

The sergeant nodded without glancing up. He made a note of the large, round brilliant on Jack's hand. It filled one page and part of another. He did a good job of steadying his fingers.

"Do you know of any others he has?" he asked Kelly without turning.

"No. I'd like to get Lyla here. She'd know. It's a lot to be responsible for."

The doctor came toward Kelly and the sergeant. "Hello, Marshal," he said to Kelly. Kelly was always surprised to be recognized. Maybe it was his height.

"Hello, Doctor."

The doctor then introduced himself to the sergeant. "James W. Carrow, M. D., Skagway!"

He turned back toward the body. "In the name of God, make some room!" he cried. "Get away! Go outside. Open the doors. If this man isn't dead now, he'll die of suffocation!" When the torso was completely stripped, he ran his fingers along the wounded side. The man had been shot and there were entrance and exit wounds, both. The bullet, which had to have been a large one, had torn out an exit wound big enough to hold four fingers. The doctor wiped his hands on damp cheesecloth. He looked to see whether a bullet might be caught in his clothes, or fallen to the ground. It often happened, but Kelly could recall the slap of something against the rise of the muddy canyon wall.

After a consultation between the doctor and the sergeant, Sergeant Lockwood said: "This absolves you, Marshal . . . if you needed any absolving. No thirty-two made this exit hole. Thirty-two twenty or otherwise."

"It looks like an old time forty-four or forty-five," the doctor concluded. "Somebody must have been out there by the river, or on the ferry platform. I'd find the old ferryman and ask him."

"The clothes have no burn marks," Sergeant Lockwood said. "Somebody stood out there on the walk or beyond, and shot him with a Colt forty-four or forty-five. You must have seen it, Marshal!"

"No, I was turning in the other direction. His Derringer bullet almost tore the parka off me." Kelly stripped off his parka and showed the holes. "There and there! And, Jesus, look at that! It turned me half around. So I took a shot at the light. The globe was a foot wide. I couldn't miss. Then Jack fired again. The Derringer was loaded and primed. Black powder. The powder was still burning when it got to me. See the canvas . . . it's scorched."

"Would an autopsy serve any purpose?" the sergeant asked the doctor.

"No," the doctor said. "He was hit once, and the bullet was going fast enough to tear off a big piece of shirt. It lodged in the mountain, from what I judge to be his position. If you ask me, somebody. . . ." But he did not finish. Then: "I'm just the doctor. And coroner, if asked to be. I'm not of British or Canadian citizenship. I stick with medical aspects only."

"I'll have to contact White Horse," the sergeant said. "We're dealing with a very important person here."

It shouldn't make any difference, Kelly thought, but nobody seemed to find the comment out of line. The fact was it did make a difference.

A third policeman arrived. He, too, was a sergeant, but apparently with more authority than the other man.

"I'd like to talk with Miss McGowan before proceeding further," he announced. Then the appearance of the wound seemed to change his mind. "We'll take him down to the police house and fix him up a little first. I don't want her to see this." He looked at Kelly. "Would you like to go along and talk to her, Marshal?"

"Oh God, no! After all, I'm a suspect. I'm a party to this."

"Why was he looking for you, Marshal?" The second sergeant asked this question quietly, with Kelly drawn aside.

"I think it had to do with the pirogues. My partner, Mister Blackmore, was hiring pirogues, and Jack thought it was a stab in the back. I was at his place at the time, sitting in the lookout chair. He assumed the worst. Actually. . . ."

"I understand," the second sergeant said.

"Do you need me any more?" Kelly asked. He felt he had to get out and away. He had to breathe. He didn't want to face Lyla right now.

"No, but keep yourself available."

"I'll be across at the barge. I'm one of the partners."

Chapter Nineteen

"You know what they're saying?" asked the ferry pilot whom Kelly called "Charon." "They're saying that partner of yours shot Jack from across the river."

Kelly did not answer. He didn't pay the s.o.b. either. He didn't even bother to show him his badge. He walked the muddy path between the steep black hill on one side and the barges on the other, and went aboard. He looked for the Kid, but didn't find him. He didn't see Blackmore, either.

Woodward spoke, asking him something.

"The police say I'm not to talk, pending inquest," Kelly put him off.

Whether true or not, they should have said it. Tired! Fatigue flowed through him in a wave. He took off his parka, his mukluks, his trousers, but not his medicine bundle, fell in his bunk, and slept.

"Kelly!"

Tired as he had been, deep in sleep as he'd been, he was awake in an instant. It was Bob Nelson, one of the sailors. Nelson wouldn't have awakened him but on orders.

"Yes?"

"The Kid. You know? The Piegan Kid?"

Kelly sat up and rubbed his scalp. He still did not need a shave. It seemed that days had passed since he'd been to the barber, but he had only the slightest bristle along the jaw. His mind focused and ran a fast inventory of all that had happened in that telescoped period of time. If time was a matter of events, he'd lived weeks in the last few hours.

"Yes. The Piegan Kid. Did he send you?"

"He thinks it's pretty important."

"Tell him I'll be there."

He bathed and combed and had a look in the mirror, pulling down each eyelid to see if his eyes were bloodshot. They seemed all right. He brushed his teeth — not having a toothbrush with some very coarse, bristly sacking, using soap and soda. He rinsed his mouth, spitting over the rail, aiming at the ice floating by. The sacking left his mouth with a raw burn, but he didn't mind. It was a kind of penance. He thought about the monks of old, how they used to wear sacking and flagellate themselves.

"Hello, Kid," he said, not turning, knowing he was there.

"Hello, Kelly."

They went into the office. Kelly's eyes fell on the Winchester rifle. It stood in its old place. It appeared to have been freshly cleaned with soap and water.

"Thanks."

"Sure. You my frien', Kelly. You know what you do for me? You. . . ."

"I left the jail door unlocked. I pulled a thorn from the lion's paw."

"I don' know about those lion, Kelly. You long-tam frien'."

The Kid's black sheet-metal portmanteau stood open — the one holding all his things from the Sisters' school. Priestly vestments, scarlet and white, were out airing. Kelly knew most of them by name: the maniple, the chasuble, the cincture and cord, the big square linen napkin, with embroidery, called what? He couldn't remember.

"Corporal," said the Kid, guessing his thoughts. "All damp.

186

Smell of river. She's okay, though."

"Chalice?"

"Sure, chalice, too. This is pall. Have to keep covered. Hold blessed body of Christ! He Catholic. This camp, she not have priest. Not even White Horse. White Horse priest he pick up, go to Dawson. Many Catholic die in Dawson. Smoke from shafts. Plenty die of pneumonia. I wait for you to wake up, Kelly. I'm about ready wake you up!"

"What the hell? You don't intend. . . ." He didn't finish. It showed little gratitude for him to say the Kid shot a man and now proposed to say his requiem mass. But he didn't have to say it. The Kid put him to rights in Roman Catholic style.

"This thing, she make no difference. I read one tam how ol' Pope, you know, ol' tam Pope, Saint somet'ing, he have cardinal burn at stake! No matter. Say his mass anyhow! 'Blessed Savior,' he say, 'when two men meet together in my name, I be there also.' Holy word! Right in Bible!"

One thing Kelly didn't feel qualified to do was argue matters of Catholic doctrine with the Kid. Months, years, at Fort Shaw, the priest gone, all those Sisters whispering their sins to him through the little, grated window. What sins? "Oh, Father, I had impure thoughts?" And the Kid giving them six Our Fathers and Hail Marys, and one *acte de contrition,* and absolution.

"You go fin' those poor girl, Kelly. You tell her, papa got to have Catholic burial. She maybe ver' sad." He dropped a tear. "She maybe don' know which way to turn. You tell her Piegan Kid say mass for dead many tam'. Requiem! Holy water, whole works. Bishop say okay. You tell her *bateaux* chief, Flambeaux, he ver' fine altar boy. Do job plenty tam'. You Catholic. This you' duty tell her!"

"Oh, Christ!" Yes, Christ! Kelly actually crossed himself. Her father, Diamond Jack, was lying over there in that police shed, he supposed, dank and cold. And what next? He had to be buried.

A grave had to be opened. He could imagine what uncertainty yawned before Lyla. The Piegan Kid was right. He had to take care of things.

"Yes! You're right. We'll have to go over there."

"Sure. Big boss, Blackmore, he say I damn' fool. He say I get shot. He not real Catholic. He Eastern Catholic. Lak Constantinople. He don' know one dam' t'ing about his own religion. They cross themselves with left hand, Kelly, lak ol' *Diable!*"

"Well, I never believed that," said Kelly.

"Sure, you always believe best in people." The Kid shook his head woefully. "Gets you in whole heap trouble. We go over and see about Jack. See he have good coffin. Maybe those police help. Then we see poor girl. *Domine requiem.* This mean 'grant him rest.' *Dona nobis pacem.* You say now, *Deus per omnia saecula saeculorum, Amen.*"

"*Amen,*" said Kelly.

Kelly went on shore and climbed to look across the barge roof to view the town, the *bateaux* camp, all the other boats, and the yellow and white deck structures of the *Faro's Daughter* with banners flying. They should be at half-mast! Over the dull black roofs he could see the tent. It flew a pennant with the letters McG in a circle, green against yellow or orange, showing, Kelly supposed, that he welcomed men of the green shamrock at the orange. A steady disheveled throng moved along the walks, the sloshy roadways and sled paths. He hadn't realized there were so many dog pens. Dogs barked continuously everywhere.

The *bateaux* camp was up and stirring. Flambeaux was notable in a special garment of some sort. With a cap and feather, he looked even taller. Was that what he wore as an altar boy? No, it had to be parade garb. What seemed to be his sacerdotal garments were hanging on a line to sway in the wind. Kelly went back down the mountainside, the narrow path where water lapped near, and back aboard by the plank. The boat was unsteady enough to make him glad for the hand ropes.

"Those fella all ready?" asked the Kid. "Good!" he declared without awaiting an answer. "You lead way, Kelly. We cross over on ferry. You tell those fella, 'Charon' . . . that his name? . . . clean up his boat. We don' want get vestments dirty."

"All right. Just a minute." Kelly found a necktie, and made sure of his Tipo hat. "We'll have to see them at the police shack. Then Ho! for the tent."

It was one journey he didn't fancy.

With Kelly and Flambeaux in the lead, and the Kid walking singly, and four more of the *bateaux* men behind, they formed a strange, imposing group to the ferry; and "Charon" jostled around, mopping up water and seeing to it that things were presentable. He didn't even try to collect. It was a privilege. They moved past the scene of last night's tragedy, people standing aside for them, and on to the police shack, with its two flags flying, the Union Jack and the police insignia. It was not a shack, really, but a substantial new building of squared timbers. Sergeant Lockwood was there.

"Oh, Marshal!" he said. "Miss McGowan was here and left." He looked at the *bateaux* men in their sacerdotal finery.

Kelly said: "We were told . . ." — he began, then changed that to — "we assumed he was Roman Catholic."

"Yes. She said something. She asked about a priest. We had to tell her. . . ."

"Brother LeMo is fully qualified," Kelly assured him. "Suffragan Brother, Sisters of Charity, Mother House, Montreal. He was some years at the Saint Peter's school. He's fully qualified to act in all matters when a priest is not at hand. Brother Flambeaux, Brother Perchoir, Brother. . . ."

The others introduced themselves by Indian or French names. Each solemnly bowed and received the police recognition.

Lockwood told them, "I've already taken the liberty of choosing a plot and having the grave opened. It's only a reef at the end of town, but it's the best we have. It's as high up as possible, away from the floods."

"If Miss McGowan is pleased. . . ."

"She hasn't seen it. If you'd like. . . ."

"No, but I think the brother and his altar boys would like to bless the body." He had no idea whether this was the proper thing, but it ought to be.

Yes, the Kid and his acolytes indicated, they would appreciate the privilege.

"We have found a fairly new tool box of the right size," Lockwood explained. "We've cleaned it out, and added some fresh white cheesecloth. Really, it looks pretty decent, and we'll put some around the grave. That drift rock is pretty grim."

"I'm sure God will understand," Kelly told him, sounding not one bit smart-aleck. He caught sight of Jug Macure hustling to catch up. Jug prided himself in his Irish Catholicism, and Kelly hoped he wouldn't create a scene over the Kid, who might well have fired the shot, and the *bateaux* men whom he had once labeled "savages." You never knew with Jug, strong-arm bouncer, but with unexpected proprieties. . . .

"Would you care to view the body?" Lockwood inquired.

"If you please," said Kelly, although it was the last thing Kelly wanted to do. Of course, it was never so bad after you decided. It was easier to do than to suffer regret afterward. So Kelly followed the Kid and his acolytes inside the shed where Jack lay rigid in a plank box under a tarp. The policeman moved the tarp aside, but he didn't seem to know whether to remove his hat. He decided, instead, to step outside. Jack lay with the whites of his eyes visible, which was about as bad as it could be, his cut-away clothing partially covering him. And there was the wound in his side, making Kelly think of Christ the Savior, a person Jack little resembled despite his faith. Flambeaux managed to get Jack's eyes to stay closed.

The policeman came back in. Kelly asked him, "Ever recover the bullet?"

"No. The doctor said it wasn't a thirty-two for a variety of reasons. A three-aught-three or thirty-thirty, possibly . . . but probably a Colt forty-five or forty-four forty . . . lots of them around . . . or even a thirty-two Winchester. There's a whole flock of heavy calibers on the stampede."

"I think if he could be wrapped in the tarp," said Kelly, "we'll stand the expense."

"That's all right," Lockwood said.

"Do that and please close the coffin," Kelly said. "No doubt she'll want to. . . . Well, I'm going up there. I'll stop in on my way back."

The Kid had a small wooden crucifix, native-carved of a brown hardwood, with an INRI insignia, which he wanted to place in Jack's hands, but Jack's arms refused to move, so he laid it on his chest instead. Then he knelt and said a prayer in Latin, sprinkled the canvas and the new, crisp cheesecloth, up and back again sparingly from a vial, and nodded he was through.

"We all go up there, Kelly," the Kid said. "Group, you savvy? You tell her she don' need come this place no more tam. All go show poor girl we feel great sorrow."

However, there was no need of going to the tent. Lyla was on her way with Ed Curry and a man Kelly did not recognize but proved to be an acquaintance from the States. He was introduced as Ted Langlen. Lyla was completely composed and dry-eyed.

"Yes," she said, "I'd like to see him one last time."

They let her go in with just the policeman, and she came out after a few minutes. She had wept a little, judging by the redness around her eyes and the handkerchief clenched in her hand.

"Thank you. It was very kind. The crucifix. . . ."

191

"Those carve by Cree holy man!" said the Kid. "He ver' good Catholic. We ver' honor say mass for dead. Me, all-same lak regular priest." He had a white card and envelope, both with a crucifix impression, on which he painstakingly wrote Jack's full name. "Kid send holy Fathers in Montreal. They say ten Masses. You pay one penny. You don' have one penny, pay dime, two-bits. Okay." He took the quarter. "Holy Fathers, Montreal, mak prayers from you, good daughter, you savvy? Holy Sisters, also, say many prayers before altar. You envelope and card inside. All these prayers ver' great t'ing. Mak saints in heaven before holy throne of God ver' happy. Kid now bless you. *In memento etiam, Domine . . . ,*" and he went on, making a cross with a drop of holy water on her forehead when she knelt. "There! This mak you strong! You be ver' happy at requiem mass this day! Police open ver' nice place you papa in cemetery. What tam you have, Kelly?"

Kelly fumbled, found his watch, and said, "Five past eleven."

"Maybe two o'clock?" the Kid asked Lyla.

There was no doubt the Kid knew his business. There are times a person wants another to make the plans, and this was one of them.

"We all meet here," the Kid declared. "All walk to cemetery together. Police have choose ver' highest place of whole cemetery, you papa. This great honor! He great man. Now, *famularumque tuarum, qui nos praesserunt cum signo fidei et documint in somno pacis.* You kneel."

She knelt on one knee and he quickly made another cross with holy water on her forehead.

"There! You now ver' strong with God for this day!"

"Say, that was all right!" Kelly said when they were on their way back.

"Sure," said the Kid. "Do 'em plenty tam."

He enjoys it, thought Kelly. *He really does! He's almost glad it happened!*

Word of the funeral spread widely and what seemed to be the entire population of South White Horse was waiting at the police shed, or upcanyon at the drift of earth where a few boards and stone monuments marked perhaps forty graves. Kelly had been told how some hustler had tried to jump it as a mining claim and charge for burial plots only to be cast out by the police — but that was the year before. In the meantime the police had built a low fence, some paths, and made similar improvements. The grave had been opened as high against the basaltic cliff as was possible, limited by the shallow drift of earth. A number of small spruce trees had been planted, and there was a roof on four white pillars with a bench. Although there had been no rain, water stood in large droplets on every painted surface.

The procession came up the main street. Six men of Jack's crew were at the tump line which pulled the one-time railroad freight cart. The coffin, covered by a pall of stark white cheesecloth, was very impressive. Quite a number of young jackanapes who had come to jeer were made hesitant because of the police, and later by the Kid and his acolytes who would have been just 'breed Indians and despised had it not been for their sacerdotal garb. Still there was some snickering around the edges of what proved to be a large crowd, almost a multitude.

The Kid knew how to handle them. He explained who he was, and what. He was Louis LeMo, suffragan brother, with full powers of priest when a holy man was not there. "This holy water bless' by priest." If anyone ridiculed this holy service, the Kid would call out the hour of his death. Then he sprinkled the coffin, Lyla, who dipped her knee, and Kelly, those at the tump line, and all the others. Most dipped in genuflection, some unsure which knee, had to look to make sure. The Kid's quiet certainty made even Kelly believe he had power, and the service proceeded. There was silence as the Kid made his ablutions. The only sounds came from the distant river with its rush of cold water and the grind of ice. Many were bare-headed, although the Kid and his acolytes wore small skull caps of red or white.

The service lasted about five minutes, mainly in silence.

"*Munde cor meum,*" chanted the Kid. He sprinkled holy water on all the altar boys and on Kelly, on Lyla McGowan who again fell to one knee as he made the mark of the cross on her forehead. "Please stand."

Lyla rose, crossing herself, and the Kid looked around for any others who wished the special apostolic blessing. The Kid was very conspicuous in his scarlet chasuble, which gleamed like fire in the rays of sunshine, and in his small linen cap.

"*Munde cor meum, Deus,*" the Kid chanted. He sprinkled holy water on the coffin. The cheesecloth, somewhat dampened, hung in heavy, shining folds. It's whiteness seemed to glow as though by an inner light.

"This cleansing of all wicked thoughts," the Kid said. "*Evangelium tuum digne, per Christum Dominum nostrum, Amen.*" He turned to the crowd and cast droplets of water over their heads "*Per Christum nostrum, Amen.*"

Flambeaux, in his penetrating, nasal voice, chanted: "*Jube! Domine! Benedicare!*"

Apparently, a response was expected, so a number made the effort, and said the words, or something like them, and the Kid, advancing on the coffin, repeated a prayer in Latin at some length, leafing to different pages in his prayer book.

"You now say, 'Lord grant Thy blessing!' " and the mourners did so. Even the young jackanapes, who had been stilled by the Kid's threat to name the hour of their death, responded.

The requiem mass was almost finished. Some of the service remained. The Kid stepped back. His eyes found Kelly.

"You now say few words in English tongue, *Frère* Kelly?"

Kelly should have been given a warning. There stood, all six feet three and three-fourths of him. He heard his voice saying: "Diamond Jack McGowan!" People listened. He went on, or his mouth did, for once begun the words came forth: "A famous man. A man world renowned as showman, collector. Known to the great palaces and spas of Europe, of America. Is it not passing strange" — that was a good touch, "passing strange," and Kelly went on in new full-voiced confidence wherever his inspiration led him.

Lyla, ready for this if Kelly wasn't, had slipped a piece of paper into his hand. He glanced at it and said, "John Edwards McGowan, born January fourth, Eighteen Forty-Eight, a memorable year . . . the year before the discovery of gold at Sutter's Mill, an event that transformed America . . . in the village of New Trenton, Ohio, to J. S. and Sally McGowan, pioneer Kentucky stock, where the elder McGowan served in the Legislature." Kelly's mouth and voice went right on, unheeding of the written words: "In New Trenton the young John Edwards McGowan early clerked in his father's store, read for the law, became a skilled keeper of accounts. Leaving home to seek his fortune early, the restless and ambitious John Edwards McGowan journeyed to Cincinnati where, despite his immature years, he kept accounts for shipping firms plying the Ohio River. With the war, still a youth, the young Jack, as he was known to all, enlisted in the famed Eleventh Ohio, younger by years than the usual enlistment age. He was made drummer boy, was wounded at Arlington Heights, the Union's first advance into Virginia and, transferring to the forces under General Butler, was part of the occupying force at New Orleans, and its capture, May sixth, Eighteen Sixty-Two."

Since none of this was on the tiny slip of paper, he saw a look of surprise on Lyla's face, as if truths were only then being

195

made known to her and, as for Kelly, he thought, how do I know what I know until I hear myself say it? He was the image of surety as his voice went on and could hardly wait to hear the rest of it himself.

"Serving in New Orleans through the war, a young sergeant, doubly valuable for his skill with the French tongue and for his mathematical and forensic skills, his young mind quickly mastered French and Creole dialects . . . he left for Ohio, but soon after the end of our tragic schism, returned and he became one of the select Saint Charles Street Buccaneers, a dueling and pleasure-loving group, sons of the best old families, and enjoyed the honor of being the only Northern veteran invited to join the New Orleans Guards, once captained by famed engineer-general, P. T. G. Beauregard. Censured by some of his Ohio contingent, it was certain he did much to reëstablish the Union and put the Great Unpleasantness behind us."

Kelly looked around. A statement such as that would still have raised a few hackles back home, but the cosmopolitan Yukon audience seemed fascinated. Mercifully, Lyla had come to stand beside him, and in her quiet voice give him other vital statistics: Jack's marriage, death of his wife and son, but still there seemed much unsaid. There had to be something more, so he concluded:

> *These in the robings of glory*
> *These in the gloom of defeat,*
> *Both with the battle flags gory*
> *In the dusk of Eternity meet. . . .*

Then Kelly turned to the Kid who waited perfectly serene with his chalice to deliver the final blessing. Kelly nodded that he proceed.

"*Benedictat vos omnipotens Deus: Pater, et Filius, et Spiritus Sanctus.*"

"*Amen,*" said the voyageurs.

"*Dominus vobiscum,*" responded the Kid.

Then he gave a communion wafer to Lyla, and bits of another precious wafer to Kelly, the altar boys, to all who offered themselves, and looked around afterward. His gaze fell on Blackmore. After an instant's uncertainty, Blackmore shook his head, no. So with a prayer in Latin, the Kid commended the body of the dearly departed to the earth. A final blessing concluded the service: "*In nomine Patris, et Filii, et Spiritus Sancti. In saecula saeculorm. Amen.*"

"Kelly, that was first-rate!" said Slader, the big-time gambler, coming up and wringing Kelly's hand with tears in his eyes, as if Kelly and not the Kid had brought it off. "That was real class!"

More people came to compliment Kelly than they did the Kid, whose sacerdotal robes seemed to scare them off. They offered condolences to Lyla who, Kelly noticed, had a sprinkle of tears in her lashes. She, too, thanked Kelly and then asked if she should give money to the Kid and his acolytes.

"One penny each," he told her.

When she couldn't find enough pennies, she borrowed some.

Only Blackmore was in an evil mood. "Yes, *Dominus vobiscum!* And thanks be to God I have signed contracts for those pirogues!"

Kelly felt sorry for Blackmore, he really did. The only one Blackmore ever thought of was himself.

Chapter Twenty

Kelly wanted to be shut of the man. If there was anyone he didn't want to listen to right now, it was Blackmore. His complaints about the funeral service and about the very decent effort by Flambeaux and the French-Indians as altar boys showed that the only thing he could do was belittle. Well, Kelly was proud of the service, proud of what the Kid had done. What the *bateaux* men had done. What the police had contributed in fixing up the grave so it looked like something other than a rocky mudhole, a sodden cinder slot with the fire put out — lining it with stiff, new cheesecloth.

Kelly had to stand in line at the ferry. Boats blocked his view of the shore, the barges, and smaller craft, and the *Faro's Daughter* farther on, around the point, and he could see festivities of some sort at the *bateaux* camp. Once across, he climbed the steep streets and paths of the former town site which had been abandoned by order of the police the year before, because it was just too steep for safety. A stormy dark was settling. The mountain forced a man to climb ever muddier pathways, through a misty gray sleet that shone on the rocks and turned the sun to a ruddy spot riding the horizon.

He decided what a man needed to see his way in this was a small, bull's-eye lantern, and he resolved to make one. You could do it, using a tin can and a candle. A tall tomato can would serve. A piece of glass could be mounted inside. Such a lamp concentrated the flame and kept out the wind and sleet.

The muck was slippery, but projecting rocks were jagged enough to give footing. The path climbed until he could see above the barge roofs, only the pilot houses breaking the view. Close by, the *bateaux* men had managed to keep their fires going, underlighting or sidelighting canvas and skin shelters. *Père* Flambeaux came in view, long-legged and long-necked, like a hitchy crane, and bowed double to go inside a tent. He had been to the main barge, probably to return his chasuble for the Kid to store. It would have to be dried before being put away with whatever it was they used to give that church smell. A powdered ash of incense? He knew the Kid saved incense ash and kept it in a small receptacle after it had burned in the thurible. The Kid had had trouble in this rainy air with the thurible which held the incense and emitted the sandalwood smoke, so Kelly imagined some of the precious fragments remained. Special care had to be taken. As with the last fragments of the bread and drop of wine, body and blood of Christ Himself, which of course had to be consumed. The Kid did that, and carefully dried the golden lining of the vessel.

The *bateaux* men must have chipped fish from the ice. He could see five or six large trout, salmon, Arctic char on roasting sticks over a fire — or more like over coals which blazed and became fire when the grease dripped. It stunk, and yet it smelled good. And he was hungry! Hunger hit him now like a club. He realized suddenly he hadn't had a bite since morning.

The Chinese cook had prepared a good supper when Kelly got back to the barge. There was no sign of Blackmore and no one wanted to wait for him. Later Kelly heard from the Piegan Kid that Blackmore was down at the *bateaux* camp. The Kid was not too happy.

"Big *tyee*-boss give Kid bad talk! Say I double-cross! Say where contract for *bateaux?* I tell him Indian-French fella no sign contract. Call many bad name. Say he tak heem Indian-French fella to court! Ho-ho! This work both way. Some lawyer, he say all Indian ward of Queen . . . they her children. Ol' Canada law don' count."

"They're French!" said Kelly. "How about Quebec?"

"They French sometam, Indian sometam. All depend. You lift hand to Indian, lak so, all contract you need. Ol' *tyee* curse you plenty bad, too, Kelly. He say you mak big trouble, get French-Indian *bateaux* men say Holy Mass for Jack. Frenchmen ver' . . . what you say . . . sentient?"

"Sentimental?"

"Sure. Cry real easy. Give you shirt off his own back. You know what Blackmore say? He say ver' bad word. Say French-Indian stab him in back. Tak all his money and now cheat him on *bateaux.* This not so. Flambeaux, he bring money. You know what big *tyee* say? He say he Judas Iscariot, bring back thirty pieces of silver."

"What a damn' fool thing to say! Who does Blackmore think he is?"

"He think they back down on contract because they feel sad for poor girl. Flambeaux say maybe he agree to give boss half those *bateaux.* Flambeaux, he cry. Tears run right down his cheek when he think about that poor girl. Blackmore, big *tyee,* he rip and tear around, say he break Flambeaux's neck! Two fella, Woodward and one those sailor fella, have to hold him he so damn' mad! You should been here, Kelly. Talk sense to you' partner."

Kelly was damn' well happy he hadn't been there. "Blackmore'll have to work it out of his system."

"I don' know about that. In England he big man. Sir Studdsworth, hey? This country he black Moor. How come is this, Kelly?"

"I don't know that it is! All I'm saying, the Indians hadn't better back that fellow into a corner right now!"

"Anyhow, this ol' river, she in no shape for *bateaux*. Big ice smash *bateaux* lak egg. Still have eight-ten day. Whole thing straighten out maybe. Maybe red coat police tak over, register pilots, *bateaux*, whole works. Anyhow, weeks away. Look at ol' river! Solid ice!"

Ice or no ice, Kelly knew that he just had to cross over to see how Lyla was holding up under the pain of losing her father. Chafing at the delay, he had to wait a good half hour for the ferry.

In South White Horse the sidewalks had been awash, and great slabs of ice lay along the street. Business was booming. He stopped at Mazie's.

"That was some speech you gave, Kelly!" she exclaimed.

"I figured Jack deserved the best I had. He was the closest we had to an international celebrity."

"Well, there's still the girl! The 'maid with the flaxen hair.' "

"Yes. I wanted to ask, do you know of anything I could take to her? Back home the neighbors come around with gifts of food. If there were only flowers available. . . ."

"Just pay her a call. Do it, Kelly. I have a bottle of perfume. But no, it wouldn't be the right thing. Just go and ask if there is anything you can do for her. It's the thought that counts."

Kelly recalled another service, in Montana, when he stood at the back of the crowd — the one where none of the preachers showed up, only fellows from around town, and the girls from Madame Riddell's. Annie, the dark-eyed one, had swallowed the prussic acid. Mr. Carlyle had said: *"Le silence éternal de ces espaces infinis m'effraie."* How Kelly wished he could have remembered that during his funeral oration Pascal had said it. "The eternal silence of infinite spaces terrifies me." That was how Kelly felt now.

Chapter Twenty-One

The tent was aglow in the smoky twilight. Icy rain had turned the canvas translucent. A crowd was on hand but none of the bank games was going, only some card tables, and the dice and Rocky Mountain games. Lyla was seated at the roulette table, writing a letter. She saw Kelly and laid down the pen, putting a blotter over the letter.

There was a great deal of noise and voices inside and barking outside. Some independent entrepreneur must have rented space out back for a dogfight. Kelly knew nothing about Jack's business: his debts, the diamonds, his estate. For all Kelly knew he had carried it all in a satchel, or it could be spread from hell to Saratoga, as the saying went, wherever large sums were won or lost. If Jack had been smart, it might be that he had turned it over to Lyla.

Her eyes looked larger than usual in her lovely, pale face. Kelly wished that he could put his arms around her and comfort her, but he could not with all these people in the room. Lyla gave him a welcoming smile.

"Kelly! Why, it's a regular halo!" She was referring to the light shining around his parka hood. "It's the lamplight on that fur!"

"Lucifer, after the Fall," he said, trying to keep his voice light. "Wolverine, *bête de Diable*. That's what the French say!" He sat down. "I wanted to know if I could do anything for you.

Is there any way I can be of help?"

"That's very kind. I wanted to thank you again for this afternoon. It was very nice." She stayed his denial, laying a hand on his sleeve.

He remained only a few minutes. He felt tongue-tied and uncomfortable with all those fellows from the *Faro's Daughter* on hand. They had, of course, attended the service. Like Kelly, they wanted to be close to comfort Jack's daughter if she needed them. He counted Bob Ford, John Rowe, Ed Curry, and Rusty Phelps, Jack's pilot. Who wasn't there? One only that he could think of, Slats — Slats Hargrove, the bookkeeper. Slats had an office in the bowels of the ship, which one could identify by its lamp, a rather bright one, gas under pressure. Come to think of it he had seen a light burning there when he came across, but it was only a dull glow. A pressure light would be too dangerous to leave unattended. Somehow, it troubled him. Bookkeepers wanted all the light possible.

Outside, he watched the office window of the *Faro's Daughter* for some movement, a shadow. When the Kid was working on the books, he kept standing and then sitting, reaching for this or that. But, all was still on the *Faro's Daughter*.

He went over to the barbershop and stood in front. The window was misted over, not on the inside, as with most barbershops, but on the outside. He wiped the mist away with a parka sleeve. A man was just alighting from the chair. He took a second look. Could it be the man he'd just been thinking of — Slats Hargrove, the bookkeeper? He stood back from the window as if in shock at seeing an apparition.

He went inside, but Slats was gone.

"Hello, Marshal," said the barber.

"Oh, hello."

Kelly decided to wait for Slats to come from the inside shower room, which was the only place he could have gone. The barber was standing by a shelf, writing figures on a tablet. He finished, and used a damp towel to wipe off the leather surfaces of the chair.

"Wasn't that Hargrove . . . Slats . . . you know?"

"Yes. He kept the records for the late Jack McGowan." The barber seemed amused. "He must be on the run from you!"

Long-striding, Kelly passed down a hall, rooms where the barber ate and slept, and reached the back door. He opened it and, by habit, moved to one side. You never knew. He felt the wet breeze of the alleyway. Every building extended to its own depth. One could see the shine of rain. He was cautious. Gun drawn, he went quickly out and stood by a shed.

"All right, Slats!"

Nobody answered. The only sound was the steady drip from the roofs. Slats was either standing very quietly or had fled. He went back inside.

"Funny thing," he remarked to the barber when he was back in the shop.

"Yes," agreed the barber, "he didn't pay me. Well, that's a dollar he owes me. I wrote it down." He looked at his note pad. When he looked up, Kelly was gone.

There was a simple explanation. The man was supposed to be at the *Faro's Daughter*, but he wasn't, and he didn't want Kelly to see that he wasn't. The barbershop with its steamy window was a good place to lurk. If this were true, he'd try to hustle back, which had to be via the ferry, and up and around the mountain. The boat was on the far side, having its usual trouble. "Charon" was up the steep bank where the cable was anchored, and was tightening the tackle by one of the two blocks fastened to anchor posts.

It took about ten minutes before the operator seemed satisfied and came down the steep embankment, using a hand rope to keep from slipping. He crossed with only two passengers, strangers to Kelly.

"Hello, 'Charon,' " Kelly said.

"Hello, Marshal. Say, why do you call me that? It sounds like a girl's name."

"Your classical education has been neglected."

"So? Why do you call me that?"

Kelly told him the Greek legend of Charon, the ferryman on the river Styx who took souls across to the Underworld, and how you were supposed to have a piece of meat along to toss to his watchdog, Cerberus, who had three heads.

"If it was the Greek hell, why would anyone want to get in?"

"Well, you know those Greeks! Hell or not, it's home. Nothing worse for a man than to be homeless."

"Hell's bells, Greeks now come to America. They start soda fountains."

The conversation halted as some great ice blocks bore down on them, and it was touch-and-go whether they'd make it or not. The ferryman managed to get by, with the help of his steel-shod pike or the ice simply passed around them.

"This is going to be my final trip, at least for the night," "Charon" said. "The ice is just too thick. Some of the big lakes have broken up and we're getting it. You should see some of the fish frozen in the ice. I'm going to chain and padlock as soon as I get back to the town side."

"At least I'm on my way home," said Kelly.

"If there's nobody there, I go back empty. If you hadn't been there. . . ."

"Thanks. You're a good man."

"I could use a prayer of yours, Marshal. I tied up long enough to show respects. You should have a prayer for ferrymen. You know, you never see the one that gets you."

Kelly decided to give him five dollars. A small coin, but U. S. gold.

"You didn't have to do that, Marshal."

Kelly grinned at him. "I'll charge it up to expenses."

He took the familiar high path above the barge roofs. The fire burned low at the *bateaux* camp. Shadows moved, but quietly after supper, and a somewhat satisfying sacerdotal experience. He descended into the shadow of boats, a slick rock path, and groped with his feet for the landing stage. It startled him when he saw a man was there, waiting. He stopped short of the cleated plank and reached by instinct for his gun. He didn't draw. He didn't touch the butt, only made sure it was there.

"Hey! Hello!"

It proved to be Nelson, one of the sailors who had been rescued by the police and fobbed off on Blackmore at Bennett.

"I been waiting for you, Marshal Kelly."

"For me?" Kelly was surprised.

"Yes. Mister Blackmore . . . he left here in, well . . . he sort of sneaked off. I had this feeling you should know."

"Sneaked?" If there was one thing Blackmore never did, it was sneak!

"Yes, he sneaked, but I saw him. And he had that hatchet along. The one sharp enough to shave with. I saw the edge of it. That fresh-ground steel! He had it sort of under his coat, but I saw it. I saw it and he didn't see me. He walked by, not ten feet away. I was standing right there, right along about. . . ."

"All right. Where did he go?"

"That's the question! He went ashore. He either had to head toward the north or the south."

Kelly was impatient. "He could have gone to the pilot house on the main barge."

"He could have, but he didn't. I listened and I could hear rocks rolling loose when he climbed up there where that path runs, the one they use only going down the canyon. Toward the *Faro's Daughter*."

206

Kelly felt a grab at his guts. Alarm and fear. Yes, *fear*.

"Is Jug inside?"

"He wouldn't do a thing. He said to mind my own business."

Kelly didn't want to argue with Jug. Ordinarily, perhaps, he would have, but he had a bad feeling, a sort of sickness. In fact, ever since following that damned sneaking Slats Hargrove to the back of the barbershop, he'd had that queasiness.

"Just keep quiet about this. I'll go have a look. You're a good man, Nelson."

"I know who my friends are!"

"Don't say anything. I'll go as far as the path and listen for a while."

"You want me to stay here?"

"Yes. In case I call. I might want Jug, or somebody."

It was dark and steep, but one could feel with his feet — the mukluks were just perfect for this, and the steepness an advantage, steps in the rock. There was a faint light from the sky, and from across the river, from South White Horse. Doors were opened, letting noise out, and closed again. The higher one got, the better the sound carried. Dogs barked. There were many sled outfits from the Klondike, mushers from Carmack where the Yukon Trail left the river and cut across, via Scab Mountain and the Stick Indian villages. One could look across at a terrace where tents had been pitched, a part of South White Horse unknown to him. And the upriver camp had grown. It seemed to have doubled in size.

He followed what had once been a side hill street of the abandoned city. Some level places remained, house logs and baked-clay chimneys. Over the mountainside he could see the gold ball which decorated the mast of Jack's boat. It appeared and disappeared, and did it again. He realized it was the craft rocking to the movement of the water. Not a flat barge, it swayed wide on its rounded bottom.

Looking, he almost fell, slip-sliding down the side of a gully. He climbed again; the path was wet and difficult in the murk, but he found footholds. The *Faro's Daughter* made a rhythmical splash as it rocked and came down, sending up a sheet of water. A bell rang in short, uneven bursts. It sounded like some bird or animal in pain, not the sweet note he'd heard across river in better times. The bell, he supposed, had gathered ice, as metal will, choking the clapper. He could see the pilot house now, a captain's promenade, some Jim-crack railings — the pilot house where Jack had once liked to sit, but no longer.

Suddenly, the *Faro's Daughter* came in full view. It appeared to rise, paused for a second, then came down sending a sheet of water high up the steep shore, then gurgled as it ran back again. It made a slippery descent. If his footing gave way now, nothing would stop him from going hip deep into the river — he might even slide legs first under the boat. It wasn't tied to the shore by short hawsers like Blackmore's barges. The hawsers seemed to have been tied to the far side on mooring posts, then strung over the deck houses and down again to heavy posts on shore. The posts were set at an angle uphill from the river to keep the hawsers from rubbing up and back. The *Faro's Daughter* was thus given a considerable room to roll. No sudden shocks. The landing stage, in two sections, slid up and back. There was a sucking sound as the ship rocked away, and a slosh as it came back again.

Kelly got aboard. The cabin was there to brace him. He went hand over hand. Nothing to hold to, no cabin rail, he had to go to one knee, brace himself, then go on. He imagined he could smell Blackmore. Feel his presence. He remembered the bear cave in Wyoming. The same dark shape, incredibly powerful. He needed the gun to stop him. It was the hatchet's gleam that caught his eye. Fresh-ground, it was a wide sliver of light. Of lightning. Blackmore, back turned, was at the rail, where the hawser slanted down. He was waiting for a moment of steadiness, when the ship paused, just before its returning rock. Kelly was no sailor. He had to keep one hand braced against the cabin wall.

The hatchet was raised; a second seemed a long time. Two seconds. If Blackmore had an inkling of Kelly's presence, he gave no indication. He was there to do a job.

"No!" cried Kelly.

But with an unflinching, terrible deliberation down came the hatchet. And, by God, he cut that hawser! The ship made little response. Perhaps a vibration across the deck planking. The hawser parted; one end whipped toward the dark mountain, the other with a rough sound slid across the deck house roof. The ship rocked and Kelly felt it as an unsteadiness when he tried to walk. Yet it was still held by the second, upstream hawser. He had to guide himself with one hand on the wall. And there stood Blackmore, looking for him.

Kelly's parka blended with the wall behind him and the shadow. He was not about to retreat. He drew his revolver, but he had a gutless feeling. Like one has when he faces a knife. Warren had told him about it. There was something primitive, long known to man before guns — the sight of a drawn blade. He was reminded of this as he saw the glimmer of the hatchet blade as Blackmore stood there, tensed, trying to see him.

Kelly stood his ground. There was still one hawser holding the boat, which swung away, half free. Kelly used the deck house wall to steady himself. He had the advantage in that he could see Blackmore and Blackmore had a hard time seeing him. Suddenly there was no deck beneath Kelly's feet. He had stepped into a hatch. His foot and hand lost contact at the same instant, and he fell. There were about six steps into the storage and office area, but he caught himself on about the third step. His front and elbow came in contact with the deck. He'd hit his crazy bone, and he could hear his gun as it went thud-thud-thud down the steps. Then he heard it sliding across the floor.

His brain overcame the impulse to chase it. At least he still had one good hand; the other was dead for the moment, burning. Both hands were free, yet one could barely feel the deck house wall, and then a railing where deck chairs had once been tied. He proceeded, hand over hand, but head turned to watch. Unarmed now, he expected a charge at him by the big, crouched ape of him, with hatchet upraised. Kelly planned his move — to go down with legs forward, roll, and find the deck railing. He could even go under the bottom slat, into the river. A molding placed there to save objects from going overboard had been removed to facilitate cleaning. Trust to God he could get up the bank through the cold, cold Yukon.

Blackmore, although seeing him, did not relinquish his true purpose. Kelly realized that when he saw that he was no longer there. He had turned away to circle the deck to the forward side, to the second hawser. The boat started to swing in giddy uncertainty toward the river, through the vibration of moving ice.

Kelly was at a loss how to respond. There was little chance in following him. He could descend to the depths of the ship, perhaps find the other stairs. He was not sure of the layout. He could go around the stern end and intercept him. Then he realized that Blackmore would not go for the stern rope where it crossed the rail, but get it at its mooring post.

Kelly descended the stairs. In the faint lamplight he could not see his gun. He was aware of the various odors of a little-used galley, then the sour smells of ink and damp paper as he passed through the office. His hand was still numb but he could flex his fingers. He could make a fist and then open it. He looked again for his revolver. There was only one, dim light. A lamp, not the gas, as he had observed from across in the town. The lamp where a watchman should have been.

The son-of-a-bitch! thought Kelly, recalling Slats Hargrove and his precipitous flight from the barbershop. He wondered how much it had cost to hire the traitor. He had no time now to look for the gun, and the steps were not where he had expected them to be. He had to pass down a short companionway. The hatch was marked by the glow from town. He climbed, pausing for the briefest moment when he reached the deck. He had to steady himself against the cabin wall. The ship had started its return tug against the one remaining hawser, and this time, forward free, it was held only on its prow and by ice. He leaned against the cabin and let his shoulder guide him, leaving both arms free. He was struck by the force of the wind which coursed the canyon as strongly as the water current which carried the pounded float ice.

He paused to get his bearings. He was beneath some steps leading somewhere. The pilot house? The upper promenade? It gave him a moment of security. His eyes searched for Blackmore. At least there was no immediate attack as he had half feared.

He smelled him before he saw him. Smelled his oily perfume — the Moorish smell, the smell he used lotions and perfumes to cover. Essences of Arabia. He was a dark movement against the town lights. He was not waiting for Kelly, not at all. He'd come there for one purpose only. He had located the mooring post with its still-taut line crossing the deck house, holding the entire ship now with all its tonnage against the mighty Yukon. With its prow mooring line cut, the stern overhung the bank, providing a hurried route of escape.

Blackmore knew Kelly was there. He didn't turn, but Kelly knew that he was aware of his presence and, armed or not, he was going to cut that rope. He was on one knee for added steadiness. The hatchet rose and the hatchet descended. The hawser parted and snaked in two directions. The water end went overboard while the boat end snaked the upper deck like a serpent. One felt the sudden relaxation of the ship's tension. It remained still for a fraction of time before realizing its freedom.

"No!" cried Kelly in an anguished voice. "For God's sakes, no!"

They faced each other at about three strides' distance. The boat continued its shoreward rock longer, the deck steeper, lacking the restraining hawser. When it rocked back, it would know itself free of restraint, and the distance to shore would widen. Free, free in the power of the Yukon, in the great river entering the White Horse Rapids. Nothing could stop it now.

"Let's get off of here, Kelly!"

"No, damn you! You cut it loose . . . you'll ride it out!" The words just came. The vengeful, unconsidered intention. It was too late, anyway. With a great hiss of ice and water, the boat descended. Drifting outward and back, unrestrained, the deck went awash and came up flowing. No scuppers. None was needed on Puget Sound. Only the deck. Kelly could feel it around the thick soles of his mukluks. Blackmore was worse off, closer to the rail and wearing high-cut, laced, leather boots. He'd had them polished, and you could see the shine in the lights from town. They were still in calling distance, but a precious lot of good any calling would do now.

Blackmore paused for a fatal second. He tried to get past Kelly toward the prow, the way he had come, and nearer to shore. The ship was swinging stern first toward the channel and had collected masses of drift ice which somehow lifted it, but at the same time also caught the current. Pieces of ice were carried like thick shards of glass over the deck.

"I'll split your skull!" Blackmore said viciously. He still had the hatchet.

"Drop it!" cried Kelly, with his hand under his parka.

It took Blackmore a second to realize that he didn't have the

212

revolver. Kelly did what he had to do. He threw himself to the deck and, rolling to one side, lashed out with his legs. The hatchet swung but the impact of Kelly's legs spoiled Blackmore's purchase to the deck, and the hatchet missed and, wet, slipped from his hand. He made the mistake of trying to retrieve it. It skidded about three times and fell overboard.

Blackmore knew how to get free. He came up with both hands against the deck house. He still might have got the better of Kelly if it had not been on his mind to escape the boat. He charged with his head down. The parka baffled him. Every blow was caught by a hood, or the loose sailcloth. Blackmore turned and there he was — served to Kelly like beef on a platter. Bloody beef, because he was bleeding from nostrils, or mouth, or both. He tried desperately to grapple and save himself. He was trying to get low and toss the taller man overboard, but Kelly fell back for footing, found it with the thick, spongy moose soles on the water-sheeted deck, and God, how he hit him!

I only want to stop him making a fool of himself, thought Kelly as Blackmore dropped, hitting the deck like a pole-axed beef. Even as he swung, it was in his mind, some compartment of it. His hand and forearm went dead. When you hit a man, you're hitting yourself as hard as you are him. The boxing glove was invented not to protect the opponent, but the hand of the user. Perhaps at that final fraction of time, he turned the blow inward, like a shortened hook. He could open and close his hand. He did it twice.

Blackmore was down. He rolled, apparently trying to get up, but his momentum carried him to the edge. Kelly yelled, but there was no response. Blackmore had disappeared. He was overboard!

Kelly heard the sound of his own voice coming back from the shore, but not close by. How could that be? He steadied himself. He had a brief memory of Blackmore's sliding feet-first under the cable stretched beneath the railing although stretched was not the right word. It sagged from collected ice. Kelly seemed to recall a grasping hand, a desperate last reach as, without outcry, in a terrible silence he slid under it. Kelly followed, holding the deck rail. The ice seemed to stand still. That meant the ship was moving at the same speed. He saw Blackmore, head and shoulders and a grasping hand. He held to a deck post and reached. On hands and knees, Kelly stretched his arm to the limit. Close to losing his grip, the hand seemed only inches away. The inches increased, but slowly. Farther and farther. Later he recalled, not the hand, but Blackmore's staring, doomed eyes.

Then the eyes were gone. He was struck by the strange sensation that it had all been a dream. Blackmore had not been there at all. There were only the ice slabs and half shadows between. Those great slabs of British Columbia lake ice. He was like a dreamer. He imagined he saw Blackmore. Only his eyes. His eyes staring from the river. No reaching hand.

Kelly called to him. "Blackmore!"

A sudden grating and crashing jolted his mind back to the present reality. The boat was sidewising to the flow. He climbed the steps to the forward oar. It was a new platform, and a new oar made of cedar. He got it set between the big slabs, firm and sure, and gave it his weight. The oars were made for two men. This time, one man had to do. He worked doggedly, inch by inch, degree by degree, aligning the boat with the current. Steady pressure was what counted, he noted, when open water and foam showed between the great slabs of ice. They had speeded up perceptibly. One started glimpsing water, some open stretches one could fit a boat in. You could tell by the eddies where the reefs lay, the rocks that cut boats in half when too heavily laden, as the *Faro's Daughter* certainly was, a full cargo except what had been taken to the tent.

Suddenly, there was open water aplenty. The rapids ran with

a terrible, deadly speed. Where there were foam and turning ice, that was where to watch out. Futile strength or not, he kept straining desperately at the oar. He was dimly conscious now of a deep roar, probably an echo from the canyon cliff walls. The worst four miles in the North! The rounded, modified V-bottom worked both for and against him. It might scrape, but there was less bottom to scrape. It stayed with the current, the swiftest part. What was the old saying? The horse knows the way. Well, the ice knew the way. He felt if he stayed with the main flow, well, he would be just another block of ice. The river cared naught for man's work or man, but that ice went through.

He was not aware of crossing mid-canyon, where the great whirlpool lay. It was very rapid water here. One might see a great slab of ice strike something, give off a shower like snow, perhaps turn over or stand on its side. Hold the course! Steady! The lights of White Horse lay ahead. Old White Horse, one of the great settlements of the North. He had heard something about a bridge across the river. There were some piers but no bridge, cable or otherwise. The town had its electric plant, wood-fired steam pressure at the foot of one of the great hydro-power sites in the North.

The river slowed! It became so slow one could actually see the ice bobbing, where once it had been lunging and plunging. There were lamps aimed at the *Faro's Daughter*. The lamps had been sighted long before, perhaps kept burning permanently. The canyon, now fallen away, revealed a red-streaked sky. He saw warehouse signs and roofs, jetties, docks, other signs, and the steeples of at least two churches. The flag flew. Men were on the run. A steam whistle was tooting. There seemed to be a great deal of excitement on shore.

"Hey, it's that *Faro's Daughter* of McGowan's! They brought it through under cargo!"

215

"That's what I always said they should do! Take them through with the big ice on. Why, that old river is feet higher. The ice gets through . . . the boats get through! It's how they should bring those big barges, too!"

Chapter Twenty-Two

Kelly managed to steer the ship into some quiet water where the ice was turned by the pilings of a breakwater. Waves from a steam launch kept the *Faro's Daughter* rocking gently. The steam launch came alongside and a man shouted through a megaphone:

"Pilot! Pilot!"

He meant Kelly. "Yes?"

"Where's your captain?" Kelly thought about what to answer. "Isn't this the McGowan boat?"

"Yes." He had to remember the name it went by its registry. Shipwreck Kelly — he'd surely dispute that title now! "This is the *Faro's Daughter*."

The man had a list. "You're Patrick Phelps?"

That would be Rusty Phelps, the pilot. "No, I'm Kelly. Patrick Kelly. The Alhambra, Blackmore-Sheridan-Kelly, Limited." He added the Limited because it had the right sound in British jurisdiction.

"You the one with the four barges?"

"Right! This outfit belongs to Miss Lyla McGowan. Her father was buried yesterday. The boat got away. The ice sawed its hawsers. There was nothing to do but come on through. Mister Blackmore . . . I'm afraid we lost him, sir. He went overboard at the head of the canyon. Gave his life, actually. He was a hero!"

A red-coated policeman came in a second boat and Kelly was

obliged to repeat the story. He made certain to keep every piece of information exactly as first stated.

"Deputy Marshal Kelly?" He wrote it down. "I'm Sergeant Ellis. Inspector MacIvers spoke of you. We're to afford you every courtesy. Overboard, you say? Not much chance for him."

"No. He was caught in the big ice."

"Why Jack McGowan was Blackmore's chief competitor!"

"Deceased. Interred yesterday. Blackmore was sentimental. He took it rather hard, felt very sorry for the daughter, Miss Lyla."

"Yes, I can understand that. They may have been competitors, but. . . ."

"He was very saddened by the graveside service."

"I heard you did yourself proud there, Marshal. We got a report on the wire. And Sergeant McKay came over. We're flooded off the tramway, but there's still the goat-route . . . for the brave!"

"Well, I'll have to return, so that's the route I'll have to travel."

"We'll send one of our men along. Miss McGowan will know the outfit is safe, though. We're putting it on the wire now. But she'll like to hear it from your lips. It's well when the two main outfits have such a close relationship, tragic though this was."

"Well, we cussed each other, but, deep down. . . ."

"I understand."

The *Faro's Daughter* was towed by cable and nosed by the tug. Kelly had had no idea of the extent of the White Horse river front — at least a half mile of docks with warehouses. The town had the substance of age. Bells rang and steam whistles blew. A crowd was gathered. Another policeman came aboard. He had a clipboard and started taking a quick cargo inventory. He came from below and asked Kelly, "Is this your revolver I found on the floor? It's one of the new long-barrel Colt thirty-twos."

218

"Yes. I dropped it. You must have about three registrations of that gun. Chilkoot, Bennett, and South White Horse. Guess I felt like an interloper, a U. S. Deputy Marshal in Her Majesty's Dominion." Kelly stopped himself. He was breaking cardinal rule number one: never volunteer. Always wait until asked. The loquacious man always uncovers more bodies than he covers.

Men were still discussing whether it was the best time to run the river. The consensus seemed to be no, but "It's all right if you have the size. Early in the breakup you clear all the reefs." They argued about it. "The main thing is getting the right start." They argued over whether a canoe, V, or square bottom was an advantage. "The square scows would fit just like the ice. That old river thinks they *are* the ice." But others stuck with canoes and V-bottoms. "The pressure, man! The pressure lifts them in the ice. Ice deepens the water. A boat is lighter, or it wouldn't float!"

Kelly had to go ashore to an office and sign some papers. By slow degrees, polling the ice, by tug and cables, the *Faro's Daughter* had found a berth near the Yukon Commercial's wharf. Kelly was made welcome in the office, by the stove, and had breakfast carried in from the galley. Leanback bacon, eggs, English muffins, coffee.

"You're in Canada, now, Marshal," they joked when Kelly stared at the thick, fat bacon. "There's plenty of fuel in that bacon. None of your crispy Yankee slicings!"

And eggs, runny-centered, fresh.

"A true Northern breed of hens, Marshal! Silver wyandotte with feathers to the toenails, to keep them warm!"

There was something Kelly wanted to know — how did the hens know when to roost, since it was never really dark?

"The hens know when to get up and start scratching. When the rooster crows!"

Everyone in White Horse seemed to want a look and a word

with Kelly — the first boat through that season. It was hard, maintaining a solemn respect for Blackmore, to keep the eternal note of sadness.

At every turning, Kelly's responsibilities seemed to increase. He had to get back to see Sheridan — but he couldn't because now there was no Blackmore to deliver the barges to Dawson. Then the steamer would come with the Alhambra — the grand piano, the French beveled mirrors, everything.

"Oh, Christ!" said Kelly, viewing the tasks ahead.

"Yes, it's very sad losing your partner."

"British Army, you know," Kelly said. "Officer of Sepoys in India. Dual citizenship, U. S. and England."

"Dual citizenship?"

"Once an Englishman, always an Englishman, U. S. papers notwithstanding. He voted Liberal in England, Republican in the U. S."

"Say! Can a Canadian do that?"

Kelly spent some time at the inspector's office. He said yes, he'd be pleased to lunch at the officers' mess. He slept briefly and awoke from a couch in sudden alarm. He had been dreaming, and he thought he'd seen Blackmore walking across the water.

"Oh, Christ!" he exclaimed, and shook his head to clear it.

"Everything all right, Marshal?"

"Yes, but I have to get back to see Miss McGowan. The *Faro's Daughter* is her outfit, now. And she is really going to need help, with her father gone and her all alone."

"We already exchanged messages by wire."

Kelly had a last cup of coffee and left by the foot trail, accompanied by two police employees who made the trip regularly each day, carrying mail and supplies. There were some steep ascents with rope and slat footways, anchored from high up, dangerous to look at and best not to look down, ever — only ahead, but not a man had been lost, at least not that year.

"Slow and certain wins the day!"

"Right!" said Kelly, and looked over the river, which seemed to lie still, a rough field of gray, unmoving, with only now and then an ice block, standing on end. Once he saw a tree, with its brace roots sticking out, and there was the great whirlpool, ice slabs turning like the second hand of a watch, slowly.

"Down, down, down among the dead men. Well, that's what they say," said one of the young policeman accompanying him. "It's nothing compared with some of the log jams on the Liard. No open water, only maybe a thin strip of river. Many stories of men and canoes being sucked down and never coming up. Not ever! Said to be still down there in perfect preservation. Mother Nature's cold storage vault."

It wasn't really a very pleasant subject for conversation, but it made the cliff trail seem a pretty good place to be. At least you could look down and see where you'd get your neck broken.

Word of the *Faro's Daughter* had reached South White Horse. Everybody wanted to ask Kelly what happened.

"Let's say Mister Blackmore saw the craft had broken loose, and was much saddened for the poor girl who had just lost her father," Kelly replied. "I happened to hear his calls for help. I came to harbor in White Horse City, without losing a bottle, but he didn't. That's the size of it . . . he was knocked overboard at this end. Those hawsers are tricky things when they get to flying around."

"Is it true Blackmore cut it loose and you fought with hatchets?" asked a newspaper man from the States.

"No! I never fought man nor beast with a hatchet in my life. I tried my best to rescue my partner, but such was not the will of the river. His last and final act was to wave me good bye. I repeat, he was very deeply affected by the loss of that poor girl. He gave up his life trying to save the *Faro's Daughter*, and save it he did! All right, *we* did. The firm of Sheridan, Blackmore, and Kelly goes on, as does the enterprise of Diamond Jack Mc-Gowan."

"I been told he was carrying twenty pounds of gold belonging to the partnership, and it's what took him down."

"Mister Blackmore? Then you were told a falsehood. Every ounce of silver and gold in his possession was paid over to the *bateaux* men to get our outfit on its way through the terrible White Horse rapids. He was a hero. A true hero of the North!"

Lyla McGowan met him in the tent. She wanted to know if all she heard was true, and he said he supposed it was. "The *Faro's Daughter* is safely through the rapids. Not a scratch! Not a bottle broken."

God, but he was tired. He sat down, choosing the lookout chair at the now quiet faro spread. His fingers shook a little as he tried to roll a cigarette.

"Here. Have one of these. They belonged to papa."

"Ah, yes. PLAYERS. The English Oval, Turkish tobacco. Thank you. Sorry, my mind is wandering. I feel transported, somehow." He lit up and inhaled deeply. The cigarette did have an effect. He thought of far off London, of Fleet Street, Charing Cross, Turkey. . . . "There are so many problems, Lyla. You have some important decisions to make, with your tent and equipment here and the *Faro's Daughter* now in White Horse. You can make yourself a nice bundle here this summer, more than in Dawson. You can then sell the tent and take the *Faro's Daughter* on before the freeze-up. At least you don't have much worry about pirogues. The accident of the breakup saved you that."

"I have Blackmore's investment to think of, the steamboat from Saint Michael with the Alhambra . . . somehow, it will all have to be put together. I'll need more funds from Mister Sheridan. I may have to catch the express boat from Juneau. Good God, the problems ahead!"

"I think you need a glass of brandy."

"Yes. Why not? I haven't had a wink of sleep, but I'm not sleepy. The excitement! A busy twenty-four hours." Had it really been only yesterday they had laid poor Jack in the ground? He said, "Time! True, it's less a matter of hours than events." And he had lived a very full life in the past thirty-six hours! He could scarcely keep back the tears. For whom? Well, the poor, bereaved girl — facing the great North country, and so very alone.

She shook her head in puzzlement. "I really can't understand there being no watchman aboard the *Faro's Daughter*. I'm so worried about Slats Hargrove, our bookkeeper. He volunteered to stand watch. Could he have fallen overboard?"

"Entirely possible. He might have been tightening the mooring blocks and been tossed over the side. We just happened to see it, bucking like a bronco. Sensed there was something wrong." *A single hair can divide the false and true,* thought Kelly, *and on what, prithee, doth life depend?* He said, "I'm just so damned tired!"

The PLAYERS cigarette, together with the fresh air and big effort, and so long without sleep, had left him with a fatigue somewhat like a levitation.

"You know," Lyla said, as if just thinking of it, "McGowan, Kelly, and Sheridan could truly make the biggest thing in Dawson! The biggest outfit, atop the richest bedrock in the world! It's something to think about, if Mister Sheridan will agree."

"There'll be things to work out, but if it's big, he'll agree!"

They walked to the ferry. The sun came brightly through the clouds. It dazzled on her hair. She had to hold it with both hands when the canyon wind arose. It streamed out in the sunshine like a glorious, golden pennant.

"Try this," Kelly suggested.

He gave her his hat. His Tipo de Oro. He had been wearing it under his parka hood.

"Why it fits!" she cried, delightedly.

223

"Just my luck!"

"I'll have to give you something in exchange."

"How about the Orloff?" asked Kelly, grinning down at her upturned face.

"Well, no. I'm afraid the insurance. . . ."

"Well, give me time," said Kelly. "I'll think of something."

"Yes," she said, demurely. She took his hand for balance on the bobbing deck. She flashed him a provocative smile. "Yes, I'm sure you will."

About the Author

Dan Cushman was born in Osceola, Michigan, and grew up on the Cree Indian reservation in Montana. He was graduated from the University of Montana with a Bachelor of Science degree in 1934 and pursued a career in mining as a prospector, assayer, and geologist before turning to journalism. In the early 1940s his novelette-length stories began appearing regularly in such Fiction House magazines as *North-West Romances* and *Frontier Stories*. Later in the decade his North-Western and Western stories as well as fiction set in the Far East and Africa began appearing in *Action Stories*, *Adventure*, and *Short Stories*. A collection of some of his best North-Western and Western fiction has recently been published, *Voyageurs of the Midnight Sun* (Capra Press, 1995) with a Foreword by John Jakes who cites Cushman as a major influence in his own work. The character Comanche John, a Montana road agent featured in numerous rollicking magazine adventures, also appears in his Cushman's first novel, *Montana, Here I Be* (Macmillan, 1950) and in two later novels. *Stay Away, Joe* (Viking, 1953) is an amusing novel about the mixture, and occasional collision, of Indian culture and Anglo-American culture among the *Métis* (French-Indians) living on a reservation in Montana. The novel became a bestseller and remains a classic to this day, greatly loved especially by Indian peoples for its truthfulness and humor. Cushman's also produced significant historical fiction in *The Silver Mountain* (Appleton Century Crofts, 1957), concerned with the mining and politics of silver in Montana in the 1890s. This novel won a Golden Spur Award from the Western Writers of America. His fiction remains notable for its breadth, ranging all the way from a story of the cattle frontier in *Tall Wyoming* (Dell, 1957) to a poignant and memorable portrait of small town life in Michigan just before the Great War in *The Grand and The Glorious* (McGraw-Hill, 1963). He has just completed his next Five Star Western, a North-Western titled *Valley of the Thousand Smokes*.